I0659487

Triple Love Score

"Granett's beautifully written novel, full of twists, turns and truths about the ups and downs of life, had me spellbound from the very first page."

> — KRISTY WOODSON HARVEY, author of *Dear Carolina* and *Lies and Other Acts of Love*

"With engaging characters, romantic gestures, and one board game, Granett makes poetry cool again."

> — AMY E. REICHERT, author of *The Coincidence of Coconut Cake* and *Luck, Love, and Lemon Pie*

"A love story that is on one hand sweet, but on the other full of surprises and intrigue, set against the background of Scrabble. It sounds entirely unlikely but this is exactly what Granett has spelled out in a novel that deserves kudos and could easily become a guilty pleasure."

> — JACQUELYN MITCHARD, author of *New York Times* #1 Bestseller *The Deep End of the Ocean*

". . . a romantic pleasure with delightfully unique characters and a plot that takes you on an unexpected journey. Granett has a clear writing style that brings each scene to life and makes for a tremendously engaging read. As a fan of love and poetry, I highly recommend it!"

> — ANITA HUGHES, author of *Santorini Sunsets*

"An entertaining and perceptive story of our times."

> — KATHRYN CRAFT, award-winning author of *The Far End of Happy* and *The Art of Falling*

"Like tiles on a Scrabble board, Granett's characters unfold and connect and diverge again. Readers will be hooked as they follow Miranda's unlikely adventures—ones that take her across the country and as far away as Istanbul and France—as her long-held dreams concerning love and career are both challenged and re-defined."

> — AMY IMPELLIZZERI, award-winning author of *Lemongrass Hope*

". . . what is refreshingly different are descriptions of how and when convention fails, what causes a very quiet life to evolve into something different, and how the soul can be awakened to new opportunities. Women seeking a solid story of a poetry professor's awakening will find *Triple Love Score* a delightful romp through options Miranda never realized she had."

— DIANE C. DONOVAN, Midwest Book Reviews

"While there's nothing weighty in this fun, lighthearted book in terms of subject matter, the novel includes plenty of steamy sex scenes as well as some unexpected plot twists and turns. Granett includes an intriguing, relatable human dilemma as Miranda tries her new 'lightness' and 'no strings attached' attitude on for size. The protagonist must ultimately decide whether it is smarter to listen to the warnings of her rational brain or simply allow herself to follow what feels right to her passionate heart. An entertaining romance novel with an engrossing plot, a conflicted heroine, and a couple of surprising, poignant takeaways."

— KIRKUS REVIEWS

Triple Love Score

BRANDI MEGAN GRANETT

Wyatt-MacKenzie Publishing
DEADWOOD, OREGON

Triple Love Score
Brandi Megan Granett

ISBN: 978-1-942545-40-8

Library of Congress Control Number: 2016932379

©2016 Brandi Megan Granett. All Rights Reserved.

SCRABBLE®, the distinctive game board and letter tiles, and all associated
logos are trademarks of Hasbro in the United States and Canada, and
are used with permission. ©2016 Hasbro. All Rights Reserved.

No part of this book may be reproduced in
any manner whatsoever without written permission except in the case
of brief quotations embodied in critical articles and reviews.

The characters and events in this book are fictitious. Any similarity to real
persons, living or dead, is coincidental and not intended by the author.

Wyatt-MacKenzie Publishing
DEADWOOD, OREGON

Wyatt-MacKenzie Publishing, Inc.
www.WyattMacKenzie.com
Contact us: info@wyattmackenzie.com

Dedication

To Avram.

Without you, I wouldn't know enough about love to
write even a sentence about it.

You never realize where you are going until you get there,
where nothing is planned, nothing is known,
and you're drawn back into the heart's old orbits,
tiny as a grain, massive as a moon.

— Pat Boran, excerpt from "Moon Street"

Prologue

**E**VEN AT TWELVE YEARS OLD, Miranda knew better than to dissuade her mother from orchestrating her own funeral.

"So," Louise began, "you will wear the brown dress. Not the black. You are too young for black. Anita will iron it for you and make sure you have fresh hose. Daddy, luckily, already wears the right suit. The town car will come for you. Yes, you will sit in the back. Don't even ask to ride up front. The car will take you to the church. The big one, downtown, the one my mother loved. I didn't like it there except for the music. I loved the organ and the choir. So that's what it will be. All music. No sense in your father standing up there to speak. I couldn't do that to him." Her mother's voice quavered. She could pretend to be okay with dying for only so long.

Miranda, perched on the bow window seat of her parents' bedroom, remained silent. There was no sense in talking. Her mother valued knowledge, concrete plans, and making sure everyone knew exactly what to expect.

Louise leaned back against the floral print chaise lounge

and gasped for breath before continuing. She picked up the gold chain she wore around her neck. Her engagement ring, a single emerald cut diamond, hung from the chain, and caught the light. Cancer robbed her mother of the simplest of things like wearing this ring; all of her joints swelled from the treatment while everything else shrunk. The ring at once could not fit and could not hold. Louise let the ring dangle in front of her for a moment before tucking it back into her blouse. Miranda stroked the Hermes scarf on her mother's head.

"Randa," she said, "it makes me feel better to know you are prepared. Tell me which dress you will wear."

Miranda knew what the doctors said and didn't argue. Her mother smelled like death, sickly sweet like overripe fruit. Her thick hair, a chestnut brown and wavy, like Miranda's own, abandoned her shortly after the first treatments. Her arms could barely manage to lift a full glass of water. And Miranda's mother was always right. If Louise said knowing about the funeral would make it better, it would.

The funeral turned out as planned. The brown dress, which Anita ironed. The car where she sat next to her father. The big church downtown. But her mother hadn't mentioned the flowers. The smell of them: waxy, sweet, green. Yet the scent of their wilting decay hung in the air, too. Miranda clung to her father's side as he moved up the crowded aisles. Her parents, both lawyers and popular ones at that, served on committees, argued cases, and taught at the law school. Throngs of people came to say goodbye. Each bent low and tried to look Miranda in the eye, but she couldn't match their gaze. Their eyes ringed red from tears didn't mirror her own grief. They hadn't known what was coming; they hadn't sat in that sunny room and discussed death and funerals with her mother. Miranda spent her own tears long before the funeral.

Finally, they made their way through the crowd to the front where Linden, Bunny, and Scott sat. Bunny, her mother's best friend, knew the drill. Bunny hired the organist and booked the church. Linden arranged the car service. Even though they weren't related, they were family. Miranda slid over next to Scott as she always did. He was her brother and best friend rolled into one. He would play video games with her and sometimes let her win or picked her for his manhunt team. They watched movies together and re-enacted scenes for their parents' applause. They took turns reading to each other on long car rides to the shore where they would swim and play Frisbee while their parents perfected the margarita with many failed but consumed batches. But today wasn't like that. Miranda suspected no day would ever be like that again.

Of course, they sat in the front pew. Miranda knew that. Her mother had stressed that point. "I know you don't like being front and center, my girl," she said, petting Miranda's hair, then sun-streaked from the summer spent by the pool watching her mother try and fail each day to swim like she used to. "People expect you up there. Funerals are for everyone, not just the family. Try to remember that."

But in the front row, they were closer to the flowers. And their smell. It began to stick to the back of her throat and reach down deep into her lungs. Her chest constricted. The Reverend signaled for everyone to stand. The weight of this day and all the days of her mother's illness pressed down upon her. Miranda went to move, but her legs gave out from under her just as the thunderous noise from the organ began. She saw her father's gaze transfixed on the cross over the altar and was grateful he didn't see her falter. She tried again to stand. This time a hand around her waist lifted her. Scott looked down at her, his own eyes brimmed with tears. He lifted her up and then took her hand, pulling her arm close to his. He kept his arm tensed and flexed. She leaned into him, gripping his fingers so tightly that the knuckles on both their hands turned white. Embarrassed, she moved to let go.

"No," he whispered, squeezing her fingers tightly back.

He didn't let go. He kept her upright for the entire service of music and through all the goodbyes in the foyer of the church. He held her hand until the driver opened the door to the town car and ushered her inside.

"Thank you," was all she said to him.

He only nodded in reply.

CHAPTER

1

IRANDA STOOD ON THE STREET CORNER admiring the brightly dyed flowers arranged in so many buckets in front of the bodega. With the dreary gray of fall about to be winter hanging in the sky, the flowers struck her as even more improbable, even more abstract, something her undergraduate students could write a poem about. She snapped a picture with her phone and emailed it to everyone in her afternoon section of Intermediate Poetry. "Bring a pencil and paper to class," she added.

The campus already felt empty with the approach of Thanksgiving as she took the long way from her car to the classroom. The fitness tracker she kept clipped to the inside of her belt, hidden from view, reminded her that her foot-step count for the day lacked about five thousand steps from her ten thousand goal. Miranda didn't want to go crazy about the exercise thing; too many women her age did that as if exercise could stop them from turning thirty. They took Pilates and spun, did yoga and now Zumba. She couldn't bring herself to really even say the word, such an ugly-hybrid, nouveau word, commercial speak, let alone put on skin-tight spandex and "have so much fun" you will forget you are exercising. Nothing about dancing under fluorescent lights in a musty exercise room sounded like fun.

Dancing, however, a rumba proper or a tango, or some other Latin-flavored, romantic dance under the light of the moon or the black lights of disco in Ibiza—now that sounded fun. Miranda let her thoughts wander as she stepped carefully on the damp cobblestones, slicked with leaves. She imagined phoning Avery, her stepmother, and saying, "No, I'm not coming for Thanksgiving this year. I'm going to Ibiza."

But she remembered Avery's email all too clearly. "The Cramers are coming! Scott, too!" Only Avery used about twelve exclamation points, excited to have everyone back together again. But Miranda didn't share her enthusiasm. At least not anymore.

After her mom died, Miranda tried everything possible to be someone else, but with Scott, she had no choice. He already knew who she was. With him, she could relax and stop pretending to be fine or to like horses or to love school or even to be happy. She loved how he listened to her stories. She loved how he made everyone laugh. She loved how he made her feel like everything would be just fine after a round of Frisbee. And Scott liked her; Miranda knew that. But not liked her-liked her. He was a big brother, an older cousin, a family friend. Even if she had once hoped it could be more than that.

Like when she was sixteen to his eighteen and finally filled out her red and white Polka-dotted bikini, and he didn't take his eyes off her all day, not even while he was eating. Or the time they both got drunk on cheap beer on the back deck of his parents' house in Rhode Island after her seventeenth birthday party and sat under a full moon listening to the waves in the distance, their fingers dangling centimeters apart, electricity flowing across the slight divide. Or the time he came to her place at NYU unexpectedly, bringing takeout Thai and Scrabble, six years ago. She buzzed him up to her apartment, and he walked in as if he visited her all the time, flinging his coat over the back of the futon and pulling a bottle of wine from a paper bag, while she tried to act casual and set about picking up stray hair-ties and empty soda cans from the tiny area she and her roommates called the living room.

"I hope you have a corkscrew," he said.

"Yes, but I hope you don't mind serving a minor. My birthday isn't for another two weeks."

"I thought it was the twelfth," he said.

"Reverse that," she said. "Twenty first." She fidgeted through the kitchen drawers looking for the corkscrew. Suddenly it seemed like nothing in the kitchen belonged to her. He shifted her entire world off its axis just by showing up.

"Oh," he said.

"It's not my first or anything," she said, pointing to the rack of wine and assorted liquor behind her. "And you know that. You gave me my first beer when I was only seventeen."

"No, it's not that. I just wanted to do it right."

"Do what right?" She moved as if in a dream, still fumbling with wooden spoons and mismatched yard sale measuring cups, until the sharp tip of the corkscrew pricked her index finger.

"Nothing. I brought Scrabble. Let's play."

With the wine opened, they settled down on either side of the coffee table. Well, at least he settled down. He sat on the futon, his basketball-playing body taking up the full space with knees spread wide. She sat on the floor across from him, wishing for all the world that she had washed her hair that morning; she felt a few escaped strands from her ponytail press against her cheeks. She hoped it wasn't too greasy; each year it grew darker and darker, the blonde of her youth disappearing to mouse brown. Grease only amplified the effect.

But he didn't seem to notice her hair or that she was in her pajamas. He handed her a container of Pad Thai and shook out his seven letters.

And after a few minutes and few sips of wine, she stopped caring, too. He launched into a story about selling bonds that ended with a bad joke about handcuffs.

She laughed at his joke. With him, she didn't have to be so grown up.

"So," he said, "has this writing program made you any better at Scrabble?"

They played with focus, only stopping to pass out a second round of spring rolls and to steal a bottle of wine from her roommates' personal stash.

Miranda played mystery on a double word score with a blank tile. "Bingo," she chorused. "Fifty points." She hopped up to do a victory dance. As she did, her foot clipped the table, and the tile bag toppled over.

They both bent to pick them up. He smelled like Old Spice, the way her father did before the chemo made her mom's nose too sensitive. "You," Miranda started to say, to ask or to explain why she couldn't stop staring at him.

"You," he said in reply.

Then he leaned in closer and pressed his lips against hers. His eyelashes stirred against her cheeks as he closed his eyes. She leaned in closer. And neither one moved to stop. For a very long moment, lips slightly parted, they breathed in the same air, as they hovered in the sweet spot right after a kiss.

Then his phone went off, startling them both.

He snapped backwards and patted down his pockets for the source of the interruption. He stared at the number. "I think I have to take this," he said. "Some kind of hospital."

As he stood up, his pant leg caught on the edge of the board, bouncing all the letters out of place as he slipped out of the apartment and into the hallway.

For what felt like an hour, she strained to hear his footfalls in the hallway outside.

When he pushed back in, she almost didn't recognize him. He ran a hand through his hair, leaving it standing on end like a man electrocuted. The color in his cheeks disappeared.

"I have to go." He kissed her cheek and grabbed his coat. "I'll be back after your birthday," he said.

Too stunned to say anything, she just watched him go.

She expected him to be back. Her birthday came and went. Her emails and calls went unreturned. She thought for sure that he would show up at Avery's next party with some excuse about work. She would pretend to be mad, but knew she would get over it just to talk to him again. If he didn't want to kiss again fine—well, not fine, but she would deal with that—but it wasn't okay to walk out on their entire friendship.

"Where's Scott?" she asked as Bunny enveloped her in a hug at the front door.

"Scott?" Bunny asked.

"Don't be funny," Miranda said. "You know, your son? I saw him a few months ago, but lately he's been MIA."

"Dear," Bunny called over her shoulder, "do we know a Scott?"

Before Linden could say anything, Stanton stepped into the foyer. "Scotch," he announced. "Did I hear someone request Scotch? I just so happen to have the best bottle right this way. Come along."

Linden shrugged his shoulders at Miranda and followed his wife and best friend into the other room. For the rest of the party, no one mentioned Scott at all. Before she left to go back to the city, Miranda cornered Avery. "Seriously," she asked. "Where is Scott? Why is everyone being so strange?"

Avery put a manicured finger up in front of her lips. "Quiet. Don't let Bunny hear you."

"Why not? What is going on?"

"They say he quit everything and flew out to Oregon. But don't ask. They refuse to speak about it. Linden even talked to your father about redoing his will."

"But why? Why would Scott quit everything?"

"Some trouble with a girl. Drugs."

"A girl? Drugs?"

"It happens," Avery said. "I never expected it from him, but well, sometimes you never know what's going through a person's mind. Please just don't mention it. Let's just hope it blows over."

But it didn't blow over. Or hadn't for the last six years. Until that email from Avery announced his return.

She tried to conjure up some righteous indignation at the email. A few times, "how dare he" escaped from her lips with barely a whisper as she paced around her apartment the night before. But she wasn't mad at him. Mad, the burning feeling mixed with embarrassment and shame, was an emotion she reserved for herself. What if she was the reason he left and never spoke to them again? What if some girl meant her? With her needy groping of a childhood crush? What if he spared them both further embarrassment with his disappearance? Once again coming to her rescue by being a gentleman. She longed to get on a plane and run far, far away.

She pushed these thoughts from her mind as her students filed into the room. She expected a smaller batch because of the holiday, but this was ridiculous. Out of the eighteen assigned to her section only six sat around the table.

"Hello," she said. "Let's just give everyone a few minutes to arrive."

Clementine, a girl who favored brown sweaters and overly sensible Earth shoes, sat at one end of the table. The red-headed Ronan took up occupancy two seats over from her. The stoner hippie kid who went by Tad sat two seats over from Ronan and so on. No one talked. They pulled out their phones and stared deeply into their radiant screens, content to ignore her and each other.

"Did everyone bring paper?" she asked. This was her fault if they hadn't. At the beginning of the semester, she declared her classroom a paper-free zone. She held her hands over her head, her cell phone sitting majestically in front of her on the table. We will "ping" each other our poems in real time, she proclaimed. The students just nodded, undergraduates, already jaded. Now she could never tell if they were reading the poems their classmates had just sent or if they were surfing for porn or Facebook memes.

"Paper," she said again, waving a few pieces that she pulled from her purse.

Everyone but Tad produced the required sheets and pens. She handed Tad the stack from her purse.

"Pen?" he asked.

Ronan flicked one at him across the table.

"Thank you, Ronan," she said.

"You're welcome," he said, his brogue thick with just a few scant syllables.

Sometimes she picked him to read aloud just to hear him speak. When he did, she could close her eyes and imagine a weekend in Dublin, sitting in a pub, ordering a round of pints for mates and watching football on the television. They cheered in all the right places. When the home squad captured the final victory, the bloke next her let out a whoop in his brogue before sweeping her up for a kiss. When she leaned back to look into her Irishman's eyes, his face always transformed into Scott's.

She shook her head to pull herself back to the present moment. "So did you get my email about the flowers? Let's use those to free write. Open form. Twenty minutes."

She pushed the timer on her phone and left it at her place at the table. Normally she wrote with them, using the exercises to push herself, maybe even to compete against them. But today, with just these six, her heart wasn't in it.

Instead, she stood by the window and contemplated the growing darkness of the evening. Again, the lure of cancelling on her family and just showing up at the airport pulled at her. She could just book a ticket right there for the next plane out, even if it was headed for someplace unexciting like Cincinnati. She wouldn't have to think about Scott Cramer in Cincinnati.

Ronan coughed the kind of cough you get from a multiyear cigarette habit. Miranda turned her head slightly, catching his eye to make sure he was okay. He pointed with his pencil toward Clementine who had drawn herself up into a ball. The hem of her skirt opened around her like tulip petals. Miranda saw the torn and ripped crotch of her tights. Tad angled himself for a better view, completely ignoring the blank paper and pen in front of him.

"Don't forget time of year, now. Are these flowers natural? Tad? Your thoughts?"

"I don't know," Tad stammered, still not taking his off Clementine.

Miranda strode across the room and placed a hand on Clementine's shoulder, pretending to look over her work. She stood there a bit too long, just enough to make the girl shift uncomfortably.

"Good, good," Miranda said. She hadn't read a word from the girl's page, but it probably was good, usually was good. And frankly it was just an exercise, what did it matter anyway?

The twenty-minute timer sounded, and all six promptly put down their pens, breathing a sigh of relief.

"You know," Miranda said, "we should probably wrap up. That is if you all don't mind. I know a lot of you are probably leaving town, maybe even have plans to go out tonight."

A few nodded; no one offered any complaints or protests about the early dismissal.

"I'll collect the exercises and read them over break."

They handed her the papers and left the room as

quietly as they had come in.

"Ronan, could you stay a second?" she asked.

"Yes, ma'am," he said in a way that came out more like marm, which somehow made it less insulting than being called ma'am.

"Thank you," she said. "About, you know, before."

"Thank you?" he asked. He took a few steps closer to her. He smelled like pine trees and Ivory soap. Miranda fought the urge to inhale deeply; it wouldn't be professional.

"With Clementine. And Tad."

"Oh, him. Yes, well, anything to help a lady."

"That's nice of you, Ronan."

"It's not just nice. I mean it. Anything to help a lady."

Miranda set the stack of papers down and caught his gaze. He locked his blue eyes on her, a regular Irish Rob Lowe.

"Anything," he said again.

Her cheeks flushed; bowing her head, she rifled through the papers, pretending to organize them. "Oh," she squeaked out. She wished herself some ingénue in a BBC production of Jane Austen or one of the Bronte sisters with flaxen hair neatly arranged instead of perpetually slipping from a ponytail. "Well, have a good Thanksgiving."

"You, too, Miranda," he said. He stood there for a minute, but she fought the urge to look up. After a few awkward moments, he turned and left the room, leaving her with her stack of poems to be graded.

"Good," she thought to herself, "work for the weekend." She would be able to whip them out of her bag and walk off into another room. "I have papers to grade," she imagined calling out over her shoulder. "I really, simply must get this work done to enjoy the break properly."

Her father would nod mutely. Bunny and Linden would understand. A family of lawyers expected people to work all the time. As for Scott, if he did magically re-appear, well, she didn't know what Scott thought, at least not anymore, and frankly, she wished she didn't care.

CHAPTER

2

T₁HAT NIGHT INSTEAD OF PACKING, Miranda opened a bottle of wine and pulled out the Scrabble board and her cell phone. It was the same board that Scott had left some six years earlier, but she didn't really think about that. Well, she did, but only in the back of her mind. Tonight's agenda was work. Serious stuff. Before granting her Ph.D., her committee chair admonished her to play with form. "Be creative and less stiff. Fight the rigidity," he said, the vodka and tonic sloshing over the rim of his noon refreshment. He approved the committee's recommendation to pass her, but added, "To publish, you must be more than what you are." This stung.

At least she graduated, she reasoned with herself, just as she had planned. And she would teach. Also as she had planned. One couldn't expect magic; for someone like her, someone rigid, or as the chair said, stiff, to become a Poet with a capital P, an important person of arts and letters. Just finding poetry would have to be magic enough.

Her poems could be about broken coffee cups on ceramic tile floors, and no one needed to know the shattered mug had been her mother's favorite. When she included an allusion to the dance of the seven veils, chemotherapy danced for death instead of Salome for Herod. But no one else needed to know that—at least not until her drunken committee chair member pushed the issue. He was right; as much as she revealed herself on the page, she also held back, using the metaphors and images to hide her bruised insides.

After earning her doctorate, Miranda didn't touch poetry. She wrote articles on teaching poetry. Started groups that put snippets of poetry in unexpected places like bus station restrooms and interstate rest stops. She read her students' work because she had to. She read her colleagues' work because she had to, but she didn't let poetry seep into her. She didn't let it touch her soul. With her advisor's words, poetry joined the long list of things that failed her, things that couldn't be trusted to remain the same.

When she moved into this new apartment in May, she struggled to stow this Scrabble board in the top of the closet. The box, after years of benign neglect and being transported to six different yet equally squalid apartments, now ripped, and board and letters tumbled to the floor.

She bent to pick up the letters and was startled to find the p, o, e, and m tiles lined up next to her left foot. She lifted them up carefully and placed them on the board. From the m, she added a "y." From that y, she add an "s"; above the "o" an "n." Poem, My, Yes, No. The board spoke for itself. Or rather it spoke for her. Instead of shoving the box up high behind her tennis racquet and indoor soccer shoes, she left it out on the coffee table.

The next night and the night after that, she played with arranging the letters into little free verse poems. Strings of words built together to show something. Each day, she pushed herself. Then the stroke of genius came. Photograph the results. Using Instagram on her phone, she played around with documenting both the words on the board

and the feel by messing with the filters. They were uploaded under the screen name, Blocked Poet. Joy, actual kick-up-her-heels joy, filled her. She raced home each day to play again with the words on the board and the picture. The years of tempering her expectations fell away, leaving her just the pleasure of creating something and sending it out into the world.

She even gained a few followers on the site, those people who attached themselves to any and every early adopter. After a few weeks, they started sharing her word sculptures. Then she linked the Instagram account to Twitter, and her numbers of followers and fans grew even more.

During the first week of the summer term, she looked over Amanda's shoulder as she was supposedly reading Christine's poem on self-harm and shockingly saw her own poem right there on a Facebook wall. Amanda quickly clicked on like and then returned to Christine's work.

Her concentration abandoned her for the rest of that class. She wanted to get online and see exactly where her word sculptures had travelled.

That night, after a hasty dinner consisting of a slice of cold pizza, Miranda logged into the email address for Blocked Poet. She hadn't used her school email address to sign up for Instagram and Twitter—too many horror stories about people being denied tenure or otherwise just embarrassing themselves with pictures online.

She never expected Blocked Poet to turn up among people she knew in real life. The posts were just for fun; some of them might even be embarrassing. But the only way she could see what the people in her life saw was to rejoin Facebook. When she earned her Master's degree, she deleted her Facebook account and all memories of Stephan, the man-boy hybrid she had shacked up with during her last year there.

So she bit the techno-bullet and signed up, as her real self, and walked through all the steps. She even let the computer search her email contacts for friends she might "know." A smattering of current and former students came up, like Amanda and Christine, her father's law firm, and some classmates from high school who kept trying to organize off-year reunions. She hovered the mouse pointer over each one, deciding each time to click. It would be pathetic to have a Facebook account and no friends. She flipped through several screens of these people she may know until she saw it—Scott's picture beaming up at her.

She didn't hover for very long. Friend request sent.

Five months later, and he never clicked on accept. The others accepted, though. And from what Miranda could see, many people she actually knew on Facebook found her Blocked Poet sculptures from Instagram or Twitter and shared them. After the fear of embarrassment wore off, watching them spread across the internet brought her great pleasure; how many poets can watch their works being read in real time? How many poets get their work read at all? Sure, they weren't Nobel Prize-winning caliber confections of words and emotions, but people liked them and shared them with their grandmothers and boyfriends and best friends alike. And for Miranda, that worked better than ignoring poetry altogether. Plus no one ever made the connection between her and the Blocked Poet; she could post whatever sappy word sculptures she wanted without fear.

Miranda took another sip of her wine and began rooting through the tiles. Friend, she laid down, with request off the r. Then sent off the t in request. Waiting, she added from the n in friend. And still from i as the final touch. She photographed it and added a black and white effect before posting.

If Scott wasn't going to respond to her friend request, maybe there would be someone else in the universe who would.

UST ON THE OTHER SIDE of New Haven, the traffic broke up. Miranda's phone kept binging, almost in time to the Christmas music they inexplicably start playing on all the radio stations the day before Thanksgiving. Every time someone shared one of Blocked Poet's sculptures her phone chimed in notification, or as Miranda liked to think, appreciation. Thank you, she said, thank you for making me feel like something I do matters to someone, whoever you are, bluefroggie_2112. She resisted the urge to pick up the phone and look at the recent list.

She swung into the driveway and almost rear-ended a station wagon. Bumper stickers covered the entire backside of the car. Miranda couldn't imagine Avery being friends with anyone who wanted to Visualize Whirled Peas or vote for the Green Party. Maybe the housekeeper had a new car.

She walked through the front door, not knocking, though each time she returned here she felt more and more like she should knock. The blare of some television program from the den hit her; her father, almost deaf, was obviously watching some nature documentary.

"Avery," she called out. "I'm home."

The house smelled clean like every surface had just met a rag soaked in Lemon Pledge.

Avery strutted past on the balcony over the foyer, waving with one hand, cell phone clutched in the other.

With Avery indisposed, Miranda decided to rouse her dad from his television stupor. If he wasn't at work, he liked to be in front of the television. Financial reports, sports programs, and the occasional crime drama. Typical stuff. Though once or twice, she and Avery had come home early and caught him watching Oprah. Sometimes when he gave her advice like, "you should always let the man call back first" or "never wear a short skirt on a first date," Miranda and Avery would chide in unison, "Did you learn that on Oprah?" Her father's rich olive skin would grow pink on the tops of his cheeks and nose, a trait of blushing that both he and Miranda shared.

"Dad," she called out, loudly as she entered the den. Walnut bookshelves lined the room; an espresso leather sofa and plush easy chairs circled a massive, sixty-two inch flat screen, Stanton's only request when Avery redecorated the last time. One room, he said, one room completely arranged to his likes instead of the whim of the latest designer. "A man cave," she said. "How cliché." But she told the designer to do it anyway. Though Avery may look every part the wicked, gold-digging stepmother, she had loved Stanton since the first time they had dinner together at a legal conference two years after Louise passed away. It didn't help that Avery looked much younger than Stanton. For every bit of exercise he avoided, she did double, making their seven-year age difference appear to be fifteen or twenty. After she hit sixty, her hard work really began to show. Their mutual friends got soft in the middle, lost their ability to walk in heels, and started getting their hair cut in very short, manageable dos. Avery instead took up Pilates and started green juicing.

"Dad," Miranda called out again, stepping down into

the sunken room. The plush carpet mimicked walking on thick grass in a forest. She studied the big screen for a moment. A scene from some nature movie where the female penguin gives the male penguin the egg to keep warm played out in full high definition and Dolby sound. The sweeping views of the frozen world and James Earl Jones' heartfelt commentary swallowed Miranda whole; mesmerized, the scene held her transfixed.

"Hello," said a voice that was clearly not her father's.

Miranda looked down. A short girl about six or seven with a chin-length brown bob sat on the chair, a bottle of Coke balanced between her knees. Her eyes were the most stunning shade of green. "Who are you?" the little girl asked.

"Hello," Miranda said. "I'm Miranda. I live here. Well, used to. My parents live here."

"I'm Lynn. They said you were coming soon."

The screen changed to a scene where a polar bear is beaten back by a walrus. Lynn and Miranda turned in unison to stare at the screen. When the polar bear finally stalked off, leaving the walrus pups unharmed, they turned back to each other. "Is my dad around?" Miranda asked.

"Yeah, he's outside with my dad. Golf."

"Oh, golf. Your dad likes golf, too?"

"Just started. Right now he says he is trying to find his Zen with the clubs and just enjoys the walk. I think that means he sucks."

Miranda smiled at this girl, liking her spark. "I just can't get the hang of it. Does your mom golf, too?"

"I don't know."

"She hasn't tried yet?"

"No, I don't know. I don't know her that well. She isn't around."

"Oh," Miranda said, the sting of her own childhood hitting her. "I can understand that. My mom passed away when I was twelve." She regretted saying this immediately. But before she could take it back, the girl spoke.

"I'm sorry," Lynn said. "That's really bad. My mom isn't

dead, though. Almost though I think, but I'm not supposed to know that."

"Oh, oh—" Miranda said. She remembered the limbo of her mother's illness and how hard they tried to hide it at first; her heart ached for this cute button of a girl.

"No, it's okay. I just don't know how you say it. It's not like I don't know who she is. It's more like she doesn't know who I am. She doesn't come around. It's just me and my dad."

"Oh," Miranda said, desperately wanting some other adult to stop this conversation. "Does your dad work with my dad?"

"I don't think so. He said Grandma and Grandpa Cramer wanted us to come here. Something about family friends from way back."

"Cramers? Your grandparents are the Cramers?"

"Yup, me, too. Lynn Louise Cramer."

"Louise was my mother's name. Your grandmother was my mom's best friend."

"Oh," Lynn said, shooting a glance toward the door. Miranda could tell that now Lynn clearly wanted someone to jump in on this conversation, too.

They both heard the back door close and the stamping of feet to warm up.

Stanton's voice boomed out. "I'm just going upstairs to check on Avery and see when Miranda is due."

"Sure, sure," the other man said. "I'll go watch more nature with Lynn."

The light from the rest of the house framed him as he entered the darkened den.

"Scott," she said, pulling herself up straighter.

"Hey," he said. "They said you would be here later."

"It's been a long time," she said. She made a sweeping gesture with her hands to encompass the whole of the room. Lynn didn't notice; she turned back to her video. Butterflies migrated and filled the screen. A soft music to echo what their wings would sound like filled the room.

Miranda hopped up the two stairs to exit the den, but Scott still stood in the doorway. She moved to the left to get past him, just as he moved to his right. They collided. She could smell his cologne, still Old Spice of all things. Neither moved for a very long minute.

"Ah," he gasped. "I can explain."

"Explain, really? I don't think that is even possible," she said, ducking under his arm.

Grabbing her bag from the hallway, she took the stairs to the second floor two at a time and quickly shut the door to her room behind her.

She barely thought Scott would actually show up, and she never expected he would show up early. With a kid. His kid. A kid who didn't have a mother. Or did. But didn't. Miranda shook her head to clear her thoughts. She had wanted him to call her for so long only to find out that he was off starting a family of his own and cutting them all out. Cutting her out. In what universe was that even possible? And what on earth was she supposed to say now? She thought about all her childish fantasies. She cringed, remembering all the times she had imagined him coming back after that night and kissing her again and how many nights she had stayed in, hoping that it would be the night he finally returned her calls. She burned now with both embarrassment and rage. She could have accepted him walking away from his parents, from the Wall Street job, and the life they had always planned for him. It made sense; people rejected their parents' values and joined communes or the Peace Corp. But to run off and start a family? Why did any of them need to be cut out of that part of his life? It didn't make sense. This required answers, but she didn't want them from him; she didn't want anything else from him ever again if she could help it.

She found Avery in the kitchen reading the house-keeper's directions for how to reheat the Thanksgiving dinner that lay spread about the kitchen covered in foil.

A stray blonde hair fell from Avery's bun at the nape of

her neck. Miranda reached over and tucked it back behind her stepmother's ear.

Avery leaned over and kissed Miranda's cheek. "I'm glad you came. Did you meet Lynn? Isn't she just divine? Quite the surprise, but a lovely one!"

"You're taking this very well."

"How else can you take it? Look at that girl! Don't tell me she doesn't make you melt."

"Sure, she's a cute kid. But what on earth is going on here?"

"Dear, it's Thanksgiving, you know that. We're celebrating like we always do."

"No, it's like we used to, only plus one. I thought Bunny and Linden didn't know anyone named Scott. I used to think I did, but I was told not to ask about him anymore."

"It was a very hard time for everyone. You can understand that."

"No, Avery, I can't. All you said was some trouble with a girl. And I'm sorry, but that little girl doesn't look like trouble. You just said so yourself."

Avery sighed. "Please don't be difficult. I have a hard enough time keeping up with Bunny's mood swings through all this. Something changed, and they patched it all up; it's not polite to probe. Bunny asked me to invite them. And I'm glad she did. I missed him, too."

"Seriously? We are just going to pretend the last six years didn't happen."

Avery put down the directions and looked up at Miranda. "Surely, you can't hold a grudge? There's obviously more to this story than we know."

"I can. He was my best friend."

"He still can be. Sometimes you have to forgive."

"Was he married?"

"I don't think so. Bunny and Linden don't really talk about it. You've witnessed that first hand; it's no different for me, either."

Stanton's booming voice filtered in from the foyer.

"Avery," he called.

"In the kitchen," Avery called back.

"Avery, I sure did witness it, but that didn't make it any easier. How can he just show up like nothing happened?"

"I thought you emailed her about this," Stanton said.

"I told her he was coming."

"Miranda, dear, you knew he would be here. Why the fuss?"

Before Miranda could roar back, "why the fuss," a crashing sound came from the den. Avery rushed to the hall. "Is everyone and everything okay?" she asked.

"It's okay," Scott called out. "We're playing Jenga. Come play, too."

Avery returned to the kitchen. "That is not my cup of tea. Speaking of which, Stanton, would you like one? Miranda?"

"I believe I will, dear, and I will stay in the kitchen. Miranda, you go play with them. I can't fathom any game that makes a sound loud enough that I can hear it."

Miranda looked at them. "Are you serious?"

"Come on, Randa Panda," Scott called out from the family room. "It's only a game."

Randa Panda. She thought it wouldn't still feel like this. Like a helium balloon in the place of her stomach, lifting her feet off the ground. She wanted to be angry. Gnashing teeth and sharp words. Or even better, calculated silence and pointed stares. Instead, she felt sixteen again.

"Miranda, I understand you might have feelings about this," Stanton said. "But we should set those aside to enjoy the holiday. This isn't open for discussion. Please be a good host."

Lynn and Scott sat side by side on the floor beside the leather ottoman under the giant television screen. Instead of scenes of butterflies or battling polar bears, college football players ran back and forth. They balanced the Jenga tiles on the teak serving tray that turned the ottoman into a coffee table of sorts. With all the lights on, the den gelled seamlessly with the warm butters and creams of the rest of the house. It was like being inside a carton of caramel swirl ice cream. And Scott and Lynn only completed the tableau.

Lynn leaned over and pulled out a particularly difficult piece from the side near the bottom of the tower. It wobbled slightly but did not fall.

"Whoa, I don't want to go next," Scott said. "Randa, you do it."

"Randa Panda, go on," Lynn said.

He didn't deserve to call her Randa Panda any more, and it certainly wasn't right to use Lynn to smooth things over.

Then Lynn erupted in a fit of giggles. She burrowed her head against Scott's chest to stifle them.

"What's so funny?" Scott asked her.

"Miranda doesn't look like a panda at all," Lynn finally announced after catching her breath. "But I like the way it rhymes. Like a poem."

Miranda felt some of the melting Avery mentioned. "Okay, I'll play," Miranda said. She took a deep breath but didn't move right away.

"Come on, then," Scott said. He locked eyes with her and then turned away.

She took a seat on the opposite side of the ottoman, placing herself in front of Lynn. "So, Lynn, what happens when the tower falls? Do you have anything riding on this game?"

"Riding?" Lynn asked.

"Any wagers or bets." Miranda said.

"Oh, like Daddy and the Gators. He has big money on them tomorrow."

"Oh, sugar, you aren't supposed to mention that," Scott said.

"Mention what?" Miranda asked.

"Daddy's gambling problem," Lynn said in a serious voice before breaking out into more laughter.

"I guess some things never change. Has he told you

about the marshmallow eating bet?" Miranda reached over and pulled out the block opposite the one Lynn just took. The tower now hinged on a single brick, but it did not fall.

"Marshmallow bet?" Lynn asked.

"Yup, your dad wagered my cousin that he could put more marshmallows in his mouth at one time without swallowing them."

"But how do you know if he didn't swallow them?"

"Count them! I counted them going in and then again as he spit them out."

Scott surveyed the Jenga tower very carefully. His hand hovered over piece after piece, backing away from each choice after a few moments.

"You did that?"

"Gross, huh?"

"No, cool! Do you think Mrs. Avery has any marshmallows?"

Scott finally settled on a piece. The tower gave way before he could get the block free. Blocks flew everywhere.

"Loser buys the marshmallows," Lynn and Miranda said at the same time.

"Jinx," Lynn said to Miranda.

"Jinx?"

"Yup, you owe me a Coke. Only I already had a Coke today, and Daddy says only one soda once in a blue moon."

"Blue moon, eh? I think our first meeting deserves some celebration. Maybe I can get him to bend a little?"

"That was quick," Scott said. "I knew you would side with Randa Panda, sugar, I just didn't think it would take all of ten minutes. Girls always stick together, eh?"

"It's not like boys stick around."

"Touché," he said in a whisper. "Who is coming to the store with me to get marshmallows?"

Lynn sprang to her feet. "Shotgun," she said. She quickly added, "But not really, I'm too short. It's back seat city until I break four feet nine inches, if I break four feet nine inches!"

"I don't know," Miranda said. "Your dad's pretty tall. You might make it."

Lynn shook her head. "My ma was really short, though, four eleven. Right, Daddy?"

Scott winced a little. "Yup, sugar. Four eleven. Are we getting these marshmallows or what?"

Lynn galloped toward the door of the den. Miranda watched her, hanging back. "I'll just wait here," she said. "I don't think I'm ready for this. There's a lot I don't understand."

"I told you I could explain," Scott said, looking down.

"I want to believe that, Scott, but I can't even imagine a reason that it would be better for you to stop talking to me, to all of us, especially a reason that included Lynn. Why wouldn't you have wanted her to be a part of our family?"

Lynn bounced back in with her puffy winter coat zipped all the way up. She bounced around Scott's feet, making a circle around him.

"It wasn't my choice," Scott said. "But give me a chance. Later?" He shifted his eyes toward Lynn.

"Daddy, are we going? Are we going? Are we going?" Lynn began to chant.

Miranda nodded to Scott.

Miranda found Avery and her Dad watching television in Avery's den, a room decorated to look like a Victorian tea parlor. Several tea sets littered the room on strategically placed antique tables. Their last housekeeper took one look at this room and asked for a raise. But in the middle of the room sat an oversized chair. Avery curled up next to Stanton, her legs in his lap. Tiger Woods and his caddy filled the television screen.

"So," Avery said. She shifted in the chair to be more upright.

Miranda knew it was coming. The cross examination.

"You honestly had no idea about Lynn?"

"None."

"You mean to tell me in this time of instant communication, all this social media and what have you, you and Scott never once even emailed?" Avery asked.

Stanton picked up the remote and muted the television.

"I tried. He wouldn't write me back. And you both made it clear that this subject was not to be broached. In this day and age of tolerance, did Bunny and Linden really disown their son for having a baby out of wedlock? Did I lose my best friend because of some Puritan ideal?"

Her father chortled. "Well, that's putting it square on the nose."

"Yeah, but why did we have to spend the last six years pretending Scott never existed?" Miranda asked. "What happened?"

"I don't really have the full story, but it wasn't just Lynn. It was something about the mother and drugs. They didn't want the woman using his trust fund for drugs, so they cut it off. Then Scott blew up and vowed to never speak to them again," Stanton said. "Ugly, ugly, ugly, but somehow some common sense finally sunk in on both sides."

"I still don't understand how we got disowned in the process, too."

"Drugs do terrible things to a person, and I couldn't be sure Scott wasn't using, too," Stanton said. "I thought that it might be for the best."

"What do you mean you thought it might be for the best? What did you do, Daddy?"

"I always knew that boy had eyes for you. I teased him constantly. I warned him to keep his distance until you were of legal age. But I am not daft. I saw the way you always followed after each other. I knew it would happen sooner or later. But when this unpleasantness happened, I asked Linden to deal with it. I couldn't have you caught up in that mess, too."

Avery stood up and joined Miranda staring at Stanton in disbelief. "Stanton, you never told me this. You told him

BRANDI MEGAN GRANETT

not to talk to her? How could you?" Avery asked.

"You couldn't trust me? You went behind my back and arranged things?" Miranda asked.

"He was spiraling out of control. I did not want you to lose out," Stanton said.

Scott entered the room with Lynn up on his shoulders. She held the bag of marshmallows up high. "Who is losing? Tiger Woods again?" Scott asked.

"Just a case," Stanton said. "You remember, sometimes you find yourself on the wrong side of the jury."

"It's been a long time since I was in that position," Scott said. "Can't say I miss it much."

"Well, I for one must go back to it right now," Avery said.

Stanton's phone rang as if on cue; he waved as he followed Avery out of the room.

Miranda and Scott stood there staring at each other. After what she had just heard, she had no idea what to say. Her father made him leave her alone. And Scott let them do that. Part of her wanted to grab her things and leave the house. She couldn't imagine staying here with any of them. She eyed the door just behind him.

"Don't leave," Scott said. "I don't know what they told you, but don't leave."

Lynn said, "Miranda, don't leave! We have the booty!"

"Booty? Are you a pirate?" Miranda asked, trying to change the subject.

"They celebrated 'International Talk like a Pirate Day' at school. What can you do?" Scott said.

"But Daddy, it was your idea! You told Mrs. Jean all about it."

"Oh, what can you do, eh?" Miranda said.

"Aye, Captain, but I come only for hospitality and merriment. No plundering or pillaging in sight save this bag of marshmallows," Scott said.

"Arg!" Miranda said, deciding to play along. She crooked her finger at Lynn. "And you wee lass, you come to plunder

26

the kitchen of turkey on the morrow?"

"Urgh, captain, no siree, I come for thee sweet potatoes. The candied sweet potatoes."

"Good choice, good choice."

Lynn slid off Scott's shoulder. "Shall we do the marsh-mallows now?"

"First go take your vitamins. They are in your bag upstairs. Grab a bottle of water from the fridge where Mrs. Avery showed you."

Lynn heaved out a heavy sigh. "All right. I knew that was coming." She slunk out of the room defeated.

"She'll only be gone a minute, and I really can't talk about this in front of her," Scott said.

"I just don't understand, Scott. What happened? Why didn't you talk to me?"

"My father made it pretty clear you didn't want to talk to me. He made it sound like you thought I was a deranged drug addict."

"A drug addict? I didn't know anything about that. I sent you all of those emails. I called."

"Emails? That was my address at the firm. I wasn't allowed to forward anything. I couldn't afford the phone, so I had it turned off."

They heard Lynn start down the top of the stairs.

"Can we talk about this later?" he asked, looking over his shoulder.

"You keep saying later. Just tell me this. What changed? Why are you back now?"

"She needed a family," he said. "If it's what she needs, I can forgive them. For our sake, I'd ask you to do the same. Or at least pretend this weekend."

She studied his face. He looked older and probably a little tired. But she saw the face of the person she always believed to be her other half. He balanced out every ounce of her seriousness with unadulterated enthusiasm. For all of his wild schemes, she held the set of detailed plans to make them happen. A pair. A team. At least they once were.

She knew in her heart she could never deny Scott.

"Vitamins all taken," Lynn announced. "Now for the challenge. Randa Panda, you go first. How many can you fit into your mouth without swallowing? Daddy will count since he made you do it last time."

"Me?"

"Yes, taking turns is fair."

"That's right, taking turns is fair. Do they teach you that at school?"

"Yes. We have to take turns at each of the stations, and we take turns with the different teachers. But I don't get a turn in Daddy's class because he is mine."

"Daddy's class?"

"Yup. Third grade!"

"I'm a Montessori teacher now," Scott said.

"Yes, everyone loves him. Even my teacher, Mrs. Jean! But she's a Mrs. and not a student so she can't love him like everyone else. He even coaches the soccer team. I'm the manager."

"Manager, that's an important job."

"I make sure everyone shows up on time and has the right equipment and eats a healthy snack. We aren't allowed to have chips or cookies."

"Lynn, don't talk Miranda's ear off—are we going to do this dare or what?"

"She's not talking my ear off; I like hearing what she has to say. I'd love to know more about your life now. Clearly, I've missed a lot."

"I'd love to know more about your life, too," Scott said. He lifted his eyes to meet hers.

One glance took her breath away. "Sure," Miranda finally said. "Where are those marshmallows?"

ATER THAT NIGHT AFTER A DINNER of takeout Chinese food, Miranda slipped upstairs to her room, leaving everyone to retire to Stanton's den to watch another nature video. She wanted to get a few more poems posted before Thanksgiving. Responsibility to her followers tugged at her. She liked the idea of making someone smile while they basted the turkey or sat through an uncomfortable meal with a tipsy aunt. Even with the door shut, she heard Avery's pretend complaint that, "Oh, animals are gross." And the whispers of Lynn's insistency that, "No, they are not."

Something about Lynn being there made the whole holiday seem better, more like a holiday should be. Something about her easy laugh and endless excitement reminded Miranda of her mom and how they had celebrated holidays before everything ended.

Miranda pulled out her Scrabble board from home. She dumped the tiles out on her bed and swirled them around. She made random words and tried stringing them together. But nothing made sense. Nothing gelled. They just sat there looking back up at her. On a good night of "writing," she could fill the board connecting thought after thought in a Scrabble free verse. Today nothing. She leaned back into the plush pillows and closed her eyes. She must have drifted to sleep because when her eyes fluttered awake, Scott was peeking his head into her room.

"Miranda?" he asked.

At first, she couldn't answer. The whole day slipped from her mind during her rest. Then she remembered. Him. Here. Lynn. "Hey," she said. "What time is it?"

"Ten thirty. I just wanted to know if you were up for an adventure."

"An adventure?" She still wasn't fully awake.

"Wear warm clothes," he said. He ducked back out of her room.

Downstairs, she found Lynn in her puffy pink parka clutching a long stainless steel thermos.

"Cocoa," she said holding it up. "Daddy says we're going to take the train. Mr. Stanton gave us his pass."

"The train?" Miranda asked.

Scott came up behind her. "We're going to Central Park."

"To see the balloons," Lynn squealed.

"Have fun," Avery called from the foyer balcony. She had finally switched from her lawyer uniform to a purple terry cloth robe.

"We will?" Miranda asked.

"Yes, we will," Scott said. He put his hands on her shoulders, giving them a squeeze before spinning her around toward the door.

The walk from the train station was crisp to say the least. Something about the wind whipping through the tall buildings and the concrete losing all the day's trapped heat quickly at dusk made walking in Manhattan like walking in a refrigerator. Lynn huddled between them as they walked. Her thick coat and warm boots gave her a wobbly bop; she alternated between bouncing into Scott and bouncing into Miranda.

"You sure you don't want to take a cab?" Scott asked her.

"I'm sure. Then we wouldn't see the diamonds," Lynn said.

"Tiffany's?" Miranda asked. "You're a little young for that aren't you? Though you are Bunny's granddaughter."

"Not like Grandma Bunny's diamonds! The diamonds on the sidewalk. Look!"

Sure enough, the concrete in front of them sparkled. Four or five runs of sidewalk shimmered with mica flecks, then it went to plain for a block or two, then more that sparkled.

"I want to know what makes them different," Miranda said to Scott, pointing at the abrupt change from sparkle to non-sparkle on the sidewalk in front of them.

"But knowing the difference would ruin it," Scott said.

"You'd rather think it was magic?"

"I like the idea of magic. Don't you?" he asked.

"I don't take much stock in that," Miranda said.

"Daddy, look!" Lynn said.

And there in front of them was a huge elephant balloon with a circus ball balancing on his trunk. The ball wasn't all the way inflated yet; it wobbled a little and the sides of the elephant shuddered some as the helium pumped in. But an elephant as tall as a house at Central Park was a sight to behold no matter the size or amount of helium left to go. The crowd around them seemed to holding their breath in anticipation as the ball slowly rose.

"See," Miranda said, "to people watching on television that's magic. But it's not magic. It's a year of planning and then people working all night on the day before a family holiday to pull it off."

"But it's magic to her," Scott said.

Lynn strained at the barricade, craning her neck to see down the street and the rest of the balloons staged there.

"Sure, it's magic to her. She's a kid. Kids have to believe in magic. When you really grow up, it's different."

"I guess I'm not really grown up then," Scott said. "And maybe I don't want to be."

"So you haven't changed?" she asked.

"Whoa, that's a little unfair. But maybe I haven't, not on the inside. You haven't either, Randa. We're still like yin and yang, don't you think?"

She did think so, but she didn't want to admit that, at least not out loud. At least not yet.

They rounded the corner, and there was Kermit the Frog, face forward with a huge fisherman's net weighing him down. The air inside the balloon shifted, and it looked like Kermit was breathing. For a second, Miranda imagined him lifting up his head and saying, "Hi ho, Kermit the Frog here."

"Wow," Lynn said. "Look at Kermit. He's bigger than a bus. Two buses!" Lynn rushed forward to the barricade and the mass of people congregated there. "Look they have to hold him down. It's just like trying to keep your balloon at the carnival. Only, bigger. A lot bigger." Lynn bounced up and down and clapped.

Miranda couldn't help herself; she clapped, too.

"Turn around, you two," Scott called. He held up his phone and snapped a picture of them clapping in front of Kermit.

They moved up the row. Hello Kitty, only partially inflated, incited a sort of polka from Lynn. She galloped around Miranda and Scott spouting facts about Hello Kitty and her twin sister, Mimmy.

"I didn't even know Hello Kitty had a sister," Miranda whispered to Scott as they moved up the row to Sonic the Hedgehog.

"You learn lots of things when you have a kid," he said.

"About Hello Kitty?"

"Yes, and other important stuff. Like this." He gestured to the space between them. "I'm glad you came tonight."

"I'm not allowed to play that," Lynn said pointing one mitten-covered hand at Sonic. She didn't dance, but instead turned her nose up at Sonic and kept going.

"Who is that?" she asked, pointing to the Pink Panther.

Scott started to hum the theme song and slink up the sidewalk, looking side to side like a detective on the watch.

Lynn watched; her brow furrowed as she looked from her Dad to the balloon.

"He's a detective," Miranda said.

"A pink cat detective?" Lynn asked.

"Yup, it's hard to explain. You have to see it. Maybe we can watch it together one day. As you can tell, it's one of your dad's favorites."

"Really?" Lynn asked. "I'd like that."

Lynn's pace slowed, and the crowd surrounding the balloons started to thin out. Almost all the balloons were inflated. The workers even started to break down some of the barricades and head home for a few hours of sleep before the big day.

"Tell me a story about my dad," Lynn said, snuggling next to Miranda on the train home. Scott sat across from them, holding his head in his hands, faking concern.

"You don't want to hear any of her stories," he said.

"But, Daddy, you said she tells the best stories. You said she was a writer. A real writer, exact quote!"

"She does tell the best stories, but not about me."

"Really? Not about you?" Miranda asked. "Let me find a good one."

"I knew you would do it, Randa. You're my best friend."

"Best friend? I like that. Shake on it." Miranda extended a gloved hand.

Lynn shook off her mitten. "No glove," she said. "We have to do this for real."

"Okay, for real," Miranda said, removing her glove and accepting the shake. But it wasn't any ordinary handshake; Miranda remembered it clearly. Lynn first moved Miranda's hand up and down, then curled her fingers into a fist. They tapped their fists together, first Lynn's on top, then Miranda's on top. Then they flipped their hands and touched the backs of their hands together before wiggling their fingers over their heads.

"That's a story I could tell you about your Dad. I could tell you where that handshake came from."

"I remember that," Scott said. "We were just kids."

"I was eight," Miranda said. "I had just gotten back from that disastrous summer camp with the horses."

"Horses," Lynn chimed in. "I love horses."

"I love horses, too," Miranda said, "But I don't love jumping over things while on a horse."

"They made you do that?"

"Yup, until I fell off and broke my arm."

"Wowzer," Lynn said. "That smarts."

"Smarts indeed. And it meant I couldn't go swimming that summer when we went to the beach. But your dad, even though he loves swimming, he stayed with me on the deck the entire trip. We made a fort to keep out of the sun and everything. Your dad named it Randa's Cove. We demanded Oreo cookies and portage to the ice cream store for passage to the other side of the deck and the propane grill."

"Like a pirate's fort?"

"Exactly, but we needed a secret handshake to protect it. You can't let just anyone into your fort, you know."

Lynn's head started to lean more heavily against Miranda's shoulder. She nodded a little. "Uh huh," she mumbled.

"So we worked out the handshake. It didn't use to have the wiggling fingers at the end though; we added that when your Grandpa Linden started to figure it out."

Lynn's eyes closed, and her breathing shifted to the slow rhythm of sleep. Miranda looked up to see Scott smiling at them.

"How did you wind up with this magical kid?" Miranda

asked. "Eventually, you are going to have to tell me."

"Shhh," Scott said. "We don't want to wake her. It's late." He reached across and squeezed her knee. "Thank you for tonight," he said, before leaning his head against the window and closing his eyes.

Miranda steadied herself; she didn't want to move and break the spell.

At the house, Scott carried Lynn out of the car. He waved to Miranda at the top of the landing and disappeared into the guest room furthest from hers. She watched the door close softly. With no other sounds in the house, it was easy to pretend this night didn't just happen. Maybe it was better, safer even, to believe that there was no magic in the world, nothing exceptional, nothing worth noting year to year.

The Scrabble board remained out on her bed. She pulled out some tiles and spelled out magic. Magic, cannot, hold.

5

N THE MORNING, Lynn knocked twice, then leapt across the hardwood floor, to the Persian rug, and landed in the middle of Miranda's comforter.

"Best friend," she whispered, "it's time."

Miranda glanced at the clock on the nightstand. Too early, much too early. "Time?" she asked.

"The parade. We must see our new friends from last night. Please come."

"Lynn," Scott called out, trying to whisper, but failing. "Lynn," he said again, this time a hiss.

Lynn burrowed under Miranda's duvet, signaled a shush with one slender finger over her beautifully pink lips. Miranda sat up, grabbed her phone, and stared at it, pretending to be keying a vital, supremely urgent text. Scott poked his head in. Without knocking.

"Randa," he said.

"Umm," she said. She held up the universal symbol for one minute. Luckily, pillows filled the bed. Lynn could hide, and if no one saw her arrival they wouldn't know. If she stayed as still as a pillow, that is.

"Oh," he said. "Sorry." And he pulled his head back out of the room.

Miranda and Lynn both took a deep breath. They let it out with a flurry of giggles.

Scott quickly poked his head back in. "I knew it," he said. "The parade starts in ten. I'm making French toast, not that you sneaks deserve any."

"I'll help," Lynn said. "I'll cut the shapes." She climbed out of bed and marched toward him.

"Take your vitamins," Scott called out.

"No," Lynn said.

"Take them or no parade."

"No," she said again.

"Scott, it's a holiday. Relax," Miranda said.

"Randa. Don't. Lynn, vitamins now."

Miranda heard her heavy footsteps across the hall.

"Wow. You're tough."

"Not now, Miranda."

"No really, an ogre routine before nine in the morning? She was just waking me up for the parade. I didn't mind. You don't have to be so mad at her."

"I'm not. Just drop it, okay? I'm not mad at her. She just needs to take her vitamins."

"Vitamins? Really?"

"Yeah, okay, can you drop it? It's none of your business." Then he turned his back to her and shut the door to her bedroom. The hollow thud filled the room. Something caught in her throat.

When Miranda finally got downstairs, the marching bands were in full swing. Lynn sat in the middle of the den, staring up at the screen, her plate of French toast untouched in front of her.

"Eat, sugar. It will help," Scott said.

"It never helps," she said.

Scott put his arm around Lynn, who started to cry.

Miranda stepped back from the den, afraid to interrupt.

When Bunny Cramer arrived, the whole town knew it. Maybe all of Connecticut knew it. Perhaps the earth tremors with the anticipation of her every word just as Bunny Cramer believed it should. Today, she appeared in the foyer, an old-school fox stole draped around her shoulders and her outfit a splendor of russet wools and earthy plaids like something from a British hunting catalogue. "Darlings," she called out. "I am Thanksgiving, and I am here."

To Miranda, Bunny would have made an excellent drag queen. Her impeccable taste, over-the-top attitude, and ability to captivate a room made her a star of whatever constellation she orbited. She and Louise joined sides at a girlhood summer camp and never once let anything get in the way of their lifelong friendship. Despite her fancy clothes and big personality, Bunny held Louise's hand through vomiting after chemo, helped her shave her head, and tried to teach Miranda that the world still had light even though Louise had left it. For this, Miranda would always love Bunny Cramer, even though at the moment she would like to scream at her. And Linden. And her father. Still, she got up and went out to the foyer.

Lynn apparently had the same idea. "Grandma Bunny," she squealed.

"Granddaughter Lynn!" Bunny squealed back.

They stood face to face and jumped up and down.

Bunny raised a hand out like a stop sign. "Let me see your outfit," she said.

Lynn stopped bouncing. She wore a pink sweatshirt with a yellow star in the center and pink sweat pants with a rainbow stripe down both legs. Her rainbow socks had slots for each individual toe. She wiggled her toes, her energy and desire to move barely contained.

Bunny looked her up and down. "Really, Miss? Don't you think you'd rather try on this?" From a bag at her feet, Bunny pulled out a gorgeous green velvet dress with ivory lace trim. Even on a hanger you could tell the skirt would be perfect for twirling. "You brought tights, right? I told you to on the phone."

Lynn resumed bouncing. "Yes, yes, yes. I did. I brought the tights. New ones!! Can I go change?"

"You certainly may. But hug me first."

Lynn flung herself at Bunny, crushing the dress and burying her face in the fur stole. She pulled back a little, and then reached up a tiny hand to pet the fur. "Real?" she asked.

"Do you need to ask?"

"Oh," Lynn said, taking the dress.

"Go change, I'm dying to see my pretty granddaughter done up right."

Lynn rushed past Miranda, holding up the dress. "Randa Panda, look!"

Before Miranda could respond, Lynn rocketed up the stairs.

"Randa Panda," Bunny said. "I see Scott is still as suave as ever and passing it on to the child."

"I don't mind," Miranda said. "She's a neat kid."

"Of course, she is! Would my grandchild be any less?"

"Never, Bunny." Miranda stood amazed at this transformation. How could you go from denying a child's existence to insisting on her excellence?

"Well, then Miranda, give me a hug."

Scott emerged from the den. "Mom," he said; his tone bordered on cool. Then he ducked back into the den, and the sound of football announcers poured out of the room.

"Men," Bunny said. She shrugged a little, and the head of the fox appeared to be winking at Miranda. She hoped Bunny would ditch the fox sometime before dinner.

Scott and Lynn watched football and the nature video on the split screen. They were oddly juxtaposed. A lion rushed a herd of zebras as a Clemson Tiger running back split through a Texas Longhorn defensive line.

"Hey," Lynn said. "Technology compromise."

"Those are big words," Miranda said.

"Daddy's," Lynn said. "Anyway I like football, too. Sometimes they show the marching band."

Scott flicked off the picture in picture. "Sugar, you can have the television. I'm going to go upstairs and check some emails." Miranda watched him go, wondering how many times you could miss someone before you stopped caring.

"Will you watch with me?" Lynn asked. "I promise this is a good part."

The comfort of the den and soothing sounds of the animal kingdom won out over the sounds of dinner being prepared in the kitchen. Miranda listened to Avery and Bunny bicker about the temperature for reheated foods until finally Linden boomed, "Just make the gravy really hot, and we'll put it on everything."

"Girls, dinner," Stanton called. "Scott?"

"Come on, Lynn—let's get while the getting's good."

"I love turkey," she said. "We try to be vegetarians, but Daddy said we could skip it this weekend. We skip when we go out for Italian food, too."

Vegetarian, Montessori School Teacher, vitamin crazy, Subaru driving, Oregon living. Hipster, she thought, a health-nut hipster. A far cry from the boy she remembered. And until this morning, she thought she really liked him. Not that she had ever stopped liking him. It was more that she forgot about liking him for a while. Forgot about waiting for him to come back. Sitting home her entire twenty-first birthday just in case he showed up again like magic or even just called.

She sat at the table and passed the food around and scalded her tongue on the hotter than hell gravy, which did indeed do the trick as after that it didn't matter what temperature all the other food was. She watched Scott spoon food onto Lynn's plate and refill his mother's wine glass. Every time his glance caught hers, she looked away, asked for the salt to be passed, or dropped her napkin. The others probably talked, probably said something about the weather or the news or what's going on in the stock market, but Miranda didn't hear them.

"Can you pass the wine?" she asked Bunny.

"So, Miranda, what's new in the poetry world? Anything to write home about?" Linden laughed at his own joke. Avery and Stanton kept eating. They never really understood why she picked poetry over the law.

"Well, actually, I'm doing this thing. Online."

"A thing? A poetry thing?" Bunny asked.

"Yes and no. It's poetry and pictures. I'm creating word sculptures on a Scrabble board, then I photograph them and share them online."

"Oh, your friends must like that," Linden said. "Can you pass the pearl onions?"

"Not just my friends, really; it has kind of taken off."

Scott pulled out his phone and started typing.

"Honestly, Scott, not at the table. It's Thanksgiving. You're as bad as your father about work. What kind of school emergency could there be on Thanksgiving?"

"Thanks, Mom," Scott said. "Like this?" He held up his phone to Miranda.

"Not like that. It *is* that."

"You're Blocked Poet?" He typed in some more and held up it up again. "This is you?" He held up her overly sappy tribute to an unanswered friend request.

"I want to see," Lynn said. "Oh, what did you do to make the picture look so old? Did you drop it in water?"

"No, it's a feature on the camera." Miranda said. "I just want the pictures to match the mood."

Scott took his phone back from Lynn. He flipped to another one of her poems. "This, too?"

"Yes, I'm the Blocked Poet. It's just me. No one else. I didn't think anyone paid much attention to it, but—"

"You have fifty thousand Twitter followers. Fifty thousand." He shook his head.

"Yes, and more on Facebook and Pinterest and Instagram. So?" She didn't want there to be a tone in her voice, but there was.

"That's a good thing, no?" Avery asked. "This work is popular?"

"Yeah, it's a good thing," Scott said. "If you have the right team in place. You can even make money on it."

"Money, how? I'm a poet, remember?"

"You know—ads on your website, links that point back to it, tie-in products. Some of this would sell great on the side of a coffee cup. A friend does this. You know the cat with the angry face? He did that. And most of the deals for that duck-hunting family, too."

"The ones with the beards?" Avery asked.

"The cats have beards?" Bunny asked.

"No, Grandmom Bunny, the cat is grumpy. The duck hunters have beards. And toilet paper with their faces on it at Wal-Mart."

"Scott, are you saying that people would be wiping their asses on my daughter's face?" Stanton asked.

"No, it's not like that. The products match the brand. Miranda, you understand, right? Give me your email, and I'll send you his stuff. Or just look him up on Facebook."

Facebook. The mention kind of stung. Miranda just nodded.

"I never use mine," Scott explained. "Too many teachers get in trouble for that. But look up my friend, Ambrose Reed. I think he puts a Q in as a middle initial, as if there are a ton of Ambrose Reeds in the world he needs to distinguish himself from."

"Thanks," Miranda said. "It's probably not that important. It's just me and a Scrabble board. But thanks."

Scott rolled his eyes. "Whatever," he said. "You should think about it."

"Well," Stanton said, "I must be getting old. I don't even understand the concepts being discussed. Nor do I care to, but congratulations to Miranda anyway. Now young people, clear the table and bring out the pie."

She followed Scott and Lynn to the kitchen. Miranda

began unwrapping the apple pie, while Scott and Lynn pulled out the ice cream.

Scott struggled to make a dent in the vanilla ice cream.

"Is there an ice cream scoop?" Lynn asked.

"I don't think so," Miranda said. "Avery doesn't eat much ice cream."

The tablespoon bent under the force. "Shit," Scott said under his breath, before quickly adding, "Don't listen to Daddy, sweets."

"Here, let me help," she said. "I know a trick."

Scott looked up. "No, that's okay," he said. "I got this. I don't need any help."

He pulled out another spoon. This time, he scrapped a little off, dotted the slice of pie Miranda set in front of him.

"Seriously, if you just run the spoon under hot water it melts the ice cream some."

"I'll do it, Daddy. I'll heat up the spoon."

"I said I got this. You aren't the only one who doesn't need any help, Miranda."

Miranda watched him chop at the ice cream, making more shavings than scoops. He refused to meet her gaze.

"Okay," she said, "Fine. Please tell them I didn't I want any dessert."

She turned and went up to her room. All she had hoped for was a little bit more of last night: some of their old friendship, a little bit of conversation, a chance to catch up about the last six years. But maybe the less he knew about her the better. And vice versa. She didn't need anything more Scott Cramer-related to think about. In the morning, she would pack her small bag and leave, chalking this holiday up as a wash. Belize looked better and better for next year.

CHAPTER

6

ACCORDING TO THE WEATHER ALERT on her phone, the forecasters were calling for an early and heavy snow. She packed up her stuff before she went down to find Avery and Bunny having coffee in the tea parlor, television tuned to the weather station.

"Glad we're in for the weekend," Bunny said. "I would hate to be out in this mess."

"I hope Scott and Lynn didn't have any traffic last night," Avery said.

"Good thing they left," Bunny added. "But I miss being with Lynn this morning. Even with all that drama, I love that little girl."

"They left?" Miranda blurted out. "I didn't get a chance to say goodbye to Lynn?"

"He knocked, but you were asleep," Avery said. "Said he didn't want to bother you and that he was really worried about the storm, but I think he just didn't want to play golf this morning."

"Silly men, going out on a day like this." Bunny picked up her coffee and took a deep sip to finish it up. "Miranda, can you be a dear and get me a refill?"

Miranda took the cup and headed into the kitchen. She filled Bunny's cup and her own. She listened to the empty house. Stanton and Linden off golfing or smoking cigars in the clubroom, Bunny and Avery cocooned in front of the television on the storm watch, Scott and Lynn gone. She played yesterday over in her mind. Why did he even bother to come back?

They used to tell each other everything from their imaginations about undersea voyages to what made them afraid about growing up. How many hours did they spend just talking? Being in the city together reminded her of how good it felt to just be with him like he was still her best friend, the one person she could say anything to. But time changes everything. She took a sip of her coffee only to find it had gone cold. She dumped both cups and started the process again.

"We were starting to worry," Bunny said.

"But not enough to come and check," Avery said.

"Had to brew a fresh pot." Miranda hated lying, but there was no point in telling them what she was thinking about it. There was no way to form the questions she wanted to ask. And no guarantee they would even answer, given the history of Scott as a subject in this house.

"I'm going to head out then. Get back to town before the storm."

"But dear," Avery said. "It won't be safe."

"Look, they say it won't really start to snow heavily until three. I'll be home well before that."

Outside on the dashboard of her car, she found a note on pink paper. Lynn, she thought, a smile crossing her face. Instead of a crayoned drawing, though, she found a name: Ambrose Q. Reed. She crumpled up the note and tossed it into her purse.

Traffic crawled through the snow that arrived earlier and heavier than predicted. After searching in vain for normal music, Miranda punched the radio off. It was still

November, too soon for Christmas carols, and she felt like a bah-humbug anyway.

She eased her car off the highway and down the winding main street to the tiny parking lot in front of the apartment. She lived on the first floor of a once grand Victorian now carved into apartments. Aside from the beautiful windows, the house's main charm stemmed from its location next to a liquor store. She stood outside her car for three full minutes just staring at the sight of her snow-covered town, grateful to be off the interstate and into the silence that descends with snow. Snow muffled everything, though not her hurt feelings. She would need alcohol for that. Turning to walk toward the store, she kept her eyes focused above her, watching the fat, fluffy flakes fall, until her shoulder collided with something solid.

"Miranda," a familiar voice said.

"Ronan?" she asked.

"Me in the flesh. And in the snow."

"Good Thanksgiving?"

"Don't really celebrate. Irish and English. My people booted your pilgrims out."

"Oh," she said. She moved to step around him. "Well, see you in class next week."

"What are you doing tonight?" he asked.

"Tonight?"

"You know, like today. Later."

"Um, well to be honest, I had a bit of a day yesterday. I was thinking about getting home and drinking. You?" she said.

"Drinking sounds like a plan. I'm Irish."

"You keep saying that."

"How about I prove it? Let me take you someplace."

"Like a bar?" Miranda asked.

"Yes, yes, a bar. Have you ever had a car bomb?"

Instead of turning into the liquor store, Ronan led her up the sidewalk, heading out of town. The shops became more sparse, giving way to houses packed tightly together.

He made a left turn, led her down another block, to a building shaped like all the other houses on the street, only instead of siding, the lower half featured rock-studded cement. Glass blocks lined the top and served as windows. In one, neon advertised Miller, Made the American Way.

"Here?" she asked.

"Trust me," he said.

I don't think so, she almost replied, but instead she ducked under his arm as he opened the red padded door. She wanted a drink. Two drinks. Maybe more.

A few people sat at the far corner of the bar under the Pronto Lotto screen. They didn't look up. They barely moved except to flick away their losing cards and draw another set.

Ronan eyed the group. "Let's sit here," he said, pointing to the far end of the bar. He placed his hand on the small of her back and guided her toward two open stools. A quick spark passed through him into her; goose-bumps ran down her arms, making her grateful that she still wore her coat.

The bartender, an older lady with her gray curls in the classic wash and set, slowly made her way over to them. "The usual?" she asked.

"Not tonight, Lucille," he said. "Car bombs today."

"You know I don't make that crap," she said.

"Let me."

"It's not even Irish," Lucille said. "That's just some American crap."

"Yes, woman, I know. But that's beside the point."

"And the point is to get drunk, I suppose," Lucille said.

"This is a bar, isn't it?" Ronan asked, a smile broad on his face.

"If you weren't cute, I wouldn't let you in here. But you start singing, Jesus, Mary, and Joseph, I'll kick you out again."

"Again?" Miranda asked.

"Ssshhhh," Ronan said. "Let's not speak of it. Guinness, Jameson, and Baileys please."

Lucille cocked her head at him.

He put a twenty up on the bar.

She still didn't move.

Miranda reached into her purse and put another twenty on the bar.

"Oh, so it's not a date," Lucille said, swinging around to grab the whiskey bottles.

"Not a date," Miranda said. "He's my student."

"Oh, so you're one of the ones that teaches him those fancy words he uses. You watch out, he might just use them on you." Lucille poured out two glasses of Guinness, put out two shot glasses, and walked away.

"She's right," Miranda said. "We really shouldn't be doing this. You're my student."

"But we aren't doing anything. We're just drinking. Even the bloody poetry department serves wine at functions. This is just a small function."

He poured the Baileys on top of the Guinness and then dropped the shot glass of Jameson on top. "Drink fast," he said, sliding hers over. "It curdles."

"Curdles?" she asked. "What kind of small function?"

"Yes, curdles, now drink. Any kind of small function. You're a poet, be creative."

She took two sips and then set it down. "You're a poet, too. What's your reason for this gathering?"

"I thought you were good with language," he said. "Drink, woman, the whole thing." He picked up his glass and downed the whole thing.

"All right," she said, doing the same. She set down her glass, and then said, "Another?"

"I thought you'd never ask. Lucille—two more?"

"You still didn't answer my question," Miranda said. "Why did you ask me here tonight?"

"You said you could use a drink," he said.

"That's all?"

"Can't a man just want to a drink, too?" he said. "Now do you want to talk or drink?"

Lucille brought over two more glasses of Guinness; he

poured out the liquors and passed hers over. This time she didn't need prompting.

There are certainly rules about being with students outside of class and probably a few about inviting them into your home along with a bottle of Baileys you bought on the walk home. But after three Irish car bombs, Miranda certainly couldn't remember them.

"Don't worry," Ronan said. "I am a gentleman."

"A gentleman, what good is that?" Miranda asked.

"That's just the drink talking."

"Funny, I don't hear it talking," she said.

Ronan chuckled. "You have clearly proven you're not Irish."

"WASP. We aren't supposed to drink this much or at least not admit to it."

She pulled out the Scrabble Board, not to show off her Internet meme-creating self, but to play.

"Who's your favorite poet?" she asked him.

"You'll laugh if I tell you," he said. "They will take back my degree if they find out."

"I doubt that. Spill it."

"Shel Silverstein," he said as he picked five more tiles out of the bag.

Every time she put down a word, he quickly put down an even better one.

"Shel Silverstein? Where the sidewalk ends, Silverstein?"

"Yes, well, not the whole thing. The Unicorn. This band my mum liked, The Irish Rovers, had an album, The Unicorn. She used to play it all the time. She'd get this dreamy look on her face and dance me and my sisters around the room. I found out the band took the lead track from Silverstein."

"But why that? There're lots of songs in the world and not all of them come from a poem."

"But not all of them made my mum dance like that. It was the first time I realized that words could be something that make people happy. I wanted to find that person and be just like him."

Ronan handily doubled her score. Doing the poetry sculptures threw off her gift for two-letter Scrabble words with maximum score value placement. The drinks didn't help. He kept pouring until she finally said, "Okay, I get it, you are Irish. I am not. The room is beginning to spin."

"That was the answer I was looking for." And he picked her up and carried her into her bedroom.

Whenever a scene like this played in her mind, she imagined a room in a bed and breakfast with a brass headboard and coordinating linens, gauzy curtains on the windows, a fire going.

She never imagined a man carrying her to her three-week-old sheets, rumpled and unmade, on the same mattress she has had she since was nineteen with no headboard at all, just a squeaky metal frame that came free with the purchase of a box spring.

In her fantasy, though, after being carried to the well-made bed, the man settled in, too, pressing himself against her, brushing aside her hair, kissing her gently as he unbuttoned her shirt or skirt or jeans. Her imagination always featured a lot of buttons and slow kissing. Kissing everywhere.

However, reality didn't match the vision here, either. Instead, Ronan set her down, then stood upright, slipping both his hands into his pockets.

"Well, Prof," he said. "Happy Thanksgiving. See you in class on Tuesday." He placed a fist over his heart, thumped it twice with a bowed head and left her there.

She listened to the click of the lock and the door thudding shut. He locked it from the inside before leaving. Courteous. Gentlemanly. Gone.

In the morning, only the headache and the bottle of Baileys in her recycling bin reminded her about the night before. She shrugged it off. A one-off. Something that could have been a mistake but wasn't. She sighed heavily and looked through her medicine cabinet for aspirin. Maybe most of all she wanted a mistake, something to shake things up, make them different.

CHAPTER

7

IN THE LONG DAYS BETWEEN their night at the bar and her Tuesday class, Miranda found herself replaying the evening in her mind. She laughed again at his admiration of Shel Silverstein and winced at memory of her hangover. Sometimes, well, maybe even more than sometimes, she reimagined the end of the evening, letting it come much closer to her fantasy with the buttons. But modesty and good sense prevailed, making her cheeks burn if her thoughts went a little too far. Still, she kept returning to the image of him standing over her next to the bed and to the question of what if.

On Tuesday, she finally stood before the door to her classroom, and Miranda feared her body would similarly betray her. She didn't want to think about Ronan that way. He was a student. Her student. But she couldn't erase the images from her mind. And part of her didn't want to—but she didn't need anyone else to guess at that—most of all, Ronan.

The full group sat arrayed around the table. Everyone

back to their usual, pre-holiday places, eyes glued down to their phones. Ronan caught her eye, nodded slightly, and then returned to whatever flickering image passed over his tiny cell phone screen. She sighed inside. It was indeed no big deal. She ran through class breezily, letting them spend too much time harping on Clementine's latest poem, a villanelle about Justin Bieber. They were riffing about other words that could rhyme with Usher.

"What do you think?" Clementine wailed.

Miranda refused to join in, waving her hands in front of her. "This is a student-led space. Listen to your peers, listen to your heart."

Clementine shrugged her shoulders and returned to taking notes of her classmates' whimsical selections. The two hours chugged by, and Miranda barely needed to speak a word. Any awkwardness she feared between her and Ronan failed to materialize. Relief flooded Miranda. She smiled brightly at them as they gathered their things and left. She even waved, chorusing in a singsong voice, "See you all next week."

A few turned back and looked at her with slight scowls on their faces.

Her fears were unfounded. It's not like anything could come of her and Ronan. But still, she remembered the electricity that had passed through her as he guided her to the barstool. That little zap felt so good, so right that the rules didn't matter. But they do matter, they lurk behind every small touch, every smile. Rare is the relationship unbound by some sort of custom. "Wait until she's at least twenty-one indeed," Miranda startled herself by saying aloud.

She took out her phone and emailed herself the word electricity. If someone put down city, first, you could get electricity down in a Scrabble game. She liked her sculptures to follow the rules—everything must make a word, and you can't use more than seven letters at a time. At least she would do that. It would give her something to do tonight. Something that would make someone out there in the in the world of the Internet notice her. Like her. Even if only through a click on a little thumbs up.

Her mind toyed with possible combinations for electricity or maybe just electric. Did the board have two "y" tiles? Could she somehow get body on the board? She walked with her eyes fixed upward; not on the sky, but inward, the way a person does when trying to do multiplication with carrying over in their heads. She pictured the Scrabble board just above eye-level as if space and time had another dimen-

sion hovering right above her. She walked on autopilot to her regular parking spot, nearly tripping over the last curb, rearranging the tiles in her head the whole time.

"Be careful, mind you," Ronan said.

Miranda snapped from her reverie. He stood leaning against the hood of her car.

"I was just about to give up."

"Give up what?" Miranda asked.

"Waiting on you. I just wanted to make sure we were okay."

"We?"

"You know, you. Me. After the other night. I left you in a state," he said.

"Oh, yeah. Well. Thanks. I'm all good. It was nice of you to lock up and all."

"I didn't trust myself not to."

"Not to what?" she asked.

"Let myself back in. Leaving was hard enough." He stood up and took two steps to cover the space between them. "Can I come over?" he whispered into her ear.

This time the electricity passed from his voice to her neck and down her arms and up her spine in the most delicious shiver. Suddenly, she couldn't imagine why anything that felt like that would be wrong. She handed him the keys to her car. She didn't trust herself to drive.

He knew the way to her apartment without even asking for directions. The snow still hadn't melted, and many streets still lay under a coat of dirty, packed-down snow. He kept both hands on the wheel, his eyes straight ahead. They did not speak. She listened to his breath between gasps of the engine; she watched it escape his mouth in little puffs of cold smoke. The car heater wasn't on. She didn't feel the cold, though; her skin burned.

He pulled the car into her neighbor's spot. For a moment, she thought about correcting him, then just hopped from the car and walked to the door. He passed her the keys, and in a miracle, she found the key on the first try and popped the door open. He followed her quickly inside, pulling the door shut with such force that it rattled the framed Matisse print that hung next to the front door.

"Have you been drinking today?" he asked.

"No. Why?"

"I wanted to make sure this is all free will." He put a hand behind her neck and pulled her in close for the longest and deepest kiss of her life. He tasted like cinnamon and coffee. He tilted his head in just the right way and moved his fingers up through her hair. She placed her hands on either side of his waist, pulling him closer to her. She felt his need stiffen against her.

He pulled his lips away from hers, bringing his mouth to her ear. "I want to go slow," he said. He picked up her hand and led her to the couch, her own couch, as if this wasn't her place but his. He sat and motioned for her to sit next to him. She pressed against him, leaning her head up to kiss him again. He returned her kiss lightly. "Tell me something," he said. "Tell me your middle name."

"My middle name. Ellen."

"Ellen. Nice lilt. Where's it from?"

"I don't know. My mom liked it. Why are we talking about this?"

"Mine is Andrew. Named after my father's father. He died the week before I was born." He kissed her; his tongue stroked lightly against her lips.

She pulled back from his embrace. "Wait, what? That's terrible."

"Him staying around would have been worse. Don't stop." He kissed her again, this time harder, more insistent.

"You didn't answer me. Why are we talking about this?" she asked.

"We are getting to know each other. We are taking this slow."

"I don't want to take it slow," she said, reaching for the top button of his jeans. She couldn't stop herself. Some great hunger welled up inside her. She licked at his lips, letting her tongue slip into his mouth before he pulled away.

"But I do." He picked up her hand and put it back into her own lap.

She felt herself pouting. It felt foolish, but so did she. She didn't understand. "Why the big production of waiting by my car then? Why the kiss?"

"I couldn't stop myself."

"And now you can?"

"Barely, but yes. Talk to me, Miranda. Tell me something about you."

"Are you serious?"

"You don't want to talk to me?" he asked.

"Not really. Not now." She stood up. She felt her composure returning. "Listen, I am not in the mood for talking.

I am in the mood for other things, and I thought you were, too. If you're not, then get out. I've had enough mixed signals in the last few weeks to last a lifetime. You are catching me at the tail end of a really long trip down that road, and I don't want to double back there with you. You are a nice guy, a good poet, and an amazing kisser, and yes, an Irishman who can hold his liquor. But I need to be blunt. Put out or get out." Miranda could see herself saying these words, hear her voice saying them, but she couldn't believe that she had just said all of that. Out loud. To a student. A current student.

He didn't say anything.

"Please just go. Thank you for the kiss. It was the highlight of my year. I shouldn't say that because it means I'm pathetic, but truly, thank you. I'll see you in class next week."

"I'll stay," he said.

"What?"

"I'll stay. I'll put out, as you so romantically requested."

"What?"

"Are you deaf, woman? You just told me to put out or get out. I choose put out. Listen, I don't do this often. I was only trying to do it right. If you don't want right, that's fine with me."

"Good. Take off your pants. I'll get us something to drink."

When she came back to the living room with a bottle of white wine, he sat there, jeans on the floor, and his tight boxer briefs highlighting the muscles on his thighs. She set the bottle of wine down on the table and moved to stand in front of him. She pressed both palms against his thighs and stroked her hands upward. She lowered her face to kiss him. This time, she leaned in deep, letting her mouth cover his. He moved his hands to either side of her lower back, and with one deft motion, flipped her over onto the couch. She let him, eagerly wrapping her legs around him as he lowered his lips to her neck, to her breasts. She tugged off her shirt, then reached behind herself and unclasped her bra. He never let his lips move from her chest. Arching her back, a moan escaped her lips.

Without asking, he unbuttoned her jeans and pushed them down, taking her panties with them. He slipped from his own shorts. She shivered a little more from the cold, but quickly pushed herself up and against him. His penis, stiff and firm, pressed against her, so close to slipping in. She shifted her weight a little. He entered, and the air rushed out of his lungs.

He wrapped an arm around her body and held her tighter, their movements more concentrated, the connection of his body to hers more solid. On each movement out, his penis fluttered out of her, licking at her clitoris. The physical sensation overwhelmed her mind's ability to fight it. The sensation drove through to her core until she finally shuddered underneath him. He felt her orgasm and quickened his pace. He buried his face in her hair, biting her neck as he erupted in climax.

She traced a finger over his shoulder, willing her breath to return to normal. Miranda didn't know what to say. So she chose to let the silence sit between them. He shrank inside of her and finally slipped out. She shifted her body, moving some of his weight off her. He mumbled something into her ear. But it wasn't words. Snoring. He fell asleep. Slipping herself sideways, she managed to free herself out from under him. He still wore his tee shirt. She stood, her pale skin glowing from the streetlight that flooded her living room. His eyes fluttered, almost waking, but then he settled into the space she had just occupied, his reddish blond hair curling in sweaty ringlets around his forehead.

She found her shirt and jeans and panties, collecting each item carefully and quietly, not willing to wake him up

She turned the water up in the shower as hot as it would go. She scrubbed extra hard and let the scorching hot water cascade down around her. Lines from Sharon Olds' poem came to her, and she spoke them aloud using her best poetry reading voice.

come to the
still waters, and not love
the one who came there with them, light
rising slowly as steam off their joined
skin?

"Sex Without Love, is it?" Ronan said from the door to
the bathroom. "One catnap and you write me off entirely?"

Startled, she dropped the soap. "It's just a poem," she
said.

"Come now. You know better than anyone it's never
just a poem."

"It can be if you are just reading it." She swatted at her
skin, eager to get the soap off and her clothes back on.

"But you aren't just reading it. You are reciting it. From
memory. After making love to me."

"But I didn't write it. And we didn't make love."

"We didn't?"

"No, we had sex. There is no love."

"How do you know there is no love?"

She pulled open the shower curtain and grabbed at
her towel. This was not a conversation to have naked.
"Listen, there just can't possibly be love yet. We've known
each other for what fourteen weeks? And only really
exchanged one conversation before today, and that was
while drinking." Miranda slipped past him and into her
bedroom. He followed, taking up a position on her bed, as
she rifled through her drawers trying to find clean sweat
pants or something, anything that she could get on quickly.
She felt his eyes like laser beams on her.

"Are you in love with someone else?"

"No," she said. Miranda turned to face him. "Why would
you say that? I haven't dated anyone in two years. Since I
moved here."

"I didn't ask if you were dating anyone else." He scooted
back and sat up like someone waiting for a servant to bring
in breakfast. He tucked his feet under the quilt she kept

folded at the foot of the bed. Her grandmother had made the quilt for her mother's hope chest. She fought the urge to snatch it away and put it away in the closet, someplace safe, where no one could touch it.

"Well, I'm not in love. Not really."

"Not really?"

"No, well, it's complicated."

"Now we are getting somewhere. Can you stop foraging around and sit down with me for a minute? I really do want to get to know you. Remember, I was the one who said let's take it slow."

Miranda sighed, finally finding the right pair of yoga pants. She pulled them on and picked up a tee shirt from the floor bedside her bed.

He patted the place next to him. "Come on," he said.

Unsure what else to do, she climbed in next to him.

"What's his name?" Ronan asked.

"Scott. But it's not like that."

"Like what?"

"Love or anything. We never dated. Our parents are friends. And now he has a daughter, this awesome little girl. He says it's complicated, but he didn't explain. I just always thought—"

"Thought you might be meant for each other?"

"Yeah. Pathetic, right? Fairy tale stuff."

"Normal, I'd say. My childhood girl's name is Lucinda. She was my grandmother's neighbor. We spent every summer together until she got sent to girls' camp for the summer holidays. We still send letters. Only hers include pictures of her kids and husband now and mine are post-cards from places in America I pretend to visit."

"You pretend?"

"Yeah, pretty much. I started out not pretending, but compared to what she has going on at home, I don't have much to say. Wrote a poem today. Tried to write a poem today. Didn't write a poem today. Variations on a theme."

"I hear you. So is this what you meant about taking it

slow?" She let herself settle against him.

"Pretty much. Listen, I like you. I have since the first day of class. I was trying to wait out the term, but when I saw you at the liquor store in the snow, I took it as a sign."

"I never noticed."

"Good. I didn't want to be that guy. Some moony teacher's pet."

"Too bad, I think I'd like that. You could bring me apples."

"They have laws against that now." They both laughed. He brushed her hair away from his shoulder. He picked up a lock and kissed it. Then moved his lips to her shoulder and kissed that. Then her neck.

Miranda paused. This should be harder. She should stop it and control herself some. But this was exactly the kind of roller coaster she longed for. It may not be a trip to Ibiza or Belize or even Bermuda, but it felt damn good and very, very bad all at the same time. She kissed him back, pulling up his tee shirt and throwing it on the floor. He responded in kind, lifting hers off her quickly, nipping at each of her nipples with sharp little bites that made them stand at attention. She quivered with anticipation as he then fingered her nipples, tugging and twisting them until they swelled with desire. Then he slid his hands lower, under her yoga pants, tugging them down. She wiggled to free herself from them. He wrapped an arm around her back and pulled her against him in one rapid movement. He stroked her pubic hair, flirting with her clitoris with each downward motion, each time, going lower and lower. She felt herself flush. He finally moved his hand to have his thumb circling her clitoris and two fingers stroking the inside of her vagina. From this position, all she could do was hold his back and run her fingers through his hair. He moved his fingers faster and faster until she thought she couldn't control it any more, then he lay back, pulling off his shorts and guiding her on top of him. He slipped in easily, plunging himself deeply into her. She sat on top of him, grinding slowly, watching his eyes fight to stay open. He wrapped his arms around her, pulling her body flat against his. His chest hair tickled her nipples, sending sparks throughout her body.

She felt him tense and shudder.

"This is so much better than apples," she said, just as she climaxed again.

This time they both fell asleep.

Noise from the upstairs neighbors finally woke them. "Do we sound like that?" Ronan asked, pointing at the ceiling and the obvious source of the bedspring noise.

"I don't know. We should try it again sometime."

"See, I'm growing on you. You said again."

"I did," she said.

"I still want to get to know you more."

"What else is there to know?"

"What do you keep in your refrigerator?" he asked.

"What would that tell you?"

"It would tell me what I am going to eat right now."

She scrambled eggs and made coffee. He buttered the toast. They sat in the living room without any lights on and ate without talking. They finished the plates and then made another round. "So tell me a story, Ronan," Miranda said.

"About what?"

"How did you wind up here?"

"Here? I stood by your car for a really long time, and then you invited me home, and we made love twice, and naturally we were hungry and so we ate in the living room because your dining room table is a little crowded with papers."

"We didn't make love."

"Are we going to have that conversation again?"

"We will if you keep saying love. This can't be love. But that isn't what I meant. I meant here, in the States."

"Nothing exciting. I followed a girl."

"A girl? Now I can ask you, do you still love her?"

"Yes," he said.

Miranda felt her stomach flip a little.

"My sister," he said. "She was following some bloke, and my mother paid for my application to graduate school if I went, too. Chaperone kind of."

"What graduate school? You're in my undergraduate section."

"There is more to me than meets the eye, Miranda. I wanted the structure of a workshop while I finish my thesis. I audit your class. It's on the website."

She never looked at her roster on the college website. She figured if someone wanted to sit in on her class without paying for it, who would it hurt? Who steals poetry classes? "Oh," she said. Then she brightened. "So you aren't my student?"

"I am not. See we should have talked first. It might have saved you some anxiety."

"I didn't have anxiety."

"Really? I saw the way you scurried for your clothes."

"You still hungry?" she asked.

"Changing the subject. But, ah, anyway. I need to go."

"It's like two in the morning."

"Graduate student—this is when I get my best writing done. And after today I have a lot to write about."

Miranda felt herself blanche.

"Don't worry, non-guilty, non-anxious parties will remain nameless. I'm serious, Miranda, you don't seem to want to hear that, but I am. I don't just do this sort of thing."

"Neither do I."

"Good." He leaned over and kissed her on the forehead, bending down to retrieve his jeans from the floor where they had fallen so many hours ago. He slipped them on, found his hoodie, and left, again locking the door on his way out. Miranda stared at the door. She couldn't tell if she was hoping for a knock and for him to come back and spend the rest of the night. She couldn't tell if she wanted him to come back the next day. All she could tell was that she was confused. And tired. Very tired. She closed her eyes, but her mind wouldn't let anything settle. Instead, she picked up the phone and dialed Danielle, her best friend from high school. With the time difference between New York and Turkey, Danielle was the perfect person to call in the middle of the night.

"Guess what I just did?" Miranda said. She knew how Danielle would respond.

"What or who?"

Miranda relished that she could finally answer who. It had been many years since a who. "Who. A student."

"What? A student. Are you crazy? Is this Miranda?"

"Well, not really a student, he's auditing the class. But I didn't know that until after."

"After?"

"After the second time." It felt good to finally have juicy details.

"Okay, spill."

So Miranda did, telling her everything.

"And you were like prepared for that. You had condoms just sitting around. Or did he bring them? And ewww—he brought more than one. What does that mean he thinks about you?"

"Condoms. No, I'm still on the pill."

"Really? You let some random guy go bareback. You, Miss Straight and Narrow just said, ah, fuck it?"

"Ah, well, not really. I wasn't thinking about it."

"Are you thinking about it now?"

"I guess so." Miranda regretted this phone call. She wanted to go back to just being proud of herself for doing something that didn't require a five-year plan, something that just felt good and to hell with the consequences. "Tell me about your students. How's their English coming?" She hoped to change the subject.

"They are doing fine, really fine. But I want to talk about you. What brought this on all of a sudden? Random sex with a student? Oh, and Happy Thanksgiving."

"Thanksgiving, ugh."

"Why ugh? You like the holidays. How're Avery and Stanton?"

"They're fine. The holidays are fine. Okay. Scott was there."

"Scott?"

"Thai food and Scrabble Scott. The Scott I grew up with. Scott Cramer."

"The one and only? Mister gone and lost forever?"

"Yeah, that one. Oh, and he has a daughter. She's like six or seven. And perfect. Lynn's her name. I have to tell you, though, she says she's my new best friend. We even shook on it."

"Replacing me are you? Hmmm. We'll see. What about the mother?"

"No mother. Just them."

"So the guy you crushed on is still single, with a kid. You like kids."

"I know I like kids. I like this kid. She was fun to be with. We went into the city to see the Macy's balloons the night before, and then in the morning Scott and I had a thing, a spat really, then zip, cold shoulder."

"Cold shoulder? Nothing?"

"He only broke his silence to me at dinner. He told me I should look up some guy to help me market Blocked Poet."

"You told them about that?"

"Yeah, I wanted Avery and my dad to know. It's not like I can win a big legal case and protect the wheels of justice or anything. It's just nice to have something to show for myself, you know."

"Yeah, I know. I just thought you were keeping that on the down low."

"I am. It's just them. And Scott. But they don't know anything about it really. They wouldn't rat me out; they don't have anybody to rat me out to."

"You should contact the guy."

"What guy?"

"The marketing guy. That stuff is good. You should

make something out of it. Make it big."

"Hmmmm…," Miranda said.

"Don't hmmm me. Do it. I gotta go, though; it's time for class to start. We're doing Valentine's Day today."

"But it's November still."

"But this is the order the textbook goes in. It covers all American holidays. Last year, I had an Arbor Day unit. We studied the vocabulary of trees."

"Vocabulary of trees?"

"Not everyone can be a famous internet poet."

"Ha!"

"Ha, yourself. You should call the marketing guy and not the student."

"I don't even have the student's number. And he's not a student. His name is Ronan. From Ireland."

"Wow, you nailed the foreign exchange student?"

"Graduate student."

"But gee, you just said he wasn't a student. Stop confusing me, okay? Call me later, but honestly, be careful."

"Thanks, Mom. It's not like I've ever done this kind of thing before."

"Exactly. That's what has me worried," Danielle said.

HEN RONAN DIDN'T TURN UP at her apartment the next day or the day after, Miranda fought the urge to be upset. Maybe it was a one-time thing. Maybe he didn't mean anything by it. She experimented with being the type of woman who enjoyed a one-night stand. She found herself striding across campus, hips swinging in a wide sashay to teach her mandatory Thursday composition classes, where she tried in vain to steer them away from plagiarizing their final research papers through a mixture of humor and begging. She smiled. A lot. The Friday department meeting was canceled and not rescheduled again until after the Christmas break. The end of the term was in sight, and somehow, she was suddenly a woman who knew how to have a good time. No strings attached. This lightness, the new attitude she tried on for size, sparked her creativity. She posted a dozen new works, all of which spread through the Internet like wildfire. She tracked their link-backs and trackbacks with glee. When her Instagram gained another ten thousand followers overnight, Miranda dug out the paper marked Ambrose Reed from the bottom of her purse.

Ambrose Reed, she entered into Facebook. Nothing. Then she remembered the Q and up he popped. Zero security settings. She could see his entire page. Each picture linked to some product or person. She recognized almost all of them. The mouse cursor hovered over the link to his email address. Click. Scott Cramer sent me, she typed in the subject line. Then she sat there, staring at the blank message area. She wasn't sure what she needed to ask. She wanted something in her life to go somewhere. She wanted this new attitude to be about more than having sex with a hot guy. She wanted it to be about how she lived her life. She didn't want to be afraid to make things happen. She wanted to stop waiting. But none of that would matter to Ambrose Q. Reed anyway. From the look of it, he mainly cared about selling things; perhaps a means to an end? If her work for Blocked Poet was something you could sell, he would be just that. Finally, she copied in the links to her Instagram and Twitter accounts and added the word "interested" with a question mark. Then she closed the email with her cell phone number.

The weekend stretched before her like a blank canvas. Finding no coffee in the cupboard, Miranda headed into town. She brought a notebook and a plan to sit in the café and write something. She wanted to watch people and eavesdrop. Research, she called it.

This town suited her in a thousand different ways, but the ability to walk to get a cup of coffee always ranked high on the reasons she listed for other people. But she really liked the anonymity and fluidity of living in a college town—small town living with none of the guilt. You saw the same people, but every year a whole bunch filtered out and a new bunch filtered in. By the time the coffee girl knew your habits well enough to ask you with true concern how your day was, she was off to Boston to work in finance or attend law school in Manhattan or move back into her parents' basement on Long Island. You could smile and wave, make polite conversation, but the transient nature of things meant you could sit and stare for hours without anyone trying to interrupt you.

Miranda looked at her watch. Ten-fifty. Not quite time for lunch. Not quite time for breakfast. She stood there staring at the chalkboard behind the counter still advertising last week's turkey noodle soup. That can't be good, she thought. Someone brushed up behind her, so she stepped forward, mumbling, "Excuse me," under her breath.

"Can I help you?" the counter girl asked.

Before Miranda could speak, she heard the Irish accented request for two coffees.

"Ronan," Miranda whispered. The air left her lungs. Goosebumps pricked up along the back of her neck. "Hi," she said. But it came out squeaky, two syllables instead of one.

He pressed his hand against the small of her back. "Hi," he said into her hair just above her ear. "I was hoping to find you."

"You knew where I was."

"But I wanted a sign," he said.

"A sign?" Miranda was grateful for the conversation. She felt her skin returning to normal. She turned to face him. His smile, for a moment, disarmed her, but she shook it off. "A sign? What about a phone call?"

"Exactly. You didn't call me."

"Call you?"

"Yes, Miranda, you could have called me. You have my number the same way I have yours."

Her cheeks flushed. The text messaged poems in class. She did have his number. "Oh," she said.

"Barring that, I wanted another sign. I wanted the universe to tell me that it wasn't just one great night, that I wasn't crazy for thinking about you, all of you, every minute for the last three days."

"And this is a sign? Here at the coffee shop?"

"I am a desperate man. I will take whatever sign I can. And I hate this coffee shop. I never come in here." He said this part a little loudly. The counter girl slid their two cups across the counter with a heavy hand. Coffee slurped over the edge leaving a brown watery stain like a slug's trail. He made eye contact with the counter girl. "See," he said. "No customer service." He put five dollars on the counter, picked up both cups, and walked toward the tables in the front. He set the cups down on the table. Miranda moved to sit. Stopping her, he picked up her hands. "I can't do this. Let's go somewhere else," he said.

Miranda felt her head actually spin. His hands felt so warm around hers. Her body tingled. "Yes," she said. "Let's." Her mind immediately leapt to a replay of their night together as she tried to guess whether he would lead them to his place or hers.

Instead he led her to the corner store and bought her another coffee in a to-go cup; she tried to not be disappointed both in the location and the weakness of her own flesh. Then without asking how she liked it, he put in the right amount of cream and sugar. A sign, she thought, not saying it aloud, though, for fear of encouraging him in that direction.

"Thank you," she said, when he handed her the cup.

He tipped his head to her and held open the door for her to pass.

"What, you aren't talking to me?" she asked.

He shrugged and clasped her free hand, tugging her down the sidewalk in the opposite direction of her apartment, toward campus. When they got to the main gate, a classic affair with stone pillars and wrought iron arches, Miranda stopped walking.

"I don't know about this," she said.

"What? What this? You come here every day."

"Exactly. I work here."

"Remember, I'm not your student. I'm an auditor."

"Is there really a difference?"

"Yes."

"Really?"

"I looked it up. The day after we had drinks at your place. I'm not some kid, Miranda. I might even be older than you."

Miranda scanned his unlined face, the thin reddish stubble, his beautiful blue eyes. He looked like a sixteen-year-old who just figured out how to shave.

"You don't think so," he said. "I'm thirty next year," he continued.

"Thirty?"

"And you? Am I right? Am I older than you?"

"I'm twenty seven. Well in a few months, I will be." It was weird wanting to be older all of a sudden.

"So have we fully established that we are both consenting adults and allowed to enter university property together?"

She shrugged. No words came. Traitors, she thought.

"Shall we?" he said. "I have something I want to show you."

Ronan led the way through the campus, not heading toward the liberal arts building, but toward the other side that housed the gym and the defunct football stadium. He stopped at the door of a small stone building marked Aldridge House.

"Have you been?" he asked.

"No, what is it?"

"Ah, let's go in and see."

A student sat in a chair right in the center of the small foyer, next to a tiny table with a guest book. She nodded in time to the music on her iPod. She wore the standard uniform of the bored undergraduate girl, hoodie and yoga pants with shearling boots. The student slipped out a single ear-bud. "Sign in," she said.

Miranda could hear the music, tinny, and small. Something poppy like Katy Perry or Britney Spears.

"What is this place?" Miranda asked.

"Go in there," Ronan said. He pointed to the black velvet curtains to their right.

"Curtains for a door? What kind of place is this?"

"Not very trusting are you?" Ronan asked.

"Past experience," she said, shrugging her shoulders. He bent down and kissed her nose. "I like you," he said. "A lot. Follow me." He parted the curtains. Inside the darkly lit space stood rows of low tables with glass tops. Inside the cases, sat books opened with pinpoint lights from the ceiling shining down on them. The gold paint glowed under the light.

"It's the Canterbury Tales. Early 1400s. The exhibition just opened. With the low lights this was one of the few places on campus suited to host it."

"I love these," Miranda said. "How did you know?"

"You mentioned the gap-toothed wife as an example once."

"Once?" She looked up at him, taking stock of his face again. She didn't understand this turn of events. No one ever paid attention to things she said. Certainly not things about Chaucer. Not even her literature students preparing for a quiz paid attention like that.

"I pay attention, Miranda. Well maybe not to everything. But to you—you have my full attention."

This time she leaned up to kiss him, before turning to the beautiful books showcased around the room. While you could barely make out the words on the page, Miranda could tell the tales by the embellishments. She looped around the room a few times; she kept being drawn back to her favorite page with the Wife of Bath sitting astride her horse.

"You know," Ronan said, "the Wife of Bath is the first of the marriage tales."

"And such a view of marriage Chaucer provides."

"It may be an economic view, but sometimes that can work," Ronan said.

"How could that work? Oh, marry me, and I'll be faithful because I am unattractive? And I have money? Very romantic."

"So you believe in romance?" Ronan asked. He smiled a Cheshire grin at her.

Her face flushed. "Look at this gilt work," she said, pointing to another page in the case. "Isn't it beautiful?"

"I could say something cliché here, like not as much as you are, but surely a poetry professor wouldn't let that slide."

"I might," Miranda said, "if you meant well."

"I mean well," Ronan said. He stood behind her, wrapped his arms around her waist, and pressed the length of his body against hers. He kissed her neck and whispered, "Your beauty could never compare to anything printed."

"Is everything okay?" the student attendant asked, poking her head through the curtains.

"Quite fine," Ronan said.

"Whatever," the student said, "but this is a museum."

Miranda turned and pummeled Ronan's chest lightly, unable to suppress her laughter. "Let's go," she said.

Outside, she picked up her pace and took big strong strides. Ronan, however, kept up with her.

"I can't believe I wasted three days," he said.

"Wasted? What do you mean?"

"Not calling you. I wasted three days."

"Two and half really."

"No matter," Ronan said. "I only have twenty-seven days. I leave on the first of the year."

"I'm travelling, too," she said. "I go to my father and stepmother's on Christmas Eve; I stay until the first. It's not like we can't see each other next term. It might be better anyway. Then you won't be my student anymore." She tried to pick up his hand, but he pulled away, shaking his head.

"Now I feel even worse. Twenty days then. I have twenty days until you leave."

"Don't be strange. I'm not leaving. I'm just going to Connecticut. For a week."

She stopped walking and looked at him. "Seriously, I'll

be back."

"But I won't."

"What?"

"Student visa is up. Time to go back to Ireland."

"Back? Back to live?"

"Pretty much. Hard to get an H-1 visa when you are a no-name poet."

"Oh," she said.

"Indeed," he said. "Let's get a drink."

CHAPTER

9

M₃ ISS MIRANDA, two calls in one week. You must have been a naughty girl," Danielle offered in greeting.

"Having a date is not naughty. We went to a museum and looked at illuminated manuscripts. Chaucer. Then we had drinks."

"Just drinks?"

"Well, no. But that isn't naughty either. This isn't the 1950s; I don't need to save my virtue for marriage. If that were the case—"

"You would have been damned freshman year with Tommy Keenan."

"Yes, um, Tommy." Miranda sighed heavily. "It had to be someone."

"That seems to be a theme with you."

"Geesh, Dani, I called to giggle not get a lecture. What theme?"

"The 'he'll do' theme. You go with whatever presents itself instead of going after what you want. Like that Scott guy. He just walks in and out, and you never do anything about it."

"You are being blunt about this."

"I haven't had my coffee. And I love you. And I have to go to work, so I figured I should be quick about the dispensing of friendly advice. You don't even know this guy."

"I know him."

"He was a student in your class. And you didn't even know he was an auditor. And what about him being Irish? Like an immigrant or just his great-grandparents came over on the boat during the potato famine?"

"No, he's from Ireland. He is going back right after the New Year. Student visa is up."

"His visa is up, and he is romancing you all of a sudden? Red flag much?"

"What? What red flag? It's just a thing. This is just for fun."

"And what does Mr. Irish say about that?"

"That he's serious."

"And there's my point. And seriously if I don't go now I won't get coffee before class, and then it will be your fault if I teach them English profanity instead of the terminology of Spring."

"They already know how to curse in English. They have YouTube."

"True, but still, I gotta go. Please think about what I am saying. All this really isn't like you, and I am a bit worried. Okay, more than a bit. A lot worried."

"Dani. Don't. I'm fine. Really fine. I really like this. Him."

"Just think about that, Miranda. This or him?"

Miranda hung up the phone; the second time a phone call to Danielle made her want to hide under the covers instead of laughing. What's wrong with having some fun? Especially with a guy who has a one-way plane ticket? Isn't that the liberated woman's dream? Friends with benefits? All of the fun, none of the guilt? It happened in books all the time. She didn't want it to matter; she wanted to see what it felt like to be one of those women who just did things—consequences be damned. Danielle didn't want a lecture when she followed Omar all the way to Turkey. And Danielle was wrong about Tommy Keenan.

Yes, a part of Miranda just wanted to lose her virginity to get it over with, and to stop Danielle from giving her the once over every time she came back home from her dates and to stop her own brain from imagining Scott Cramer's face on every other man's body.

It was the summer after their freshman year, and they took an apartment near the University to stay for "summer" classes and the quick drive to the beach that didn't involve checking in with their parents each day. Miranda felt guilty about the arrangement given the ratio between how high the rent was on the apartment and how low her grades were, so she went home to make amends and help Avery with her Memorial Day party, a small affair for about one hundred people around the pool in the backyard. Miranda swore Avery only kept the pool for this very purpose, her three summer parties a year—Memorial Day, Fourth of July, and Labor Day. Otherwise, Avery doesn't swim; the chlorine would damage her color-treated hair. It does, however, make the perfect backdrop to an early summer evening. After people are done swimming, she and Miranda would launch floating candles just as the jazz quintet began to play and the appetizers emerged on the wait staff's gleaming silver trays. But that summer, a snafu involving the vegetarian quiche mixing on the same trays as the tenderloin on toast required Avery's command of detail in the kitchen.

"Scott, you help with the lights," she said. "I must see to this." Avery held the offending quiche Lorraine between two well-manicured fingers.

"Yes, ma'am," Scott said. He handed his beer to one of his friends and quickly stepped over. No one ever said no to Avery.

"Miranda, at least a hundred," she called over her shoulder.

"Hey," Scott said. "How's school? I've been meaning to

ask you all day."

"It's great," she said. She fumbled with the matches.

"Here I'll light them, you hand them to me, wicks up."

"I'm staying at the shore for the summer session."

"Stanton didn't mind?"

"Why would he?"

"I don't know. He just always struck me as the over-protective type."

Miranda laughed. "Over-protective about what?"

"You know, parent stuff, like curfews and—"

"And what?"

"You know, boys. Men. That stuff," Scott stammered.

She punched him lightly on the arm. "There's nothing to worry about in that area. I haven't been out on a single date at school."

"Liar," he said. "There's no way you stay home and study on Saturday."

"I didn't say I stay home. I go out with the girls from my floor."

"Oh. And men just don't factor into this equation?"

"Sometimes the girls go home with guys after. But I don't."

"You don't?" Scott looked up and caught her gaze.

"I don't," she repeated.

"Ouch," he yelped. The match in his hand burned down to singe the top of his thumbnail.

Avery picked that very moment to re-appear. "Ten," she said. "You have only launched ten?"

"We were having trouble with the matches," Scott said. He held up his hand as evidence.

"Matches indeed," Avery said. "Stanton, Stan—ton," she called out across the pool. "I need your lighter. And don't pretend you don't have one in your upper left breast pocket next to the Cuban cigar I forbade you to smoke."

The men in the circle around Stanton chuckled at his expense. Stanton quickly produced the lighter and handed it to Avery. "Sorry, my love," he said.

"No sorry. Take over for these two, light one hundred. Miranda, please go put on your evening dress. Scott, please make sure Bunny has another drink."

By the time Miranda came back down, the caterer served dinner, and only one empty chair remained, next to Avery's cousin Phyllis from Long Island. She had six children and a fascination with pointing out what each one would and would not eat from the evening's menu, even though the kids stayed back in Long Island that night with her mother-in-law. Miranda watched Scott seated two tables over, surrounded by the young associates of Stanton's law firm. Their navy dinner jackets formed a solid wall around their table. Only Scott had his off. The spotlighting Avery had designed for the party highlighted the bright white of his shirt, and his smile. Miranda let the evening slip by, not touching her food once.

"Oh," said Cousin Phyllis. "You're like my youngest, Suzanne. She can never eat at a party. Too nervous."

The next weekend Miranda went out with Danielle and a few other girls from their apartment complex. Toward the end of the night, she met Tommy Keenan at the bar that sold only booze, hamburgers, and fried Oreos. He walked up and asked her if she was as sweet as she looked. She held up her fingers, coated in powdered sugar from the fried Oreos. "May I?" he asked pointing to her hand. "I have a thing for sugar."

Miranda nodded, unsure what she had just agreed to.

He bowed his head and sucked the sugar from her fingers.

She let him.

The following weekend, she told him in advance where they would be. The week after that he was driving her to the beach. Despite the finger incident, or maybe because of it, Miranda made sure that every time she and Tommy went out it was with the group or in daylight. Nothing more could happen unless they were alone after dark; at least that's what she told herself. Not that Tommy didn't try. He certainly tried. All June he tried. But Miranda would giggle and give in to little things, each time getting as close as she could without having to go all the way, without having to say the word condom or even think about going to the student health clinic to ask for birth control. No matter how much she wanted to get "it" over with, she couldn't get past the idea that your first time should be something special, with someone special.

Someone like Scott.

She wanted to see Scott again. She wanted to see him before she did anything stupid, anything with anyone else.

"Childish, childish, childish," she chided herself that Fourth of July morning, trying on her three bathing suits twelve times each to see which one flattered her enough to make an impression. Hair up or hair down? Make-up or no?

By the time she got down to the party, Scott was already in the pool playing some combination of chicken and water polo, a game Miranda typically only watched. On his shoulders was Kimberly, the newest associate at Avery's firm. They laughed and swatted at the ball. When the action stopped, she ran her fingers through his hair and didn't remove herself from his shoulders. He kissed her calf, making a show of licking the beads of water from her leg.

Miranda stayed until the evening's music started, then called Tommy and met him at a beach party with his friends from work. When the couples started to pair off from around the bonfire, instead of protesting Miranda went willingly. At least the setting for her first time was romantic, but sand and condoms don't mix. Instead of being a magical experience, it was more like a quick rubbing with some sandpaper. But Tommy seemed pleased, and he didn't stop calling. In fact, he called more. The summer continued on with more nights on the sand, in the backseat of his car, and very quietly in her bedroom at the apartment while Danielle slept. Miranda registered for fall classes. Tommy, it turned out, didn't take classes any more. Miranda would come home from her afternoon Classics course and find Tommy waiting for her on the front steps, a six-pack in a paper bag next to him, two or three already empty. She would let him make sloppy love to her in her room quickly before Danielle came home, then protest his offers of dinner because of her homework. After a few weeks, she started going to the library after class, and Tommy soon got the hint.

When she next saw Scott at Thanksgiving, there was no sign of Kimberly, but Miranda didn't really want to know anything about that. Surely, there would soon be a Caitlin or a Zoey or an Emily to take her place. Instead she hung back, watching him watch football, watching him help Avery get the bird to the table, watching him just be Scott. She learned that year that sometimes it is better to live in your head than in the real world, that it is better to let your dreams stay dreams instead of trying to make them come true.

Before she could sink too far into her reverie, the email alert on her phone went off. It was the account she used for Blocked Poet. Ambrose Q. Reed. "Call me," he wrote, "now. I don't care what time; I don't sleep."

"Well neither do I, Ambrose Q. Reed," she said aloud. She dialed the phone number at the end of the email.

"Blocked Poet," he said. "We must talk."

Before she could offer any greeting in return, Ambrose started a stream of consciousness riff on SEO, product placement, link backs, and hardcover printing. "You got that," he finished.

"No," she said, "but I trust that you do."

"No, no, no, that won't do. You must understand this one basic thing. Your pieces drive traffic. People link them, like them, share them, would buy them printed on coffee cups to send to their grannies. There is potential here to completely create a brand. Will this be sustainable for three years? Yes. Five years? Maybe. Ten years? No. But there is no reason not to try. Do you have a lawyer?"

"My parents are lawyers."

"Good, that'll do. But what about Scotty-boy? You mentioned him. Lawyer, right? How do you know him?"

"A friend, not a lawyer anymore, he just said to contact you."

"Then kiss him," Ambrose Q. Reed said. "He just made you a lot of money."

"Money?"

"Yes, dear, that is what all of this is about. Everyone mistakenly believes the Internet runs for free, but there are a lot of ways to tap into it if you know the right people. A B-lister, some Kardashian hanger-on or washed up Disney star can get upwards of a thousand dollars for the right kind of tweet. We're talking a single tweet. But again, you have to know the right people."

"And you're the right people?"

"See! You are catching on. I'll get that contract outlining my services to you by morning. Have your legal look it over and get it back to me as soon as possible. We might be too late for a Christmas launch, I don't rule it out, but we can start now and push hard for Valentine's Day and Mother's Day. Speaking of that, not to mess with your creative process, if you could whip up any love poems or tributes to mom, that would be awesomecakes."

"Awesomecakes?"

"Yes, catching on, I see. Email in the morning."

Then click and the line went dead.

Saturday morning was spent on the phone with Avery and Stanton trying to explain the Internet to them. It was hard. The contract outlined a variety of services and splits and publishing rights, and sorting through it made her own head spin, let alone Avery and Stanton's. "But you write poems," Stanton said. "On a Scrabble board?"

"Yes," Miranda said. Then she tried to explain the entire thing to them again. Finally, she said, "Can I have Scott's number?"

"Why do you need Scott's number?" Avery asked.

"He's the one who told me to start this in the first place. Maybe he can help sort it all out."

Miranda held the number scrawled on the back of her electric bill like a sacred document. Then she chided herself for being a foolish girl with a crush. She pounded in the numbers and listened impatiently to the ringing.

Then came the knock on the door. Phone tucked under her chin, she opened the door to find Ronan holding a dozen white roses. The sight of him caused her to lose her breath for a moment. His eyes, bright blue, twinkled. She looked at his sweet, sweet mouth, and remembered the things he could do with those lips and that tongue.

"Ronan," she exhaled, just as Scott picked up the line.

"Sorry, wrong number," Scott said.

"No, Scott, wait, it's me, Miranda."

"Miranda? Is everything okay? Are your parents okay?"

"Yes, yes." Miranda motioned Ronan to sit on the couch. But he didn't. He set the flowers down on the entryway table and reached his arm around her, letting his fingers hook through the belt loops of her jeans.

"I missed you," he said, nuzzling his face into her hair, his breath tickling her ear.

Miranda put a finger over her lips and tried to free herself. He wouldn't let go.

"Just take your call," he said. "I'll keep myself busy."

"What can I help you with, Miranda?" Scott said.

"Oh, sorry, someone just came to the door. I spoke to Ambrose. I need help."

"Oh, Ambrose, excellent!" Scott's tone brightened.

Miranda tried to swat Ronan away, but he held his ground. He dropped to his knees and began inserting his fingers between the buttons on the fly of her jeans. Miranda swiveled. He just reached around to continue. She stopped fidgeting and let him. "Well, yes, excellent. He has a lot of ideas and sent a contract. I need it to be reviewed."

"Stanton does that all the time. What's the problem?"

"He doesn't understand the Internet. And frankly, I'm not sure I do either."

"And?"

Miranda heard the nature video sound track fire up in the background.

"Lower it, sweets," Scott said. "I'm on the phone."

"With who?" Lynn asked.

"Miranda. Remember from Thanksgiving."

Ronan began undoing the top bottom; her jeans were tight, and he struggled some. She brushed his hands away only to have him try again.

"Randa Panda? Tell her about Christmas, Daddy, tell her we will be in Connecticut again. Tell her Miss Avery promised we would do gingerbread houses. Tell her. Tell her I missed saying goodbye to her!"

Miranda's heart did a leap. She stepped away from Ronan, this time just before he undid the last button of her jeans. "Please," she whispered. "On the couch." She pointed to the couch and stepped closer to the kitchen.

"Did you get that?" Scott asked.

"I did. But I have to say I didn't expect it. You didn't seem to have a good time. And I missed saying goodbye to her, too."

Ronan flicked on the television and flipped quickly through the channels, settling on soccer.

"You did?" Scott asked.

"Yes, I did. She's great, Scott. She's just like you. At least the way you used to be before you disappeared. I want to know the real story."

"Randa, it's not so straight-forward with me and Lynn, and I didn't want to ruin anything more between us."

"Ruin? I don't think anything with Lynn could ruin anything for anyone. You need to explain."

"At Christmas. It's easier in person." His voice was a husky whisper.

In person, she swooned. In person.

Ronan let out a roar of Irish accented expletives at the

television.

Miranda glared at him.

He pointed to the television and shrugged.

"Are you okay? Just tell me about Ambrose. What do you need?" His tone tightened. She could almost see him pulling back away from her.

"The contract. I was hoping you could review it."

"I'm not a lawyer anymore," he said. "I teach third grade."

"I know, but you were a lawyer. And you understand this stuff. And you're my friend. My oldest friend. I've known you since I was a baby. More than a friend."

"More than a friend?" he asked, again in a whisper.

Miranda's cheeks flushed. She turned her back to Ronan. "I just thought you would be able to help. I'm sorry. I didn't want to bother you," she stammered.

Ronan's team obviously did something wrong again; a new stream of invectives filled the air.

"Who is there now?"

"Someone from work," Miranda said. "Ronan."

"I see. I guess I can look at the contract, but I am not promising anything. Can you email it?"

"I don't have your email address."

"First name last name at gmail. It might take me a bit to get back to you. It's book report grading week."

"Book reports, eh? Must be nice to do something like that."

"It is nice. I like being near Lynn. I like when the kids learn something."

Another roar thundered from the living room, or maybe this one was more a cheer.

"I should let you go. Get back to what's his name," Scott said.

"Ronan," she said. "But, it's okay."

"No, I've got to get dinner started."

"Oh, okay," she said. "Thanks."

"Okay," he said.

"Yup," she said.

"Christmas," he said. "I'll see you then?"

"Yes, Christmas. I want to see you," she said, her own voice a whisper now. "I really enjoyed spending time with you. And Lynn."

"We did too, Randa. I'm sorry about how I left. It's just complicated, okay?"

"Complicated? I think I can handle it, Scott."

"I hope so, Randa, it would mean a lot to me."

Ronan let out another series of foul words even a sailor would be embarrassed by.

"Me, too," Miranda said. "Bye."

"Bye," he said.

Miranda listened to his breath on the other end of the phone line. She listened to the music from Lynn's nature show. After a few minutes, the final muted click came and then silence. She held the phone to her ear straining to hear some echo of his voice still. Ronan, distracted by the game, didn't notice her standing there. Scott's words flitted through her, danced around her. See you. Complicated. Christmas. She looked over at Ronan. Delicious Ronan. With his count down of days and desire to be with her right now, regardless of the complications.

CHAPTER

10

OU HUNGRY?" Ronan asked. He clicked the game off and with two long strides he was back in front of her. He brushed her hands away from her face. "What's wrong, my dear?"

"Nothing," she said.

"Are you hungry?" he asked. "When did you last eat? You don't look so good."

"I've eaten."

"When?" he asked.

"Does drinking with you yesterday count?"

"Are you Irish?" he asked.

"No," she said.

"Then no, it doesn't. Can I take you somewhere?"

"Sure, let me grab my coat."

"Love, I want to take you somewhere. Nice. Maestro's maybe, or Prime. You'll want to change," Ronan said.

She looked at him. The slacks, the button down shirt. "But you don't have to. Those places are too fancy. Expensive."

"Miranda, I have twenty-six days left in America. I am

teaching a class that runs until the seventeenth, so travelling to the Grand Canyon or the redwoods or the French Quarter is out of the question. I should have thought about those things sooner. I have approximately two thousand American dollars, which will mean almost nothing to me in Ireland given the exchange rate and inflation right now. I just met a woman I would like to fall deeper into love with, and I would like to have some fun before I go back to whatever awaits a poet with an American Masters in Fuck All Poetry in the village I grew up in. My choices right now are plumber or carpet installer. Plumber pays better but then you deal with shit all day. Carpet is hard on the knees. Forgive the speech and put on a dress or something, would you?"

Miranda considered him for a minute. Remembering the warmth of his breath on her body. His body on her body. The surprise of the illuminated manuscripts. The look in his eyes just now, so earnest, so frustrated with her and yet still willing to take her to dinner. This man in front of her right now. Not some other guy on a phone a state away.

"We could go to the Falls," she said.

"What kind of food is that?"

"No, Ronan, Niagara Falls. I have a car. It's only a five-hour drive, straight across the state. Have you ever been?"

"Really? That's all?"

"You never looked?"

"I never had a car. My sister didn't like touring."

"Didn't like it? Why did she come all the way here?"

"A man, I told you. We are a romantic lot. But she wasn't suited for travel."

"Do you miss her? Will you see her when you get back?"

"Miss them? They Skype me every day to make sure I haven't fallen in with the wrong sort."

"The wrong sort?"

"Catholics. Old things die hard."

"Fair enough. Do you want to go? I'm not Catholic. I'm

not anything really—that might be the wrong sort."

"You fair lady are asking me to go somewhere. Of course, I'll go. I'll go anywhere you want." He leaned in close and placed his lips on her forehead. "Anywhere."

The kiss and his tickling breath stripped her of her words. "Let me," she stuttered, pointing to the bedroom, "pack a few things. Do you, um, need to like pack?"

"I have things in my bag," he said, pointing to the back-pack by the front door. "I didn't think I was going home tonight."

"Ronan." She let the word out like a sharp cry, faux outrage. A smile spread across her face.

"Miranda," he said. "I told you I am serious."

"Oh," she said. Her phone vibrated; another email from Ambrose with an update to the contract. She didn't even read it; she clicked forward and sent it along to Scott.

Ronan slid into the passenger seat as Miranda quickly shoveled several weeks' worth of coffee cups and plastic water bottles into a loose grocery store bag that already contained a coffee cup and half of a donut. "Is it like busy hands, busy mind? Dirty car, dirty mind?" he asked.

She swallowed her embarrassment and decided to play along. "I don't know, Ronan, do you think my mind is dirty?"

"That first time we were together, maybe. You were very bold."

"I don't know where that came from. I expected you to laugh at me or leave. I think I was looking for a way out or something."

"Are you glad I took you up on your offer?"

She didn't answer right away. She put the car into gear and headed down the winding road that led to the inter-state. As the car accelerated smoothly up the on-ramp and launched itself into the travelling lanes, she placed her right hand on his knee, enjoying the way his dress trouser slipped like silk under her touch. "Yes," she said. "I'm glad you stayed."

"May I?" he said, pointing at the radio.

She nodded.

He flipped around through several stations and finally gave up and hit the CD button. Country music guitar chords filled the car with Taylor Swift singing about some exciting heartbreak. He looked at her and raised his eyebrows.

"What?" she said. "I'm a poet. I'm allowed to like romantic things. Even sappy romantic things. They are the foundation of my art form."

"Actually isn't the Bible or maybe even Gilgamesh more the foundation of the art form? Do you like church music, too?"

She pointed to the stack of CDs loose under his seat. "Gregorian Chants, count?"

He guffawed and picked up her hand and kissed it. "You are a wonderful woman, Miranda. See I told you I wanted to get to know you. This makes it so much better."

"So what do you teach? You said you teach. I haven't seen you on the roster at the department."

"So you looked for me?"

"No. The poetry department is kind of small. And well, your name would be obvious. Stop being cryptic anyway. You wanted to get to know each other."

"I teach at the church downtown. In their outreach program for kids."

"What kind of kids?"

"Kids with nothing better to do than get in trouble."

"But you made it seem like your work was worthless before. That sounds amazing."

"It would be."

"If what?"

"If it worked. Just last week a seventeen-year-old boy had to drop the program and pick up more hours at the grocery store after school. His sixteen-year-old girlfriend is pregnant. He used my class to write her love poems. I thought he was expressing himself. I was beside myself with glee that someone was writing about something other than smoking pot or playing video games. I gave him examples. He actually read them and talked to me about them. And then boom. He knocks a girl up, and it's all over."

"It doesn't have to be over, does it?"

"It sure looks that way. And I feel like if I was only paying attention, I could have said something. Offered the kid a condom, talked him out of it. Something."

Miranda shifted in her seat and punched at the button on the CD player to skip to the next song. Condom. Again Danielle's voice echoed through her. She needed to ask before she lost her nerve.

"About condoms. I notice that we haven't been great about using those, and I need to know if there is anything I should be concerned about."

Ronan turned the radio off completely. His mouth dropped open a little. "You're on protection, right? I just assumed when you didn't say anything that you took the Pill. You do take the Pill, right?"

"Yes, yes, I do. But that's not everything. And I feel like I have been really irresponsible here. Swept away as it were."

"Oh, that. I was tested when I started at the school, if that is what you are worried about."

"Yes. It was."

"Should I worry?" he asked.

"I haven't been with anyone in a long time either. Not since the last time I was tested."

"A relief then," he said.

"I feel like an idiot for not thinking about this beforehand. We aren't fifteen," Miranda said.

"No, we aren't. But it sure feels that way, doesn't it? Miranda, when you touch me I forget all about everything else. I'm sorry."

"Don't apologize. Normally, I am, well, a bit more in control of everything I do."

"And I am something you want to do?"

"Sure," she said, "I guess you are."

They drove for hours, finally stopping at a rest area for

food. Miranda patrolled the shelves pulling down snack after snack. Potato chips with bacon seasoning. Twix bars in king size. Snowballs. Green Smoothies, now with more pineapple.

"Hungry?" Ronan asked.

"Something about being with you works up my appetite," she said, leaning up to kiss him. She nipped at his bottom lip and played her tongue against his. His exhale felt warm against her face, and his breath smelled sweet, like fresh bakery bread. This made her more hungry.

"How much longer until we get there?" he whispered when the kiss finally ended.

"Two more hours. We really should see the Falls in the dark and then find a room. If you want, that is."

"A room," he said, pulling her back against him, "would be delightful, Miranda."

She liked how he said her name, the way his body pressed against hers, and the way her body responded in kind to him. "Delightful, yes. But first the Falls"

"I've already fallen," he said.

To this, she couldn't reply, or rather, maybe didn't want to reply. Fallen, she thought, as the cashier rang out her snacks and Ronan's rather meager Milky Way bar. Was it falling if the other person didn't fall with you?

"Ready?" she asked.

"Always," he said.

They couldn't have planned it better. They arrived at the Falls just as the last stragglers of tourists finished their dinner and began the staggering walk to their cars and hotels; bundled up tightly against the cold, whole families waddled like penguins in all directions away from the Falls. By the time they reached the edge, their own faces stinging with cold, they stood alone before the great gorge illuminated in its Christmas colors. The sound roared around them, and the wind caused their eyes to tear; Miranda stood transfixed at the water rushing over the edge and churning at the bottom. Ronan took up her hand and kissed it, then moved to stand behind her, resting his chin on her shoulder.

"Thank you," he whispered. "Thank you."

She pressed herself more tightly against him. They stood there until they couldn't bear the cold. When they finally broke from the railing, a lone jogger stopped to tie his shoe behind them.

"Could you take our picture?" Ronan asked.

"Cold night for it, but sure," the jogger said, taking Ronan's phone. He snapped several, turning the phone this way and that. "I wanted to get the right one," he said. "Has to be a special evening to be out at the Falls just for a look."

"Right one, indeed," Ronan said. "Thank you."

He took the phone back and pocketed it quickly, not sharing the pictures with Miranda. It was so cold that she didn't protest.

"Let's find a hotel," Miranda said. "A warm room would be perfect right about now."

"I'd be happy with just a bed."

"A warm bed?"

"Nah, we'll warm it up."

When they got inside the hotel, Ronan insisted on signing them in and paying. "I told you, Miranda, my dollars will be worthless soon. I'd rather spend them on you."

"But you don't have to," she said.

"But, I want to. Please let me."

She nodded and stepped away from the desk to examine the magazines in the lobby. She eavesdropped on Ronan turning on the brogue for the cute girl behind the counter. Then she heard him say, "my wife." Her ears burned. Wife? What was he talking about? She returned to his side.

"Here she is now." He leaned over and kissed her on the cheek.

"Yes, husband," she said, deciding to play along, though the word caught in her throat a little. She wasn't meant to be an actress.

"It's so nice that you are celebrating your anniversary here! Let me get you a Falls view room near the top."

They wound up more than just near the top; the windows of their penthouse room wrapped around the corner of the building. They could see the Falls from every angle without any wind chill at all. After gawking for a few minutes and warming up, Miranda pulled off her coat, hat, and scarf. She started to walk toward the bathroom when Ronan caught her hand.

"Come back," he said. He scooped her into an embrace and pressed her against the smooth cool glass of the window. With his free hand, he tore at her clothes, quickly removing them and his own.

"But the window," she said.

"No one can see in, but who cares if they can?" He lifted her up and moved, gently rocking into her. The glass around them fogged. When he shuddered with orgasm, he didn't stop rocking. Her legs were about to buckle, then her own release came. She collapsed against him. Before she became a puddle on the floor, he picked her up honeymoon style and placed her gently on the bed. They didn't speak, couldn't speak. Ronan dozed off, and she lay there staring at the lights in the ceiling.

It wasn't love. At least not yet. She didn't want to dismiss that possibility. A good girl shouldn't do these things without some romantic future, some possible commitment looming. This felt like eating donuts for dinner—a grand idea, all in good fun, until the stomachache hit.

After a few minutes he stirred awake. "I could really grow to love this," he said, kissing the top of her head.

"You and love. Why does it have to be that? You're leaving. This isn't some sort of ploy for a green card is it?" She let out a laugh and turned her head to look him in the eyes. Miranda felt his body tense.

"It's not what you think."

She heard Danielle's words in her head. Red flag much. It was her turn to tense. She pulled herself upright.

"What do I think?"

"You think that I am using you. Using you so I can stay here."

"And you aren't, right? I didn't really think that, I was just joking."

"But, Miranda, I am using you. Not for a green card. I've been in the States for three years. In that time, I have made no friends. Published nothing. I earned a degree that is essentially worthless unless I want to keep teaching people how to string words together themselves, so that they can be just as unemployable in the future. No offense. You are a good teacher, suited for it. But I am not, but that isn't the point here. The point here is that nothing I have done for the last three years has mattered. To me or to anyone else. I only came in the first place to support my sister, and that didn't even matter—she left me here."

"But none of this has anything to do with me."

"But it does, Miranda. You are going to be the one thing I do that matters. The one thing that makes a difference in this place that I have landed in and will soon leave. I want you to remember me."

Something shifted inside her. She reached out and placed a hand on his chest right over his heart. The thump resonated through her hand joining her own pulse. "Remember you?" she said. "How could I forget? I've never done this before."

"Surely, I wasn't your first."

"Not my first like that. But you are the first time I have given into my body instead of my brain."

"So you'll remember me, then?"

"Remember you? I don't think I will ever be able to forget. And if we keep carrying on like this, I won't want you to go. Did you ever think how unfair this is to do to a person?"

"Unfair, lady? Really what we just did was unfair? I will heartily disagree and say instead that it should be celebrated—with champagne, in fact!" He rose from the bed and put his hands on his hips in a Superman pose.

"Champagne?" she asked. "At this hour?"

While Ronan dialed for room service, Miranda pulled out a piece of notepaper from her purse, scrawling champagne, bubbly, falls. Niagara. She would have to work on it. Find seven-letter words. She felt a bit tipsy already. Maybe falling in love felt like this. She looked up at Ronan, still naked, every part of him firm and taunt. He smiled at her. She smiled back. Wherever the next nineteen days would take her, she would be happy to go. And when they ended, well, she would deal with that then. It didn't have to be love; you didn't need love to have a good time.

The next morning, woozy with champagne and late-night love making, they tumbled out of their hotel onto the boardwalk that led to the Falls' overlook. Miranda spent some time taking pictures from different angles, trying to capture Ronan in a serious pose. Every time she thought she had it, he mugged a big smile or stuck out his tongue. Before they turned to go back to her car, they stood at the edge and just listened to the Falls thundering below. The early afternoon sunlight caught the spray and created a rainbow just across the gorge in front of them.

Neither pointed it out to the other; they just stood there watching it until the light shifted, and the colors vanished from the sky. They remained silent for a little bit after that, holding hands tightly as they walked back to the car.

At the car, he took her keys from her and opened the driver's door. She thought for a moment he would drive, but instead he stepped aside and motioned for her to get in. As she slid past his open arms, he embraced her, his lips finding hers instantly. They kissed so long and so hard that Miranda thought she would lose her breath.

"Thank you," he finally said. "Thank you for building a memory with me."

By midweek, he had just about moved in. She left the apartment only briefly to attend mandatory end of term meetings and teach her Monday and Tuesday class, a class Ronan gladly skipped for once. He kept up his appointments and classes at the tutoring center. But other than that, for the next five days, they sequestered themselves within her apartment, cooking meals with ingredients Ronan ordered online and had delivered. They set the table with matching plates and the two cloth napkins she owned. They lit every candle, even the oddly shaped decorative candles, burning down snowman's hats and Easter rabbit ears. The apartment glowed from the candles and the space between their own bodies. They talked. And talked. And talked.

"Tell me about your mother," he said over a plate of shepherd's pie.

"She got sick when I was ten and died when I was twelve. She loved the law, research, planning things, the beach but not the sand, and pancakes with real maple syrup." She paused to take another sip of wine. She didn't really mind talking about her mom, but no one outside her family and the Cramers knew her well enough to ask about her; when most people found out she had died, they dropped the question and looked away. "What about you? What's your mom like?" she asked.

"It's hard to say what my mom is like. She doesn't really talk. The only time I've been able to see her, really see her, was at my oldest sister's wedding. She had a bit to drink and started dancing. She danced with my sisters, then her brothers, and finally all by herself. It was like she finally felt free. She celebrated a job well done. She successfully got a daughter married without getting knocked up."

"A big accomplishment?"

"Indeed. That's one of the reasons they sent me here after my youngest sister. As if by me being here, my presence alone could stop conception."

"Well, it worked right?"

"Yeah, but that's cause the guy was a fool and let her go running back to Ireland. She's now dating a guy that installs carpet with my uncle. I think they'll get married in the spring. And that will leave only me. Four sisters all married, and me, the bachelor poet."

"I thought you were giving that up?"

"Being a bachelor? You're not proposing are you? I said I didn't want a green card marriage. I'm really too romantic for that. Poet and all." He leaned over the still-steaming plates and kissed her on the lips. "But for you, I might consider the offer."

"Not being a bachelor, being a poet. You said you would become a plumber or lay carpet or something."

"Bah, I dunno. I'm not really serious about all that. I might teach junior school. There's going to be an opening at the school in my village."

"Junior school? Like toddlers and kindergarten?"

"Like junior high here. Early teens, like at the center. After they know something about the world, but before all the ideas get fixed. I think you can make a difference there. But not poetry. Writing is okay but not poetry. I've had enough teaching poetry."

"I like that. Before the ideas get fixed. Do you think ideas can ever get unfixed in a person?"

"Do you mean do I think people can change?"

"Yeah, can people change?"

"I hope so, Miranda. If people can change, then anything is possible."

She let the silence fall between them as she finished her meal.

"Food good?" Ronan asked.

"Wonderful, thank you," she said, her mouth still full. Her pocketed cell phone buzzed, probably with emails from Ambrose and maybe from Scott. She didn't read them and didn't reply.

CHAPTER
11

THAT FRIDAY, Ronan announced, "We need a Christmas tree."

"But we won't be here for the holidays. I need to go to my parents' house." She remembered Lynn's excited voice over the phone and Scott's promise of "in person." And while their time at Niagara Falls made her feel a little bit closer to Ronan, it didn't erase all of her doubts; part of it felt much too fast.

"I'm not asking you to skip. I'm asking for a Christmas tree. There's no rule that says you can't enjoy a tree before Christmas Eve is there? I know you Americans do things differently, but surely you wouldn't deny me a small part of a holiday celebration."

"Deny you? As if I deny you anything," she said. Then she climbed on top of him. Her hair fell from its bun around her face. He reached up and tucked it behind her ears.

"You haven't asked me to your parents. Some could say that is a denial."

"Well, I mean, it's just my family and—" Miranda stammered. Panic flooded her; she couldn't imagine bringing

Ronan home for Christmas.

"You are very beautiful when you blush, Miranda. And don't worry. I don't want to meet your parents just yet. It's too soon for that. Parents only complicate things. They're lawyers, right?" he asked.

"Yes," she said. "Why?" She wiggled free and moved to climb out of bed.

"No reason," he said. Then he reached out and placed a hand on her shoulder. "Stay," he said. "Let me look at you."

She turned and sat cross-legged on the bed. "Look all you want," she said. "Then we will go get you a Christmas tree. A small one. Okay?"

"Take off your top," he said.

"Why?"

"I said I wanted to look at you."

"It's your top actually," she said, shrugging it off. "Anything else?"

"Well, yes, you could take everything off."

"Oh, everything, okay." She wiggled free of her pajama pants. Her nipples grew taut in the cool of the room. A light freckling of goose bumps appeared on her thighs. He made no move to touch her. She shifted a little, avoiding his eyes, which moved all over her body from head to toe.

"Very beautiful," he finally said. "But that's not it."

"What's not it? Can I get dressed?"

"No," he said, reaching out to stroke the top of her thigh. "Stay like this. Let me kiss you." He tugged at her feet, making her stretch her legs out in front of her. He started kissing her toes, then her ankles, and knees, and thighs. He lingered there, teasing his tongue along the inside edge. With a light touch, he pushed her legs apart and kissed her higher and higher until his tongue connected with her body. She settled back against the pillows, unable to stay upright. He grabbed her hips and began to massage them using the same rhythm as his tongue against her. His tongue slipped inside her, first slow and then fast, alternating between penetrating and licking. Her whole body shuddered in ecstasy.

"Thank you, thank you," she said.

"I love you," he said. Then he got up and padded out of the room.

She listened to him open the medicine cabinet and brush his teeth, then the shower starting, the low hum of a song she didn't know. He loved her. Or at least he said he did. Some women dream of hearing such a confession, pull out all the stops to make it happen, and here she was, just lying there, thinking the only thing she wanted in that moment was a shower. By herself.

The Christmas tree lot stood at the edge of town in front of the VFW hall. Old school light bulbs with vibrant filaments glowed faintly despite the noon sun. Ronan bounced through the lanes of trees. Every few feet he would stop and pull out a tree. He'd twirl it like a dance partner, then lean it back up against the rope propping the trees up.

"I'll know it when I see it," he said.

"I like short ones," Miranda said. "Avery always gets the tallest to fill the ceiling, but I like short chubby ones. More homely. In a good way."

"Ah, the lady has a tree preference. Good to know." He clapped his hands together and skipped ahead. "How about this?" he said. He pulled out a tree almost as wide as it was tall.

Miranda mimicked his bounce. "Yes, yes, yes," she said. "It's perfect!"

"Perfect?" he asked. "Can't be. Nothing is better than you."

She leaned up on her toes and kissed him. He nearly dropped the tree from the force of her, toppling them both over.

"Whoa," he said. "There'll be plenty of time for that after we get this tree home, my lady."

As Ronan struggled to get the tree tied to the roof of

her car, Miranda finally took out her phone to read her emails. There were twelve from Ambrose. They all said the same thing: "I don't care when you sign the contract, but you need to keep posting. Don't let the brand die while you decide. Post more." And there was one from Scott, equally short, "Sign with Ambrose. Fair contract. Looking forward to seeing you on Christmas. Lynn says hey."

Christmas. A day that normally meant very little to her now felt like a hinge on which her life turned. Should she waste the last few days she had with Ronan by going home to Connecticut? What does it mean that Scott is looking forward to seeing her? And then there's Lynn. On Christmas. The possibility of that pulled at her in ways she didn't expect. Along with Blocked Poet and the deal and the writing. And Ronan.

Okay, she replied to Ambrose.

Tell Lynn I said hey, she replied to Scott. And thanks, she added before hitting send.

"What is it?" Ronan asked when he got in the car. "You okay?"

"I'm fine; why?"

"Your brow is furrowed. What are you thinking about?"

"Work. That's all. Work."

"Work? I thought your classes ended."

"They did. I have this other thing going. I'll show you when we get home. After the tree, okay? One problem, though. I don't have any decorations."

"I'll get them. I'm pretty sure I can afford some fairy lights. And candy canes. You can show me your work when I get back."

Before he left, Ronan maneuvered the tree into place in her living room window. Without a proper stand, it leaned against the glass completely blocking the light from outside.

"I'll get a stand, too," he said.

She pulled out the Scrabble board and put on the coffee

pot. The tree haphazardly installed in her living room window fueled boards about Christmas and glad tidings. Noel and Mistletoe, breaking the seven-letters-only rule this once. She photographed as many sculpture poems as she could.

Once she started posting the pictures, she saw Ambrose's point. The account for Blocked Poet binged repeatedly from likes and forwards and retweets and new Twitter and Instagram followers. Six or seven poems and her reach expanded. She printed out the contract from Ambrose, signed it, and slipped it into the scanner to email back. She didn't know exactly what he could do for her, but whatever it was, she was up for the journey. She dug out the bottle of Champagne from last New Year's Eve and found the fancy glasses. Ronan returned, cheeks flush from the walk to the shopping center and laden with bags containing many strands of lights, glass baubles for the tree, and candy canes in multiple flavors and colors.

She handed him a glass of Champagne as he dropped the bags at his feet.

"What's this?" he asked.

"I don't know exactly, but it might be something big. I just signed a contract for some of my poetry."

"A book? Miranda that is wonderful." He grabbed her up with his free hand for a hug.

"No, not a book. Well maybe a book, but first a web page, I guess. It's for this." She pointed to the Scrabble board on the coffee table.

He leaned over and examined the words carefully. "You had someone come over for Scrabble while I was out?"

"No, that's my poem. I do this." She pulled out her phone and scrolled through the poem sculptures saved there.

"That's you? I've seen those! You're Blocked Poet?"

"Yup, and I just signed a deal to market it. I don't fully understand, but it might get the poems out to more people. The guy with the contract, Ambrose, he seems to think it

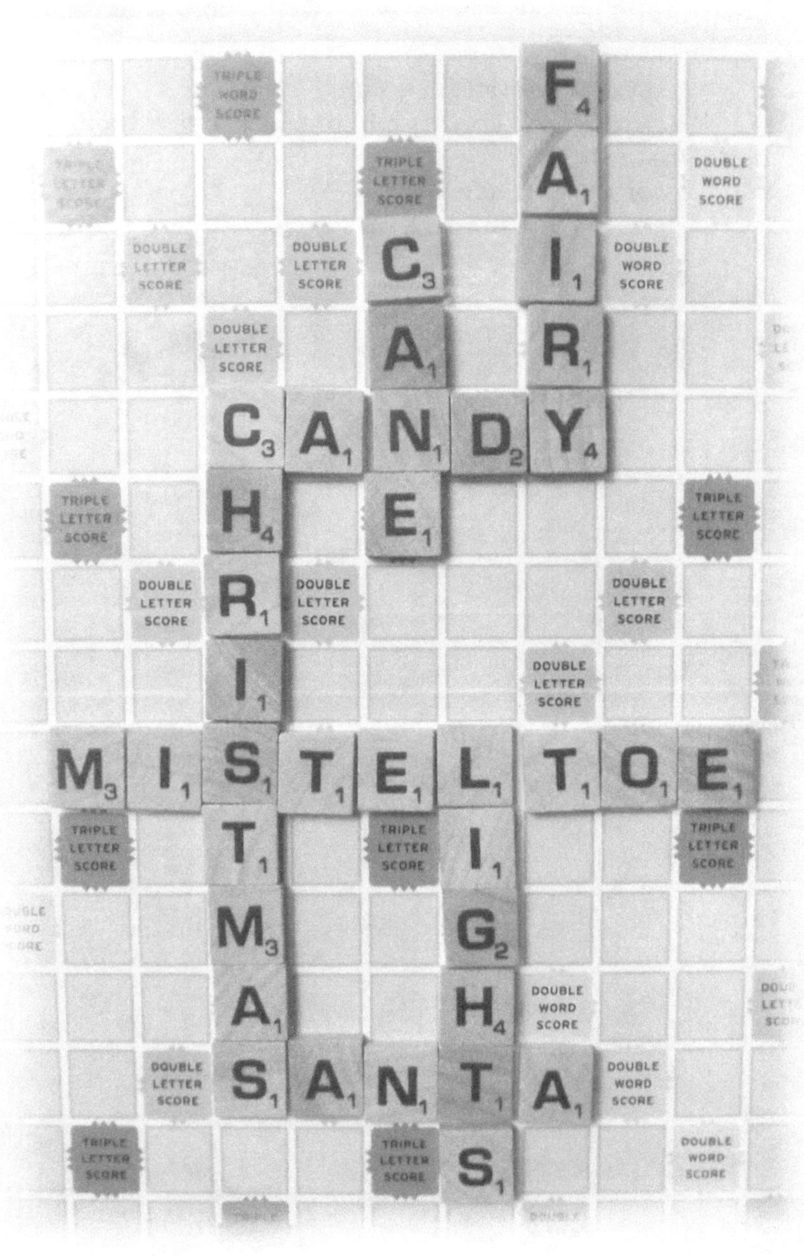
FAIRY
CANE
CANDY
CHRISTMAS
MISTLETOE
LIGHTS
SANTA

will make money."

"It's wonderful."

"We should celebrate," she said.

"We already are," Ronan said, clinking his glass against hers. "To words."

"To words," she replied.

12

T₁ HE DAYS UNTIL CHRISTMAS EVE passed quickly. Every time Ronan left the apartment, Miranda worked at her poems. New emails kept coming from Ambrose. Sign this. Curate a Valentine's collection. First book drops at the beginning of February. Maybe sooner. What about Mother's Day? He didn't sign his emails and often didn't use complete sentences. Miranda felt herself just instinctively saying yes. Yes. And then she would pull together as much as he asked for as quickly as possible. Bravo, he always replied. Do more. Then Ronan would return from the teen center, and they would tumble into bed or the sofa or the rug in front of the Christmas tree. These delicious days passed by in a rush of words and sensations.

On Christmas Eve, Ronan woke up early. "I have to go into work, love," he said. "The holidays are tough on them. There's a lot of trouble brewing on days like today. Are you sure I can't persuade you to leave later? I'd love to give you your present before you go."

"I can't get there late and leave early to get back. I

thought you wanted to see me before your flight?"

"Aye. I want both."

"It's good to want things, Ronan."

"I wish I didn't have to leave right now. There're other things I want."

"And you had those things last night. I'll be back the day after tomorrow. Go take care of your kids."

"My kids? Are you trying to give me a heart attack? They're students. Not my kids."

"Students, kids, you don't want to be late do you?"

"I wish you didn't have to go to your parents," he said.

"I'll be back in no time. We'll have New Year's."

"I'll be waiting," he said. "Under the mistletoe."

Miranda bundled herself for a walk into town to finally find a present for Ronan before she left for Connecticut. She thought about the classics like a scarf or maybe cologne, but none of those captured anything about how she felt or what she was thinking. To be honest, even after all of the time they spent ensconced in her apartment making love under the Christmas tree and in her bed and on the kitchen counter, Miranda was no closer to understanding how she felt about Ronan. She felt a lot of things with him; whole parts of her body that she never knew could feel pleasure lit up under his attentive hands, but her heart didn't stir. When he left to teach his classes, she didn't miss him. She didn't even think about him. Instead she plunged into her work creating more word sculptures in hours than she used to in months. Her entire body purred like a muscle car's engine, always ready for the next race. The work, the sex, it all fueled her and turned her on. She even walked faster. As she strode toward town, she felt her hips and arms sway, taking up the entire sidewalk with her gait. She smiled broadly at strangers who stepped aside to let her through.

It wasn't "I love you" she wanted to say. Thank you was more to the point. Thank you for these memories. For the parts of her body that now hummed with well-oiled satisfaction. For the way her brain felt clear and open. For the way she felt at ease in her own skin. For all of these things, she wanted to say thank you, yet she knew, in a way, that these things had nothing to do with Ronan and more to do with her own awakening. She had looked at him and issued it, "get out or put out." After all these years, she had finally spoken.

She wandered through the one department store still left in the decaying downtown. It mostly featured school-themed merchandise and candy, nothing unique or special or even remotely Ronan. She browsed the window of the men's clothing store and thought a nice sweater might do the trick. But inside the store, the sweaters all felt hollow, empty, just shells of things, not anything that conveyed thank you.

She hit the bookstore next. There would be coffee there, and she could sit and think about it more. Her usual latte felt wonderful on her tongue with a hint of cinnamon; she sighed at the pleasure of it. A few people milled about the aisles, and the store played Christmas-inspired jazz. Miranda tapped her foot in time with the music. Poetry, she thought, I could get him a book.

But as she scanned the familiar aisle none of the poets leapt out at her. None of them said, Ronan. Or Merry Christmas. Or I'll miss you. Instead, these volumes, these familiar friends turned their backs to her, remained silent. Or perhaps she remained silent, unable to speak. Without Ronan there, she could no longer trace the thread that connected him to her. She knew his body and what it did to hers, but she didn't know his mind. Even the few poems he submitted to her class were sparse renderings based on exercises—nothing any poet would share beyond the confines of a classroom. She tried to fix him in her mind—not the shape of him, but the inner workings and gears, only to come up blank. Quite simply, she didn't really even know Ronan. She had just spent the last few weeks having sex with a stranger. The burning realization, the full weight of it, settled in her chest; her throat parched.

She took a sip of her latte, but it had grown cold, the cinnamon now too sharp.

As she rounded the corner by the cashier stand to throw it away, a thin purple leather volume caught her eye. Diary, read the front in a thin gold font.

The cashier took her money and returned the diary neatly wrapped in gleaming silver paper, she added "To Lynn" on the tag shaped like a sleigh bell. A little corner of her unfolded as she allowed the idea of Christmas magic to take hold. Her mother had given her a diary in that exact shade of purple. Never after, did Miranda find one like it; that is until now.

As soon as she pushed in the wreath-covered front door, she shouted out, "Merry Christmas!" With the holiday traffic, the trip had taken almost the full day.

"Merry Christmas!" a chorus greeted her back from the den. Everyone was in there watching the Grinch that Stole Christmas. His big green face filled the widescreen as she entered. Lynn bounced up and flung herself about Miranda's legs.

"You came," she cheered.

"I came," Miranda said. "I enjoyed Thanksgiving with you so much that I just had to come back."

"Good! Daddy said you wouldn't. Then he said, you would. I wasn't sure which was true. Watch the Grinch with us!"

Miranda took a seat right next to Lynn in the oversized chair. Avery passed her a whiskey on the rocks, the good stuff from Stanton's private stock. "I'm glad you're home," Avery whispered.

"Me, too," Miranda said. After she said it, she realized she meant it. The last few weeks melted away from her, like they were just a movie someone else starred in, and it was Thanksgiving again, only this time a Frasier fir, fully decorated with lights and clear glass ornaments, filled the front left side of the room. Lynn rested her head on

Miranda's lap.

After the movie finished, the older generation all begged off to bed. Scott bribed Lynn into her own bed with an extra reading of the Night Before Christmas. In the kitchen, Miranda picked through the leftovers for a sort of dinner and poured herself another whiskey. She sat at the breakfast nook, reading over some emails to Blocked Poet, amazed that on Christmas Eve people would still be looking at her photos.

Then her phone buzzed. Ronan. A picture of him. Not all of him, just one key part. She blushed and put the phone down. She picked it back up. She put it down again. How could she reply to that?

"So, show me your stuff," Scott said.

His voice startled her. She nearly jumped out of her seat at the kitchen counter. Her whiskey glass almost spilled.

"My stuff?"

"The poems. What have you sent Ambrose? He told me you sent a new bunch of poems that you didn't put online yet."

"Really? You want to see them?" She took another sip of her whiskey. A big one.

"Yeah, come on. Are they on this?" He reached over and picked up her phone before she had a chance to block the screen.

"Is that?"

"Is that what?" she asked.

"A penis? You're surfing porn in the kitchen on Christmas Eve. Now that's something."

"It's not porn. It's a text message. From a friend." She grabbed the phone and slipped it into her pocket.

"A boyfriend? I didn't know. You didn't mention him at Thanksgiving."

"It wasn't a thing then. And he's not a boyfriend. I didn't say boyfriend."

Scott stepped back a little, a touch of a frown creeping at the edge of his face. "If he's not a boyfriend, why is he sending you that?"

Miranda instantly felt fourteen again. She wished Avery would wake up and breeze into the kitchen for a glass of water or Lynn to wake up looking for her dad. Anything to get her out of this conversation.

"It's not like that."

Then something darker slipped across Scott's face. "It isn't serious, is it? You're not in love?"

Miranda took another sip of her whiskey. "Not love. I don't know."

"You don't know?"

"I said it's not like that. I like being with him. But he's leaving."

"That picture doesn't look like a man who is leaving. Does the big fella have a name?"

"Ronan. And he is leaving. He's going back to Ireland. Student visa expired."

"You aren't thinking of marrying him are you?"

"No, God, no. I said I like being with him. But he's leaving. Plane ticket bought. He's home packing."

"And you're here. Without him?"

"It's Christmas, of course I'm here. I wanted to see Avery and my dad. And Lynn, and your parents."

"Exactly, Miranda, it's Christmas. Why didn't you bring him?" Scott took a step closer to cover the distance between them. He reached out and tucked a strand of her hair behind her ear. "Though I'm glad you didn't. I wanted to see you. And explain," he said.

Miranda's phone buzzed again. She looked down and fumbled to find the off button. By the time she looked up, Scott was backing himself out of the room.

"Never mind. I must have misunderstood," he said. Then he turned and left.

Miranda stayed in the kitchen for a long time after that. She kept her phone in her pocket. The ice melted in her glass, so she poured another whiskey, this time straight up. And another after that.

13

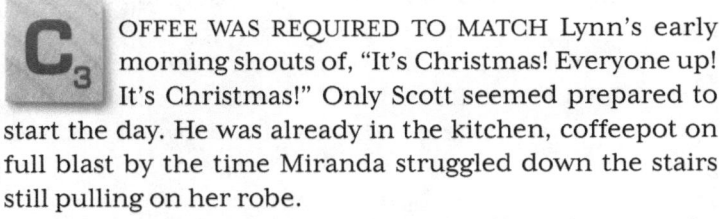OFFEE WAS REQUIRED TO MATCH Lynn's early morning shouts of, "It's Christmas! Everyone up! It's Christmas!" Only Scott seemed prepared to start the day. He was already in the kitchen, coffeepot on full blast by the time Miranda struggled down the stairs still pulling on her robe.

He handed her a cup, sugar and milk, without words.

"Thanks," she said. Then they both joined the others in the den under the tree for the explosion of presents.

Lynn tore into her presents like a tornado. Her arms wind-milled around, leaving shreds of paper in their wake. With each present unwrapped, she squealed.

Scott sipped his coffee right next to Lynn; he glanced up and smiled at Miranda. Her cheeks burned. She lowered her head, trying to ignore the buzzing of her cell phone in her pocket. Coming here made her even more confused. She had no idea what to say to Ronan.

"A Polly Pocket set. With a brown-haired Polly!! I love it! Thank you, Miss Avery!"

Next came the pink ski boots and matching parka.

"For our ski trip," Bunny said. "We can match." Lynn leaned over and pressed herself against her grandmother.

"I'm going to learn to ski, I'm going to learn to ski," she sang.

"And look good doing it," Linden added.

As Lynn's pile of gifts worked its way down to Miranda's, Miranda suspected Lynn's enthusiasm could not hold. She vowed not to take it personally. It was only a diary, after all. And Polly Pockets and Little Ponies have commercials. And cool packaging and online games you can play with your friends. Miranda shifted a little uncomfortably. She swirled her coffee cup around, thinking it might be the perfect time to get a second cup. Scott slid up next to her.

"I love this part," he said.

"What part?"

Lynn wind-milled through a Barbie and her horse from her grandparents. "Thank you, thank you!" she squealed again.

"The abandon of it. She just goes for the moment. And she's thankful for it. Right then. It doesn't take her years to figure out what things are. She sees it and loves it, and just goes for it."

"We aren't talking about presents, are we?"

"No, we aren't. I'm sorry about last night. I wasn't expecting that. I had something else in mind for this week."

"Something else?"

"I wish you weren't seeing someone."

"Why does it matter?"

"Never mind. You're right. It doesn't matter," he said, looking off to where Lynn had positioned Barbie's horse with the My Little Ponies.

Just then, Lynn exclaimed, "Randa Panda, it's perfect." Lynn held the diary aloft in both hands. "It even has a lock! Daddy, you see that, a real lock with tiny keys. Now I can write anything I want, and you can't read it."

"That's true. A diary is for your own private thoughts. Though if you ever need anyone to read anything, I'd be happy to," Miranda said.

"Of course I will. Thank you, Randa! Thank you."

"You're welcome." Miranda couldn't help but smile; the whiskey headache didn't even hurt as badly anymore.

"Didn't you have one just like that?" Stanton asked. "I think your mother gave it to you."

"I wrote my first poem in that diary," Miranda said.

"Was it purple like mine?" Lynn asked.

"Yes, it was. And I took it everywhere I went. I even wore the key on a string around my neck."

"I want to do that. I will write poems and wear the key and take it everywhere." Lynn jumped up from the pile of wrapping paper and ran to hug Miranda. Nothing could have prepared Miranda for that exquisite sensation. She squeezed Lynn tighter, inhaling the fruity scent of her shampoo and the candy cane she snuck from the tree when she thought Scott wasn't looking. "I'm glad you like it, sweetie," Miranda whispered.

"I love it, Randa. Maybe I'll be a writer just like you." Lynn said.

The breakfast of scrambled eggs and bacon helped her hangover, but the buzzing of her phone didn't. Finally, she pulled it out of her pocket, trying to think of what to text Ronan. Maybe a Merry Christmas and that she would call him later. Only she didn't want to call him later. She wanted to stay in Connecticut and make gingerbread houses. She wanted to watch Linden and Stanton play the Pretty Princess game Santa brought Lynn. She wanted to finish her conversation with Scott.

But the text messages weren't from Ronan. It was Danielle. Call me. Over and over and over again. Call me.

"Excuse me," she said to the others at the breakfast table. She saw Scott wince as she rose, then avert his eyes from hers.

The phone rang its weird overseas ring almost a dozen times before Danielle picked up.

"Miranda," she said. "Finally. I need to ask you something."

"Something? Something that required twenty text messages. Are you okay?"

"Yes and no. Just let me ask you. I want one thing to go the way it's supposed to, okay? Okay?"

"Okay." Miranda could tell by the watery sound of Danielle's voice that she had been crying. Not just a little crying, but hours of crying. She could see in her mind's eye the face of her best friend with red blotches on her forehead and cheeks, her eyelashes framing her eyes in stark, watery relief. "What is it? What do you need?"

"Will you be my bridesmaid? This week?"

At first Miranda hoped she had judged wrong, maybe those weren't tears of sadness she heard. Maybe it was all okay, just the phone connection overseas. "Yes, of course. But this week?"

"Your passport is good, right? You keep that ready. I know you keep that ready."

Miranda smiled. Danielle knew her too well. "I do keep it ready. When do I need to get there by? But wait, you aren't pregnant or something? Omar's family isn't making this a shotgun wedding are they?"

Then her friend began to wail. Not cry. Not sob. But wail. Through the breaks in her crying, Danielle struggled to get out the words. All Miranda could make out was growth and uterus.

"Wait, you have something wrong?"

"Yes," Danielle said. She sucked hard at her breath and sighed. "The doctor says there is something wrong with me, and that in my condition I can't travel or work for many months. They said I need to go to the American hospital as soon as possible. Omar is marrying me, so that I can stay in the country and get the treatment without losing my job and my visa. He says he loves me and wants to marry me, but I think it is just to be nice. But I don't care. I can't care. I'm stuck anyway."

"Oh, Dani, he does love you. He's loved you for years.

He's just been afraid of his family."

Omar's voice sounded in the background. "See," he said. "I told you. I love you. I'm sorry about my family. But please, Dani, none of that matters now."

"See, Dani, none of that matters now. Omar is right. It's going to take a bit of time for me to get to you. It's a long flight, but I will see how soon I can get there. When is the wedding?"

"I'm waiting for you. As soon as you can get here, we will have the ceremony."

"I will try. Let me go, so I can start calling airlines."

Miranda slipped the phone back into her pocket and turned to go back to the dining room. Avery would have a travel agent or some assistant who could help. She would need to go home to New York first, then drive down to JFK to fly out. Maybe there is a direct flight to Istanbul. So lost in her thoughts, Miranda didn't notice Scott waiting in the doorway to the dining room. She walked straight into his chest. Instead of pulling away, she started to cry.

"What? What?" Scott said. "What did that guy send you now?"

Miranda could scarcely catch her breath. "It's not him. Danielle. Dani. My friend. You know her. She teaches English in Turkey. She's getting married this week, and she just asked me to go. I have to fly to Turkey." She kept crying, not caring about the snot running down her face.

"Randa, this isn't making sense. Why are you crying? A surprise wedding is a good thing. A trip is nice. What else is it?"

"There's something wrong with her, some growth, and the doctor said she can't travel and needs treatment. She asked me to come."

Scott took Miranda by the shoulder and looked into her eyes. "Is it cancer?" he asked.

Hearing the word she learned to avoid made it even harder to stop crying. "I don't know," she blubbered out.

Scott ran up the hall and returned with a box of tissues

from the den. "What are you going to do?" he asked.

"I need a flight to Istanbul, but first I need to go home and get my passport."

"Do you want me to go with you?"

"To New York?"

"To Istanbul."

Miranda couldn't say anything at first.

Lynn's voice carried into the hall from the den. "Grandpa, you landed on red, so you get the red earrings to wear not the purple."

"You can't. You have Lynn," Miranda said.

"Lynn is going skiing with my parents. Let me come with you. I don't want you to face that alone."

It wasn't until they were on the interstate the next morning that she remembered Ronan. And actually she didn't remember him. Scott did. "How's the big fella going to take to this?" he asked. He drummed his fingertips on the steering wheel in time to some top-forty song that came in on the radio. He hummed and swiveled his head from side to side, checking the rearview mirror.

Miranda watched him trying to be nonchalant about the question; it quelled her own minor panic about that thought. Ronan. He would be leaving in two days, and there would be no time for her to say goodbye. No more time for her and Ronan at all. She scanned her body for a twinge of regret. Of something. But nothing surfaced. Scott accelerated around a slow-moving truck. She watched the tension in the muscle on the top of his thigh tighten and then ease as he changed lanes again. The car just glided forward, a rocket over the highway.

"I don't know. He's leaving in two days anyway. I'll call him when we get to my place. I'll tell him what happened. He'll understand." She pulled out her phone and scanned the naughty stream of texts he had sent her over the weekend. Each one more strongly worded than the last. Merry Christmas was her only reply. After everything with

Danielle, Miranda lost her appetite for Ronan. It's like her time with Ronan happened, only it was a very long, long time ago, like a memory of something you read in a book.

Inside her apartment, the cheery Christmas tree waited. Half empty wine glasses stood like sentries on every flat surface in the apartment. The sheets were still tangled across the unmade bed. "Sorry about the mess," she said, knowing exactly what it looked like. Her cheeks burned.

"No, it's fine. Nice place. You work close by?"

"Just two blocks that way." She pointed out the front window with a wine glass in her hand. She gathered a few up and put them in the kitchen sink. "I just need to get my passport and pack some clothes, okay? Make yourself comfortable."

Scott sat uneasily down on the sofa and picked at the Scrabble board left on the coffee table. "A poem sculpture?"

Miranda remembered it. Her cheeks burned again. "Ambrose asked for valentines."

"Oh," Scott said. "That would make for a good Valentine's day. Or is that night?"

Her cheeks got worse.

"It's okay, Miranda. Nothing I haven't seen. Or rather done before."

"I'll just be a minute," she said, slipping into her bedroom and closing the door. After getting her breath back, she slipped her phone out of her pocket and dialed Ronan.

"You're back early," he said.

"Yes and no," she said. "I'm leaving." She explained to him about Danielle and Turkey.

"But I won't see you?"

"No, Ronan. I have to go."

"I can change my ticket. I'll go with you."

Outside, snow began to fall. If they didn't start back soon, the roads would be a mess. "No that's okay. I'm fine. Really. I'm fine. You need to get back."

"I've been gone for three years. I don't need to go anywhere. Don't be like this. You're at the apartment? I'm coming over."

"Ronan, don't come over. Please don't come over."

"None of that now. You are being silly. I miss you. We only have a little bit of time, Miranda. We shouldn't spend that in a silly conversation."

She could hear him tugging on his coat and pulling the door shut to his apartment. She massaged her temples. "Ronan, don't come. Scott's here."

"Scott? The one from Thanksgiving?"

"Yes."

"You leave me for two days and come back with the one from Thanksgiving? What is going on here? I am coming over. This can't happen like this, Miranda. We were supposed to have these days. I love you. I thought you felt the same. Or at least you were starting to feel the same."

"It's not like that, Ronan. Please don't come. I am leaving as soon as I pack. I need to go to Danielle. She is like a sister to me. Please don't do this."

"Don't do what, Miranda? Don't be in love with you? After the last few weeks, what did you think I was playing at?"

"But you already had your plane tickets. What were you playing at?"

"I thought it would change things. I thought leaving wouldn't matter. I could come back."

"But you never mentioned that. You always said this was all it was. Just a few weeks."

"But what if we stayed together? Wouldn't you want me to come back? Wouldn't you want to be together?"

"Ronan, I never looked at it like that. You said you were leaving. I believed you."

"I also told you I loved you, Miranda. Didn't you believe that?"

"People always say that. They don't mean it. It doesn't stop them from leaving." She could feel her voice getting louder.

"Randa?" Scott knocked on the door. "You okay?"

"I'm okay," she said, "just packing."

"What's that? You're okay? Are you talking to him? You can't even talk to just one of us at a time? Maybe I was wrong about you, Miranda. I never expected you would be the type to use a person like this. And not just any person. A student."

"A student? Ronan, it's not like that. You know it. You said so yourself."

"What's it like then?"

"It's like ... nothing."

"Miranda, nothing doesn't hurt like this. I love you. Please tell him to go and let me go with you. We can forget these two days and just go on. Can't we do that?"

"Ronan, I don't want to forget these two days any more than I want to forget the last few weeks. Right now I just want to get to my friend. This isn't about you and me. I need to go. Be fair. Your plane is in three days. Don't do this."

"Too late, Miranda. We already happened. Good luck on your trip."

Then the phone went dead. She held it in her hand, staring at it. She saw her tears bubble up on the screen before she realized she was crying. She hadn't heard herself crying either, but Scott did. He opened the door to the bedroom and wrapped his arms around her.

"It's okay," he said. "You're okay here."

"It doesn't feel okay, Scott. He was upset."

"But how do you feel?"

Miranda paused at the question. Feel? She never really considered it.

"Don't wrinkle your forehead. Just stop and check in with yourself. How do you feel?"

"Check in with yourself? When did you get replaced with a hippie? What would your old Wall Street friends say?"

"It's something we do with the kids. Don't be sarcastic.

Just try it, won't you?" He stepped back.

"Honestly?" she asked.

"Yes, honestly. Have I ever led you astray?" He winked at her.

"Do you want me to answer that?"

"No, I want you to take a deep breath."

Miranda closed her eyes and took a deep breath. At first she felt weird, like there was an itch all over her skin. Then she took another breath. She heard Ronan's voice in her head. But it disappeared. She remembered Scott's hug. And Danielle's voice on the phone. How did all that make her feel, though? Resolved, she thought. She felt resolved. There were steps to be taken and a plane to catch. Scott. Ronan. They didn't matter, at least not at this moment.

After a minute or two, Scott asked, "How do you feel?"

She considered his question before answering, scanning her thoughts a few more times. "Fine," she finally said. "I feel really fine. Let's do this."

"Good answer," Scott said. "Where's your suitcase?"

CHAPTER

14

WITH THE BAGS ALL LOADED in the trunk of Miranda's car, the three fathers stood around the driveway of Avery and Stanton's house the next morning.

"Looks clear to me," Stanton said, peering at the weather app on his cell phone.

"Airline says on time," Linden said.

"Looks like there's snow in Vermont," Scott said.

Lynn and Miranda just stood there, bouncing a little to keep warm.

The men did another round of comparisons.

Miranda finally broke in. "Daddy, it's just a short trip."

"Yes, yes, I know," Stanton said. "We were just checking."

"I know." Miranda straightened the lapels on his coat and kissed him on the forehead. "We will call when we land. Miss Lynn, will you escort these gentlemen back into the house?"

"Does this mean we can go skiing sooner?"

"Not sooner, Lynnie," Linden said. "We can't wake up Bunny too early, you know."

"Oh, Grandpa, I can. She said I was the only one allowed to. Ever. Daddy, let me hug you goodbye."

Scott bent and squeezed her in a big embrace. "Lynn," Scott said, "What times do you take your vitamins?"

Lynn fiddled with the zipper of her new pink parka.

"Lynn," he said again.

"I'll be skiing with Grandma and Grandpa all day. I'll take them in the morning and before bed. I don't want to do lunch ones."

"But you need the lunch ones."

"Daddy, I am fine. You heard what Grandma said. She said I was fine. She told you to relax."

"I can't relax, Lynn-love, I want you to be okay. Please take them."

"Only if you take some, too, in Turkey."

"Okay," he said. His voice brightened. "I'll take as many as you do. And you email me every day if I don't call first. I want pictures. And stories."

"Scott," Linden said. "Me and Lynnie will be just fine. Have a good vacation. Take care of this bridesmaid. See she gets to the wedding on time."

The drive to JFK mercifully progressed with only the expected amounts of traffic. Despite the holiday, lines for checking in and security moved swiftly. Miranda wondered if the universe conspired to make this trip easy for them.

"We don't board for a least an hour," Scott said.

"Yup." Miranda said.

"A drink?" they both said together.

They found the bar closest to their gate. The bartender stood at the other end of the bar deep in thought with his cell phone. Scott pulled out his phone and started typing out a text message; his brow furrowed in concentration. She tried to bore a hole in the bartender's back with a stare; then she cleared her throat in another failed attempt. Nothing. Scott typed more, a furious clacking sound erupting from his phone. Two men. Two phones. No beer. Finally,

Miranda hopped off her stool and walked to the end of the bar. "Are you on duty?" she asked.

"Oh, sorry, ma'am," the bartender said. "What can I do you for?" He tried flashing his flawless smile.

"Scott?" Miranda asked, "A beer?"

"Sure, anything," he said, still not looking up from his phone.

"Two beers," Miranda said.

"Sure, coming right up."

"Sorry about that," Scott said.

Miranda climbed back up on her stool.

"I've never left Lynn before," he continued.

"Never?"

"Never. When she was a baby, we lived in Oregon. None of my friends there knew anything about babies. Not that I would have trusted them anyway. And my parents, well, they weren't really ready for this. Let's say it threw them for a loop to be polite."

The bartender put the beers down in front of them along with the receipt. Scott slipped a twenty on the bar and the bartender walked away, going back to his phone.

"What about Lynn's mom?"

"It's complicated. Lynn's mom disappeared right after Lynn was born. Her name is Cassadee. We met in college. We were friends. We partied."

"Just friends?"

"Well, there was one night when we were more than that."

"That is how babies happen, right?"

"Well, kind of. But not that time. Lynn's not mine."

"Wait a minute, what? She is so yours. She even has your eyes."

"Not biologically. Remember that night I visited you in New York? I got the call to come to the hospital that night. I flew to Oregon immediately and rushed to the hospital. When I got there, my name was on Lynn's birth certificate, and Cassadee refused to see the baby and me. There wasn't anything I could do. Cassadee signed herself out in the middle of the night."

"She just left?"

"Yup. She found me a few weeks later at a hotel in downtown Portland. She wanted money to score."

"Score what?"

"Anything I guess. She wasn't particular about the drugs. Or the people she did them with. When I wouldn't give her money, she told me Lynn wasn't mine and threatened to petition for a paternity test. She said that the real dad had overdosed two months before. She pulled out a stack of pictures. The last one was a guy in a coffin."

"A picture of him in the coffin?"

"This is why I don't talk about any of this in front of Lynn. This is why I couldn't just explain. I don't want to ever risk her knowing about this."

"What did you do?"

"I gave her money and tried to get her to sign a sort of adoption document just in case. She took the money and never returned the paperwork. It's been like that ever since. She asks for money; sometimes I give it to her, sometimes I don't. I didn't want her to mess anything up for Lynn, so I used to give in a lot. I haven't the last few times, though."

"Can I ask something?" Miranda took a big swig from her beer and set it down.

"I don't really talk to other people about this, but with you, it's different. So ask."

"What's up with Lynn and the vitamins?"

"She needs to take them. They're important."

"Is she okay?"

"Okay? Yes, she's great. But Cassadee. Well, she didn't stop using while she was pregnant." He picks up his beer and takes a hard swallow. "She's HIV positive."

"Lynn is HIV positive?"

"Well, Cassadee is. With Lynn, it's more complicated."

"Complicated? I thought it was just a blood test."

"It is a blood test, but her first one came back positive.

Her second one came back negative. The third was negative. The fourth was inconclusive. The fifth negative."

"Five tests?"

"The doctors think I'm crazy about it. They say the evidence is fine, she isn't infected, but there's the first test. That first test they did when she was first born, I still remember the scream she let out as they drew her blood."

"What about you?"

"My tests have always been clean. It seems that Cassadee got HIV and pregnant at the same time, sometime after we had our night together. With all the drinking and drugs, she didn't carry Lynn to full term; they told me that it was a miracle for a baby to be born so early and at such a low weight and yet have functional lungs. Even with that she had to stay in the hospital for almost a month. She was almost seven weeks early. Had I understood the math then, I would have known right away that the baby wasn't mine; I could have been spared the coffin picture. We hooked up in July. But with Lynn being that early, Cassadee must have gotten pregnant in August or September. By the time I got there, it was too late, and Cassadee was gone. And well, Lynn was there. And—"

"And what?"

"You'll think I'm crazy."

"Crazy? I think this was a rough spot to be in."

"I fell in love with her. The baby. It took two seconds. They handed her to me, and I wanted her to be mine. She was so tiny. And they kept calling her a miracle. We all did. It was the craziest thing. One minute I was working on Wall Street and drinking with friends and being everything a man from my family was supposed to be and then I was in a hospital holding a baby, a baby I suddenly loved and wanted more than anything. If Cassadee would have hung around, I probably would have proposed, made the whole thing official right then and there."

"Even with the HIV?"

"I didn't know about it right then. Cassadee didn't tell

the hospital until she signed out. And they didn't think to test her when she came in. Pregnant women usually get those tests before they deliver."

"She put a lot of people's lives at risk."

"Yes, that was her way. Still is her way. She said she never wanted to see Lynn or me again. Frankly, I don't waste a lot of time thinking about her. Lynn has me, and we are just fine together."

"You are fine together. Anyone can see that. But doesn't Lynn ever ask about her mother?"

"Not really."

"Not really?"

"Listen, Randa, Lynn knows the basics. What else can I tell her? Your mother's a junkie? Your mother left you? How do you explain any of that to a kid?"

"That has to be rough."

"It is rough. But then most of the time that stuff doesn't even factor in. Most of the time it's just me and her doing what we enjoy."

"What do you enjoy? I'd like to know more about that, too. You're the first one of my friends to be a parent. Not that I ever would have expected it."

"I didn't expect it either, but you know what? I don't regret it. Not a single minute." Scott finished his beer.

Miranda liked watching the sparkle in his beautiful green eyes. She noticed a few strands of gray hair at his temples. He looked a little older but still the same. Avery always teased that he looked like a member of the Kennedy clan. "You're a real JFK junior, all right," she said to him during one of their Martha's Vineyard vacations. "You just stay out of trouble okay." Then Scott grinned, his perfect teeth glistening like a beauty queen's. "Yeah," she said, "that just makes it worse. Go back to playing Frisbee."

The loudspeaker blasted out that their gate for the flight to Istanbul changed. Miranda consulted their tickets.

"That's in the other terminal," she said.

Scott looked at his phone. "Looks like we have to run.

Like really run."

On the plane, out of breath from the two-terminal trek, they found themselves seated in different rows. "I guess last-minute means last pick," Miranda said. Her seat came first.

"I'll see what I can do," Scott said, over his shoulder as he made his way up the aisle.

Miranda took her assigned seat. An older lady took the seat next to her. They watched the safety demonstration with rapt attention. The plane taxied to the runaway quickly and took off without a delay. Gratitude washed over Miranda; the length of the flight alone filled her with dread.

From her bag, Miranda pulled out a book from Avery's collection of mysteries. This one featured a quilting club of all things, and she tried to get past the first page while thinking about Scott.

"Good book," said the lady sitting next to Miranda. "There's even a pattern for a mystery quilt online to go with it. Do you quilt?"

"Oh, no," Miranda said. "I don't think I could. I can't cut straight with scissors."

"I have a friend with that problem," the lady continued. "They make tools for that."

"Really," Miranda said. She stretched up a bit to try and catch a glimpse of Scott in the back of the plane. "How interesting."

"Who are you looking for?" the lady asked.

"Oh, my friend. We're going to Istanbul for a wedding."

"A wedding. How lovely! I'm meeting a tour. The Byzantine Empire and Churches. Fourteen days. My daughter sent me. She's a lawyer in California."

"Wow, fourteen days of churches; that's something."

"For my birthday last year, she sent me to the Holy Land. I walked in the footsteps of Christ. That was only ten days, but they were the best ten days of my life. Just imagine walking where Christ walked."

Miranda didn't know how to respond. Her response could dictate the next eighteen hours of her life. She took a deep breath. "The Holy Land—" she started.

Just then, Scott tapped her new companion's shoulder. "Excuse, ma'am," he said. "I was wondering if you would do me a favor." He turned on the Kennedy twinkle.

"You must be this young lady's friend."

"I am, and I was wondering if you might switch seats with me. I've asked the attendants, and they assure me that if you are willing it would be just fine. They've also assured me that if you would like a glass of wine, they would happily pass the bill in my direction for your kindness."

"A glass of wine, well, I don't really drink."

"Please forgive me then."

"No, well actually, I do sometimes."

"Oh, sometimes," Scott said. "Then, well, would you mind?"

"Seeing as you went to the trouble to arrange things, no, not at all. Which seat is it?"

"35A. It's the window."

"Young man, you should have started there. I wanted a window."

"Then it must be fate," he said.

"Fate," Miranda said. "Nice chatting with you."

"You too, dear. Don't forget that quilting pattern is online."

Scott sank in next to her, pushing his backpack under the seat. His knees touched the back of the seat in front of him.

"Thank you," Miranda said.

"What's this about a quilting pattern?" he asked.

Miranda raised the book. "A murder mystery with quilting. Avery's if you can imagine that."

"To each his own. I can put on my head phones if you would rather read."

"Did you not hear me? It's a quilting murder mystery. I've never had any sort of domestic goddess fantasies, certainly not ones that involved crime fighting while making up a blanket."

"Well, you know, your taste could have changed in the last six years. Maybe you gave up on Updike and Cheever and settled for something a little more accessible. Though I must admit I always loved when you read to me. You picked the best books."

"Remember the year we read Twenty Thousand Leagues Under the Sea and then recreated it in my swimming pool?"

"That was better than when you moped about reciting *Le Petit Prince* all over Newport."

"Wait, wait," Miranda said, almost bouncing out of her seat. "I still remember some of that. 'One sees clearly only with the heart. Anything essential is invisible to the eyes.' Lord, I was a strange kid."

"I hope Lynn is just like that."

Miranda fiddled with the book in front of her, flipping through the pages like a deck of cards. "Just like what? A dork? You can't hope that. She could be something better than that. She could be homecoming queen or class president. Not some book worm."

"Not some book worm? Really? I hated when our trips were over, and I had to go back to my regular life and my regular friends. All they wanted to do was shoot hoops or play Super Mario. When we were together, you created whole worlds for us. That pirate fort you told Lynn about—that was because of Treasure Island. Why wouldn't I want her to be able to do that? You still do that. I've seen those word sculptures of yours all over the Internet. You use words to make strangers smile."

"I guess so," Miranda said. "But it makes me smile, too. I love when someone new comments on a post I made or I see that it gets shared. It's like making a difference in a really small way. But it's the only way I've got."

"Well, with Ambrose on the job you can be sure it won't be small for long."

"Yeah, well I doubt that. But it's nice to think about."

"You might want to do more than think about it. Did you even read the contract?"

Miranda buried her head in her hands.

"You didn't sign it yet?"

"Worse," Miranda said. "I just signed it. I didn't read it."

"You've got to be kidding me. Are you crazy?"

"I just trusted you," Miranda said.

"Oh," Scott said. "Well then."

"Well then, indeed."

The attendants dimmed the lights and a hush fell over the cabin. "I think I need to close my eyes," Miranda said. "It's been a long couple of days."

"Yeah," he said. "Me too, but it's been worth it."

15

THE MOST SHOCKING SIGHT when they finally landed was seeing Omar's mom, Selin, standing with one arm around Danielle, the other arm waving frantically to Miranda.

"We are here," she called out. "We are here!"

As if there was any way of mistaking the large crowd gathered. They must have taken three cars to get to the airport.

Danielle pulled herself from the crowd and ran to hug Miranda. "I told them you were like a sister to me," she whispered into Miranda's ear. "They didn't get the like part, so you are now my sister. Just go with it, okay?"

An older man, Omar's grandfather by the looks of things, walked up to Scott. "Sir," he said very formally. "May my grandson have your sister's hand in marriage?"

Scott didn't miss a beat. He put his hand to his chin and lowered his head as if he were thinking about it.

"What's this?" Miranda hissed at Danielle.

"Oh, well that. I had to tell them that you and Scott were married."

"Married?"

"It was tough for me to explain to them. I didn't even understand. And believe me, I want the full story the minute we are alone. And anyway, if I can be married this week, so can you."

"It's hardly the same thing."

"Don't be upset. It's not like you would say no if he asked. Make a dying lady happy."

"Wait a minute. You're not dying."

"You don't know that."

"I do know that. You will see the doctors at the American Hospital, and it will be fine. And don't try changing the subject. This week is all about you, not me and my love life or whatever this is."

"I'm glad you're here," Dani said, hugging Miranda tighter.

Then Scott cleared this throat. "This is sudden," he joked. The old man's face wrinkled a little. "But seriously," Scott added. "Will she be properly cared for?"

"Indeed," the man replied.

"Then I give my blessing," Scott said.

The two men shook hands and then embraced in a back-slapping hug. Omar stepped forward to shake Scott's hand.

The women, done with waiting, rushed forward to hug Miranda and Danielle. A small girl with luxurious black hair that hung in a thick braid down her back presented herself in front of Miranda, her hand extended.

Miranda shook the girl's hand. "I'm Jellie," she said. "Junior bridesmaid." Then she said something to Danielle in Turkish; Danielle beamed at her and replied. The girl skipped back to her mother.

"She's checking out the competition," Danielle whispered to Miranda. "She thinks you're pretty but that the dress suits her better."

"There's already a dress?" Miranda asked.

"Oh, you'll see," Danielle said. She squeezed Miranda

again; this time Miranda feared the waffle weave of Danielle's shirt imprinted on her cheek from the force of the hug.

The ride from the airport to Omar's house was a blur with the caravan of cars and minivans taking them all back through the city to the neighborhood Omar's parents lived in. Scott rode in front of the mini-van with the men. They immediately started talking about soccer, golf, and whether or not Scott's cell phone will work in Turkey. The women of Omar's family kept holding up swaths of fabric to Miranda's face, bickering amongst themselves about which color would suit her best.

"Like an official bridesmaid dress? I'm still not follow-ing." Miranda said to Danielle. "What type of wedding are you having in less than a week?"

"It's kind of a big deal," she said, shrugging her shoul-ders.

The convoy delivered them to Omar's parents' house. It stood two stories tall with gleaming white siding and little balconies jutting out from the second story windows. A white iron fence partitioned the manicured gardens from the sidewalk. They spilled out. The men surrounded Scott and asked him even more questions about golf from the snippets of conversation Miranda could catch.

"Omar's parents said you should stay here," Dani said. "They didn't want you sleeping on the floor at my place."

"But we wouldn't have minded."

"But they would have. Things must be done right."

"Oh, I see."

"I'll come get you first thing in the morning. Omar is staying here, too. He's going to take Scott with him to play golf. Like some bachelor party thing."

One of the women leaned out of the passenger side of the second car. "Danniiii!!!" she called. "We have to get you back to your apartment."

Selin stepped forward and placed a hand on Danielle's

shoulder. "I promise I'll take good care of your friends tonight." Then she turned to Miranda. "You must be tired. I'll have my husband show you to your room," Selin said. "I need to check on some details for the dinner tomorrow."

Roger, Omar's father, led them up the staircase to the guest room. "This is it," he said, his own accent a mix of British and Turkish. "If you need anything, I'm sure Selin will be in the kitchen all night." Then he ducked out and pulled the door shut behind him.

"So we're married," Scott finally said, whirling around to face her.

"I'm sorry about all that. This is really important to Danielle. Do you mind playing along?"

"Do you mind playing along?" he asked back. He picked up her hand and dropped to one knee. "Miranda, will do me the honor of being my wife?"

She let her eyes lock onto his. He had no idea how many times she imagined hearing him say those words.

"At least for the rest of this week," he stammered, before getting back up again.

She turned away before he could see the tears she felt forming in the corners of her eyes. It had been so long since she had spent time with him, and now all of this was too much. Even though it wasn't real, too much of her wished that it were true to just laugh it off.

But then his voice softened. "I don't mind playing along," he continued. "I would like to be your husband."

"Very funny," she said, then she moved quickly to the door and slipped out into the hallway to find the bathroom.

Sleeping in the same room as Scott was nothing new. Miranda remembered the place near Cape Cod that Bunny and Linden rented. It only had two bedrooms; one on the first floor, the other in the loft overlooking the main great room. The parents naturally claimed the bedrooms leaving Scott and Miranda to take up different corners of the great room for their own. And after a few days of staying at the beach, their new friends would spend the night, too, spreading out blankets on the various cast-off chairs and sofas filling the room. But Miranda always loved the first few nights when it was just the two of them. She was short enough to take the window seat and pretend she was really sleeping on a bunk in a boat bound for a tropical island. Scott, always tall, took the longest couch.

"What are you reading?" he would ask her.

No matter what she replied; he would then say, "Well, share. Read to me."

She began to pick books at the little library in town that she knew he would like. Stories by Jules Verne or Orson Welles or Edgar Allen Poe. The night she read *A Tell Tale Heart* they didn't go to sleep at all. Scott turned on all the lights and made them pancakes in the galley kitchen. She sat on the countertop and started to read the Little Mermaid from a fairy-tale book left as a decoration on the dusty bookshelf in the great room. Only that story didn't help to dislodge Poe from their minds; it just made it worse. They spent the rest of the night playing Rummy 500, and luckily, the next day it rained, and no one questioned why they napped all day and didn't want any breakfast.

If this week could be like that, Miranda would probably be in heaven. But you can't expect things to stay the same way they were when you were children. Things change; people change—even if you don't want them to.

Scott was already in bed when she got back to the room. The lights were still on, but she could tell from his breathing and the relaxed look on his face that he had been asleep for a long time. She climbed into bed slowly, lying on top of the blankets for fear of disturbing him. His chest rose so slightly, and the corners of his mouth turned up in the tiniest of smiles. He didn't snore as much as buzz. Even in his sleep, he was electric.

Turning away from him, she closed her eyes, certain that sleep couldn't possibly come. But jet lag and maybe the old familiar comfort of him took hold quickly, tugging her down into the dark nothing of much-needed rest. In the morning, she found a note about golf and seeing her later for the night-before-the-wedding dinner. He signed it, Love, Scott.

CHAPTER

16

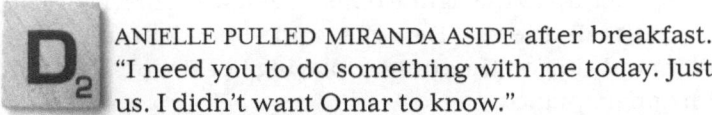 ANIELLE PULLED MIRANDA ASIDE after breakfast. "I need you to do something with me today. Just us. I didn't want Omar to know."

Miranda could tell this wasn't something about the wedding. "Of course," she said. "Whatever. Just tell me what it is."

"I have a follow-up appointment. Some kind of test to check out the tumor. I don't want Omar to go. I don't want him to be thinking about that the day before our wedding. And Omar's family, they know something is wrong with me, but I'm not ready to have his mom in on the specifics. Like how do you say vagina or uterus to that woman?"

Miranda couldn't help but laugh.

"I know, funny, right. Even though it might be cancer."

Danielle grabbed Miranda's hand. It was cold and sweaty. Miranda squeezed back. "It's not cancer. Don't say that. Can't it wait until after?"

"They said no. They said I need to have everything checked out as soon as possible. I already waited to schedule it until after you got here. I didn't want to go alone."

They went that morning to a tall shining tower of a hospital. "The VFK American Hospital" read the sign in front. "American hospital? What does that mean?" Miranda asked.

"It's for medical tourists mainly. The Turkish doctor I saw already told me to follow up here. He said only they would be willing to help me."

Inside was just like any other hospital, except maybe the staff was nicer. Everyone treated you the way a hotel clerk would. And all you had to do was show your visa. Her visa, Danielle explained, expired a very long time ago. But each time she thought about going home to the states to renew it, she realized she would be leaving Omar. So she didn't. Luckily, the marriage paperwork overrode the visa requirements. But the nurse at the check-in desk examined each document as if looking for some hole. She even held one paper up to the light to check for a watermark.

"It's all there," Danielle said. She drummed the diamond ring on the counter playing her fingers along an imaginary piano.

Finally, the nurse spoke. "Payment," she said flatly.

Danielle pushed the American Express card across the counter. The nurse bundled up the papers and gave them back without even photocopying them.

"Whoa," Danielle said under her breath as the nurse stepped away to run the credit card. "I was worried about that."

"Why?"

"I could go to jail for being here without the proper visa. And the doctor said I couldn't travel with this condition, and Omar can't leave Istanbul right now because of his job. He's about to be promoted. So getting married was really our only option."

"At the last minute."

"Yes, at the last minute."

"In a Muslim ceremony that would kill your Methodist parents, God rest their souls."

"Muslim? I knew I was forgetting to tell you something. I'm so sorry!"

"Sorry about what? I don't care that you are marrying a Muslim. I'm a little mad that Omar made such a big deal out of it and refused to tell his family about you guys, but he is really upset and doing the right thing now, so I am letting him slide some."

"Wait, Randa, wait. Get this—they aren't Muslim. They're Christian. Syriac Christian."

"Then why on earth did Omar never want to talk about it? Why all the secrecy?"

Danielle scooted to bring her chair closer to Miranda. The squeak of the chair on the polished linoleum floor startled the nurse behind her desk.

"He will be with you shortly," she said.

Danielle leaned into Miranda's ear. "You really can't talk about it here. It's like, not accepted. It's like the reverse of home. And all this time, he thought I wouldn't understand. That I wasn't really Christian because I didn't go to church."

"You never told him about your dad being a minister after he retired from the phone company?"

"It's not like I kept up with going to church after my parents passed away. It was always the last place I wanted to be."

"Well, aren't you two peas in a pod?"

"Yes," Danielle said. A smile settled across her face, the smile of a bride, a smile that extended past the gloom of this hospital waiting room. Then a man with a very dark tan and wearing a white lab coat called her name.

Both women popped up quickly, but before they could reach the door the man had already disappeared down the long corridor. They followed after him, struggling to keep up. Finally, he stopped at an open door and swept his arm out to usher them inside. The room was blank except for the ultrasound machine, the table, and a chair on the opposite side of the room. He motioned to Miranda to take the chair, leaving her seated behind his back.

"Please," he said, flipping open the chart. "Miss Townsend, take a seat on the table—they've explained this to you before, correct?"

"Yes," Danielle said. "I had an appointment last week at the health center. They told me I must come here immediately, that my condition was not good. They said this needed immediate attention."

"And that she couldn't fly back to the States," Miranda added.

Danielle's voice caught in her throat. "They did send the paperwork to you?" she asked. "They said they would."

"Yes, yes," he said. He made some notes on the chart. "You are married?" he asked.

"No, well, not yet, tomorrow."

"Tomorrow." He spoke this flatly letting his gaze fall to the diamond on her left hand. "You know this man a long time?"

"Ten years. He would have come today, but I didn't want to worry him before the wedding."

"Have you slept with him?"

Miranda stood up and crossed the room, standing next to Danielle. "Doctor, respectfully, why does this matter?"

"Ah, it matters," he said again. He pressed several buttons on the machine. "While this starts, I will leave the room; please undress from the waist down." Then he turned and left the room, the door closing like a clap of thunder behind him.

"Dani, maybe you should come home anyway. I don't like this."

"It's okay; it's just different here. People have different ideas. This is just like an American hospital. It should be okay."

"Should be? Really?"

"Miranda, listen, I can't leave. My life is here. Tomorrow, Omar and I will be married, and then this kind of thing will die down some. He'll come to the appointments and the sexist old men can talk to him the way they like. I don't mind. If I am with him, I don't care about the rest of them."

"How can you say that?"

"How can you still love Scott?"

"I never said I loved him."

"You don't wait six years for someone you just like," Danielle said, as the doctor pushed back through the door, this time with a nurse; she wore a regular set of scrubs with a floral headscarf pinned neatly back. She took the probe from the machine, lubricated it and handed it to the doctor.

"Lie back," he said. "Take a deep breath."

The monitor sprung to life with the gray swirls and lines on the screen ebbing and flowing like waves. The nurse adjusted the sound level. An even thumping filled the room.

"Wow," Miranda said, "Listen to your heart."

"It's not her heart," the doctor said. "It's the baby's."

ANIELLE WASN'T DYING. She didn't have cancer. She had a baby.

"A baby," Danielle said. "A baby."

"It's not a tumor," Miranda said.

"Four months."

"You're due in May. That's good. You miss being pregnant in the summer."

"But a baby. I don't think I can breathe." Danielle bent forward and placed her hands on her knees.

"You're breathing. Stop it. How will you tell Omar? What will you tell his parents?"

"Omar!" Danielle shouted, her voice carrying over the parking lot. "You tell Omar. Call him."

"I can't tell him."

"Yes, you can. Do this for me."

"I'm not telling him. I'll call, but you are telling him."

Miranda reached into her purse for her phone. She hadn't turned it on once since she arrived the day before. Just as she went to dial Omar's number, the battery died. "I don't have any battery left. Give me yours. I'll use that."

"I don't have it."

"Don't have it?"

"I don't carry it, and I can't have it when I'm teaching my classes—they're strict about that."

"Well, you need it now. You have to tell him."

Danielle pursed her lips together. "Can't it wait?"

"Wait? Aren't you excited? Don't you want him to know?"

"I thought I was dying. Omar thought I was dying. What if he doesn't really want to marry me? What if it is just a big mistake?"

"But you're pregnant. With his baby! Doesn't that kind of make marriage seem like a good idea? Don't you love him?"

"The baby I can handle. I've always wanted to be a mother. But, Randa, what if he doesn't love me? What if he just felt sorry for me because I was sick?"

"Dani, don't be like this. You know he does."

"Yeah, I've known that for ten years. Ten years!" Again her voice boomed out over the sea of cars. "And he never once even tried to propose. I thought surely after I moved to Turkey. I thought after I met his family. I thought after his great-grandmother passed away, and everyone relaxed a little. I thought after I had my own apartment. After he had his own apartment. But none of this mattered. He didn't want marry me, Randa. Not until we thought I was sick. What does that say?"

"Fine. You win, okay, can we go someplace to talk about this? Someplace that's not a parking lot?"

"Sure, sure. Get in the car."

Danielle kept her eyes forward and both hands on the wheel as she steered them through the streets of Istanbul. She turned the radio up loud, and music in what Miranda could only assume was Turkish poured through the speakers. Miranda studied her friend; this girl she'd known almost all of her life was about to be a mother, a wife. It all seemed like a fairy story where some magic delivered the beautiful woman from danger and waltzed her into true love's path. How was this even possible? Real life didn't work like that. As much as she wanted to believe, to think that something like Christmas magic or fairy tales could be true, Miranda knew magic didn't exist like that, not really anyway. You needed to plan for things. Especially for being a mother! Miranda remembered her own mother, how prepared she was for anything. Once, Miranda got in trouble in the third grade for something small like not turning in her math homework. When she returned home from school, she found her desk in the living room where the television used to be. Her mother, completely non-plussed, who normally would be in court at that hour, pointed to the desk and the list of rules she had taped to the wall in front of it. The list was short; homework first, it read. The television had been moved to her parents' bedroom. She didn't see a cartoon again until her mom got sick, and Miranda would snuggle next to her in their bed. But even then, even on her worst days, she checked Miranda's homework. Her mother never resorted to theatrics or threats; she simply had a plan—and Miranda knew she had better follow it. It felt like she gathered all the books about being a mother and studied them just in case, long before Miranda entered the world. In order to be a mom, you needed logic, an even temper, and a plan.

But something about this one moment defied all logic and plans. A baby. Danielle was having a baby. She wasn't going to die.

"It's really a miracle," she shouted over a pop ballad.

Danielle turned toward her. The smile started across her face again. "It really is, isn't it?"

They parked outside the entrance to Gulhane Park. Miranda recognized it from pictures Danielle had sent of the tall evenly planted trees on either side of the wide stone path. "We're supposed to do wedding pictures here tomorrow. Everyone does it," Danielle said. They took the path to the left and walked quickly to keep away from other people on their constitutionals.

Miranda watched the people; she expected more passersby in traditional Muslim dress, and while a few women walked by in headscarves, it was really no different than Central Park. The more they walked, the more she could see why her friend chose not to leave this place. "You like it here," Miranda said.

Danielle looked up. "What do you mean?"

"You seem at home here. Relaxed."

"Relaxed? Really? Right now? I am anything but relaxed. From cancer to mom in one doctor's appointment, and it didn't even involve getting laid."

Miranda chortled loudly enough that a passing couple turned to stare at her. "Stop making me laugh. I'm trying to be serious here. We should be serious, right?"

"Why?"

"You're getting married; you're having a baby."

"Maybe."

"Maybe what?"

"Maybe married, baby, yes. Like I said. We were only doing it because I was sick."

"That's bullshit. You've been together ten years. You moved to Turkey to be with him."

"Near him. We don't even live together. We can't even figure out whose apartment to keep after the wedding."

"That won't matter after the baby comes."

"And how do you know?"

Miranda looked down at her hands. "I don't. Well, maybe, I do. I just have a feeling, all right? You guys love each other. And now with the baby and all, that should be enough."

"What storybook did you fall out of, Miranda? When has that been enough? You don't sound like yourself."

"Maybe I don't want to sound like myself, okay? I get it. Lots of people get divorced, lots of marriages suck. But so does being alone. So does letting someone you love go. It can't hurt to try."

"Did you just say that?"

"Okay, so maybe that's not true—but it would hurt either way. Why not risk it?"

"What if he doesn't love me? I mean really love me. What if it is just because I am the only one around?" Danielle sank onto a park bench. "I know that's not true. I'm just scared. The cancer thing didn't scare me. I knew they could fix that. I'm young and healthy or maybe just stupid or something, but I thought, oh, it will be fine. And if it wasn't, well, I had a good run. With Omar, though, I've loved him for so long, I just didn't think it was possible that he could love me, too. I didn't think I deserved it."

"You know you are being crazy, right? How many times did he overstay his student visa to be with you? How many times did he plead with you to come to Turkey and stay? I'm sorry you were both too stupid to talk about religion so you let it get in the way for this long, but maybe the whole 'you might be dying thing' was the universe's way of solving that problem. Maybe God has your back."

"Like some kind of Greek play where the fates intervene?"

"Yeah, only it's a Turkish play because, well, obviously."

"Obviously."

"So are you going to tell him about the baby?"

"Yes." Danielle drew out the "s" in a long exhale. "But can't we do something fun first? Just something for us before my entire life changes?"

"Fine, something fun first. But only because I came all the way to see you, and now we really have this awesome thing to celebrate. And I don't mind keeping it to myself for a bit. I'm going to be an aunt, you know."

"Really? An aunt. Nice. I hadn't thought about that. You get to meet my kid. My kid. Hmmm." Danielle stood and smoothed down the front of her coat. "How about a Turkish bath then? Relaxing, touristy, authentic."

Miranda quickly stood. "I heard that they can be rough."

"That's only if you go old school. I'll take you someplace modern."

They slipped into the provided robes at the baths and struggled to keep their voices low and hushed. The waiting room looked like something out of a movie set for the Middle East. Tiny mosaic mirrors dotted the white sandstone walls, and thick woven carpets lined the floor with pillows to sit on. There were low wooden cutwork tables ornately decorated with brass overlays in patterns mimicking those on the wall and warm glass cups of strong mint tea. Shimmering candles lit the room from insets in the walls and on the tables. It felt like a sumptuous paradise, the kind of place you would imagine when you thought of the Turkish empire. An older woman with heavily drawn-in eyebrows kept staring up at them from over the top of her magazine. It seemed to be a sort of Vogue magazine with a beautiful cover girl in a pink dress with black overlay and matching pink headscarf. Every time Danielle and Miranda laughed, she snapped the pages over a little more. But they couldn't help it. Each was trying to outdo the other with baby names.

"Okay, okay, enough," Danielle finally said. "Octavia or Octavium, it is."

"You don't mean that."

"I don't, but it will be fun to see Omar's reaction when I suggest it."

"I'm looking forward to that—not Omar—but having this. I'd like to settle down. Did I tell you how awesome Scott's Lynn is? When I'm with her, I realize why people have kids in the first place. There's something about her that just lights up a room."

"He isn't already married, is he?"

"Geesh, you don't exactly have to be married to have a kid." Miranda said this a little too loudly.

The eyebrow woman closed her magazine and set it down on her lap. She didn't hide the fact that she was staring at them now. "Go on," eyebrow woman said.

But luckily, the attendants saved them. "It is time for your soak. Together, yes?" she asked.

Danielle quickly replied. "Together."

They were led to an all marble room with a platform in the center. The heat of the room caused sweat to immediately bead up on Miranda's bow.

"It's working already," the attendant said. "Detoxifying. You wait 15 minutes."

Miranda looked around. "Do we sit here?" She pointed to the platform.

"Yes," the attendant replied. "You lie down, then I come back and bathe you." The attendant moved toward the door again, but she stopped and studied Danielle and Miranda. "You're not pregnant, are you?" she asked looking at Miranda.

"Me, no." Miranda recoiled thinking about Ronan and the last month, but she couldn't be pregnant; her cycle assured her of that.

"I am," Danielle said, loudly and with emphasis. She smiled again, her lips parting wide across her face, her eyes actually glittering.

"Ma'am, I'm afraid you can't have the treatment today," the attendant said. "Didn't you see the sign in the changing room?" She pointed at Miranda. "But you can. Please in there."

"Thank you," Miranda said, "but I go where she goes."

They couldn't contain their laughter as they pulled on their clothes and stumbled out of the changing room past the eyebrow woman in the waiting room. On the street, they bought ice cream from a vendor and walked hand in hand for a few blocks not saying anything. It felt good to be there with Danielle. To be with someone who already knew your story so you could walk in silence and just enjoy the scene unfolding around you. After a few more blocks, Danielle led them back to her car. "Thank you," she said. "That's the first time I've felt normal in a while. I missed you."

"I missed you, too," Miranda said. "Are you ready for this?"

"No choice really. But yeah, I'm ready for this. Thanks for not letting me bolt."

"What kind of bridesmaid lets the bride run away?"

"A fun one?" Danielle offered.

"Nice, so you're saying I'm not fun. Travel halfway around the world to be with you, and this is what I get. Let's go."

Instead of going to Omar's parents' house, Danielle drove them to her apartment. Finding her phone, she texted Omar to meet them there and to only bring Scott.

"I don't want this to be a big family thing. You and Scott can go out for a bit, right? There's a nice hotel with a bar on the roof—you can see the Bosphorus river from up there, it's quite nice as the sun sets."

"Sure, sure," Miranda agreed. She liked the idea of time alone with Scott. How can it be that a person could be away from you for so long and then return like nothing happened? This burned just a little; why couldn't he have talked to her sooner? But then she thought of Lynn and the story of her mother; of course, he didn't want to talk about that. But maybe talking about it would have made it better. Miranda remembered her own mother's illness. All they did was talk about it. At first, Miranda squirmed and sometimes rolled her eyes, but her mother didn't give up; she kept talking. And soon Miranda settled and listened. And now she remembered her mother, not with sadness or loss, but with understanding. She knew why her mother died, and more importantly, she knew it wasn't because her mother didn't love her—it had nothing to do with her—and everything to do with the pain that wouldn't stop, no matter how much Miranda and her father loved her and wanted it to end. It seemed wrong to her that Lynn wouldn't get that same chance.

The men tumbled into the house like puppies, boxing

each other in a play fight as they spilled through the door. Miranda and Danielle looked up from the dining room table, and they straightened quickly.

"What is it?" Omar said. "Just tell me."

"What?" Danielle asked. "Nothing. Why?"

"You never sit there."

"So?" Danielle said.

"And you asked us to meet you here. You know we have to meet the priest at my parents tonight. Something you wanted to do. And you hate being late. So spill it."

"Yes," she said.

Miranda knew the stubborn side of her friend was kicking in. It was no wonder these two weren't married yet. The way Omar took one glance at Danielle and sensed something awry, gave Miranda hope for their union. He knew her and cared enough to pay attention.

"You aren't calling it off, are you? Please don't do that. I've told you before. I love you. This isn't about you being sick. Dani, I love you, and I want to marry you." Omar strode across the room and sank to his knees at Danielle's feet. "Please don't call this off."

"Hey, Scott, how about we go get a drink and come back in an hour?"

Scott caught her eyes and nodded. "Sure," he said. "Right this way." Without so much as a wave, Miranda stood from the table and walked out the door, struggling the whole time to not laugh. Danielle had Omar exactly where she wanted him without even having to say more than four words.

As soon as Scott shut the door behind them, Miranda choked out a muffled laugh.

"What?" Scott hissed. "What's so funny? He loves her. His family has planned the whole wedding. I know she's sick, but this isn't right."

Miranda jogged ahead down the stairs and pushed the front door out onto the street below. "She isn't sick," she finally managed to spit out in between gasps for air.

"She isn't sick, so she's calling it off? She was just using him to stay in the country? Why did we even come here? And how does she know she isn't sick? What did you guys do today? You know what, never mind. I thought I knew you, Miranda, but this doesn't make sense. You don't treat people that love you this way." Scott turned to walk up the street. He called over his shoulder, "He loves her, Miranda, and you're laughing about it. It's all he could talk about today."

"Scott, wait, she isn't calling it off."

He didn't stop walking. He started walking faster. She tried to catch up, but as the traffic light changed, a rush of traffic erupted on the street between them. "She's pregnant," she shouted.

Scott stopped.

"She's pregnant," Miranda shouted again.

He finally turned. "What?"

The light finally changed, and Miranda rushed across the street. "It's the best news ever. The first clinic didn't test her for pregnancy because she wasn't married. It was an older doctor. Or maybe he knew she was pregnant and didn't want to tell her, so he sent her to the American Hospital. I don't know really. All they told her before was that it was very serious and that she couldn't travel, and that she didn't have much time."

"She's pregnant?"

"Yup. I get to be an aunt, which I find very exciting. Now can we get a drink to celebrate? I am sure they won't want us back for a bit."

Scott stood there not moving. "A baby," he said. "She's not sick?"

"Nope. A baby. I don't know how this happened, but I think it is a miracle. Thank you for coming here with me."

"A baby?" he said again. Then, "A baby!" He placed a hand on either side of her face, leaned forward, and kissed her.

She felt his breath flutter her eyelashes, then his soft

lips on hers. A pulse of electricity transferred between them, and then he jerked back just as quickly as he leaned in. "Sorry," he said. Then he shook his head and stomped his foot. "Wait a minute, I'm not sorry. I can't keep doing this. I can't keep pretending that we're friends," he said.

Miranda felt her heart stop. This was too much like that summer after her freshman year of college. Too much like the week before her twenty-first birthday. Too much like Thanksgiving. She didn't want to be treated like this. She dropped her head, wishing that they were already at the rooftop bar with a drink in front of her. No, two drinks. But he didn't stop talking.

He must have read the look on her face.

"I'm not saying it right. Let me try again. I can't keep pretending that we are only friends. You are so much more to me than a friend. I need to kiss you. I want to kiss you."

Confusion overwhelmed her. Hadn't he just kissed her on the street? "You just did," she said, still not looking up.

"Not the way I wanted to. Still want to."

Only then did she dare look up. "What is stopping you then? You can't keep doing this to me. Don't you know how I feel about you?" She couldn't believe they were having this conversation in a hotel lobby in Istanbul.

"I wasn't sure you had feelings for me," he said. "Not like that. And especially with Ronan. I thought I missed out."

"But I am here with you, not him. And let's be honest, you had chances before this month. You always backed away."

"I promised I would."

"Promised who?"

"Your father. He made me promise that I wouldn't do anything frivolous with you."

"Frivolous?"

"Yes, can't you hear him say it? 'Son,' he always called me, 'don't do anything frivolous. Wait until she's an adult.'"

"When? When did he say this? I can't believe how much

he interferes in my life. Each time I think I can look past it, something new comes up."

"Don't be hard on him. I think you were 15 or 16. He caught me staring at you at one of Avery's summer parties."

"You always did have a thing for girls in bikinis."

"It wasn't like that. Though trust me, I did notice you in those, too. But not this time. You were helping Avery put flowers in a vase. She didn't like what the florist sent, and the two of you pulled them all out and rearranged them. She tucked a flower behind your ear, pulling back your hair from your face. And I couldn't help but stare. That moment something changed for me, and Stanton saw it. Man, he always saw everything. I love him, Miranda. And I respect him. Even with our differences, he laid down the law to protect his daughter. I understand that now. Even what happened six years ago. He was right to protect you from me then. I wouldn't want Lynn to get involved in that kind of mess either."

"So wait, when you showed up thinking it was my birth-day—what was that? And can we please have a drink before you answer?"

In the elevator, she held her breath until the doors opened to a glass atrium on the roof of the building. Not waiting for him, she strode forward and through the glass doors. A modern bar all sleek and stainless steel created a wall in the middle of the roof to her right. Patio heaters, long columns of blue and orange flames, dotted the space between several high-top tables. No one else braved the rooftop at this hour except the lone barman dressed in the same navy three-piece-suit uniform as the concierge.

In front of her, though, just beyond a chest-high glass railing, the Bosphorus river divided the city. As the sun started to set, lights began winking along both sides of the river, creating contrast between dark and light. Miranda reminded herself to breathe.

"I'll get you a glass of wine," Scott said, as he stepped away from her toward the bar.

She stood there watching the city unfurl into night. Everyone thinks that poets are these great communicators, so good with words. That was probably one of the greatest myths about poets. They don't realize that words dazzle some poets, capturing their hearts and interest because of their fleeting nature. What she wanted to say flitted around in her mind like butterflies while she chased after them with a net. Only the mesh of her net was woven with too wide a gauge, and every word just slipped through.

He returned with her wine.

"Where's yours?" she asked.

"I want to be sober for this. I don't want to wake up tomorrow and have it all be a hazy memory."

"What this? What do you expect to happen tonight?"

He reached his hands across the high-top table on either side of the small white flickering candle. He picked up her hands, now chilly from the onset of night. "I don't expect anything. I just needed to say something. Something about us," he said.

Us, she wanted to scream, still remembering the humiliation of that pool party and watching him with some young associate perched on his shoulders and the way he kissed her inner thighs when he thought no one was looking. Or how she waited, staying home on her twenty-first birthday, hoping he would come back again with more Thai food and another bottle of wine.

"Whenever I imagined my adult life, you were in it. Not just as my friend and not just a few times a year. At the end of the day, I always thought we would be together. I never thought it would take so long to have this conversation, for there to even be a chance for us."

But us, she thought again. Remembering how he held her hand at her mother's funeral. How he hugged her at her high school graduation, lifting her up off the ground and spinning her around like a prima ballerina. How he was here now, in Turkey, for her.

"I'm not going to push it, but could you please say

something? At least let me know that you hear me." He picked up her hand and kissed it.

A blush spread across her face. She tried to look past him, to study the waiter's shoes as he moved around the lounge lighting the candles on the other tables.

"Ah," said Scott. "That's a start." And then he smiled.

CHAPTER

18

THEY STOOD AT THE DOOR to Danielle's apartment, afraid to knock. They didn't want to interrupt, but the dinner started at seven on the other side of the city, and frankly, neither one of them had been paying too much attention to where they were or how they got there.

"I don't even know the address of the house we are staying in," Scott said. "I never thought to ask. I'll knock. We have to."

"We have to," she repeated.

Before he could finish a third rap against the door, Omar threw it open with two glass bottles of Coke, one in each hand. He thrust the bottles at them. "Finally. Come in. Finally. We need to make a toast!"

Danielle sat on her eggplant-colored couch with one leg folded on top of the other like a yogi. In that pose, Miranda could see the faint outline of her belly starting to push forward at the top of her pants. She, too, held a bottle of Coke.

"My last one," he said. "No more caffeine until after the

baby comes." Danielle held up her bottle to clink against Miranda's.

"So it's okay?" Miranda asked.

Omar spun to face her. "Okay? So much more than okay. We finally are a family. A real, honest family." Omar tapped his bottle to Scott's and then Miranda's.

"So your parents are cool with this? Wonderful," Scott said.

Danielle and Omar both looked down.

"You aren't telling them?" Miranda asked.

"Not until after the wedding," Omar and Danielle said together. This caused the smiles to return to their faces. Now it was their turn to clink bottles. "It just wouldn't be worth it," Danielle continued. "It took us a long time to get to this day; why ruin it for them?"

"Because everyone thinks you are really sick. Dying, maybe."

"Not everyone knows about that."

"Who knows then?"

"Omar's parents. And his sister. And her husband. And the seamstress."

"The seamstress is coming to the wedding?"

"Of course, how else do you think we got all of those dresses at the last minute? She loves a party. None of this will even come up. It will all be about the wedding."

"Who would mention dying at a wedding anyway?" Omar asked. Omar picked up Danielle's hand and kissed it. His lips made an exaggerated smacking sound. "It will be the best day ever. And then my family will be doubly relieved when they get the news the day after." Then he pulled her to her feet, kissed her on the lips with less comedy and more passion, and then plunged her into a dip that would rival the conclusion to any tango.

"The baby," she said. She struggled back up to her feet.

"Now that's the kind of thing you want to avoid saying tomorrow," Scott said.

"Yup, wouldn't want that to slip out right after the first

dance," Miranda added. "And don't we have to go? We aren't even dressed yet. I don't think you can wear yoga pants to a rehearsal dinner, Dani."

Danielle looked down. "It's not a rehearsal. More like a blessing. But you're right," she said. "Let me pack a bag, and we can get dressed together at the house. We need to have a fitting for your bridesmaid dress when you get there. Omar's mom just texted me that your dress is ready at their house."

"A fitting now? The wedding is tomorrow."

"How did you think they were making you a dress?"

"I thought it would be loose. One of those pant sets or something elastic."

"You didn't show her the picture?" Omar asked.

"I was trying not to," Danielle said.

Miranda didn't actually care what her dress looked like. But she loved seeing her friend like this. "It's okay, Dani, I don't care what kind of dress it is. Anyway, I'm your old, married sister, right? You met my husband, Scott?"

"That's me," Scott said, picking up Miranda's hand. "Your husband."

Miranda forgot to turn away and instead caught his eye as he said it.

"Husband," he said again.

Miranda let the word roll through her mind, remembering childish teenaged fantasies about marrying him and living in New London or Mystic in one of those huge Victorians that hadn't been converted into apartments yet. Or maybe in New York City in a tiny apartment like she had the night he visited for her birthday. Maybe that very apartment, had he come back the next day. The Scrabble board would have always been out on the coffee table, ever ready for their next game. She shook her head to dislodge the thought.

There was more to the equation now than geography. There was Lynn. Her job. His job. Their families. And the last six years. And all the years that came before that. People always accused poets of being romantic and easily swept away; Miranda wished she could tap into that for a moment and enjoy his eyes locking with hers or how good it felt to hold his hand. She wanted to entertain the thought of that apartment, a bigger one, though, with Lynn racing in after school. Lynn. Miranda could love her, too. Probably already did love her and the joy she brought every time she bounced into a room, excited about something new. But she knew enough about the world to know it didn't work this way. Life wasn't a poem. It didn't always rhyme and come out even at the end.

"Did you call Lynn?" she asked.

"Of course," he said. "when we stopped golfing for lunch, I caught her before they hit the slopes for day two— the bunny slope."

It occurred to Miranda that she would have liked to hear Lynn's voice, too.

"You have a daughter," Omar said. He tapped himself against the side of his head with both hands. "I knew that. But, man, now I have questions for you!"

"I'd be happy to answer them on the ride back to your parents' house—we are really going to be late."

Omar's parents' house stood out even more so tonight among the other houses on the block for the strings of white light bulbs illuminating the side yard and the bustle of people carrying out tables and chairs and bottles and serving dishes to the yard. Miranda hadn't appreciated how unique the house was until after seeing more of Istanbul with its modern high rises and banks of town homes crushed together on tight streets. This house reminded Miranda of the children's book about a little house that stayed the same as the city grew up around it. She knew that wasn't true, that the rest of the city was much older than this house, but she smiled at the improbably of it. Much like the improbability of this entire week.

Danielle struggled to tow her suitcase behind her and issued a thinly veiled stream of expletives under her breath.

"I'll take that," Miranda said. "Maid of honor at your service."

"Matron, remember?" Danielle said, handing over the suitcase. "And what's the deal with that? I thought you said you guys weren't an item. But all I see is him staring at you."

Omar's mother saved her from answering the question. "Come girls, come. Yonca is waiting for you. Randa, you must try on the dress."

Danielle stood up a little straighter when Omar's mother spoke. Selin was a woman who demanded attention, and tonight, in a midnight blue crepe pant suit dotted with matching seed pearls and heels higher than most Jimmy Choo's, Miranda could see why. Selin was poised, beautiful, and smiling. This wasn't the monster protecting her youngest son from the ugly American that Miranda had expected.

"I'm glad you are here," Selin said as Miranda passed her. "Dani needs to relax and enjoy this. She's marrying my son. Why shouldn't she be happy?" She said the last part loud enough that Danielle blushed.

"Selin," Danielle said softly, trying not to chide her almost mother-in-law too much.

"Mother," Selin said. "Please get used to that. No excuses. Yonca is in Miranda's room already. We shooed the men to the attic." And sure enough if you stopped to listen over the din from the kitchen, you could hear the laughter of strong men and the stomping of feet radiating down through the ceiling above them.

"Turkish Super League," Selin said. "Football. Omar's father may not forgive him for getting married during the season, but the priest promises to keep the ceremony short tomorrow."

"Nothing short about a marriage. I'll not hear of it. It should all be long. Bad luck to do less," Yonca said. "Try this." She thrust an emerald green pile of chiffon and satin toward Miranda. It reminded her of a 1980s prom dress. Miranda caught Danielle's gaze. Danielle looked down at the bedspread and began picking at imaginary lint.

"I couldn't decide, so I let Omar's cousin pick."

"His cousin?"

"You met her at the airport. Jellie."

"But she's twelve."

"And a junior bridesmaid. The only other bridesmaid. Someone needed to pick."

Yonca sighed. "Just put it on. Can't fix it if you don't put it on."

The word sculpture for this moment would use satin, lace, and somehow Molly Ringwald.

But the dress wasn't that bad. Nor did it need any fixing. The skirt fell right to the middle of her ankle at the most dainty spot. The satin bodice with sweetheart neckline and slightly off-the-shoulder long sleeves formed to her body like it was sewn on. She chose to ignore the skirt, an explosion of ruffled layers of chiffon with peaks and swirls like frosting on a cake. The crystals, all hand sewn as Yonca pointed out, dotted each ruffled layer every few inches, making ignoring the skirt a tall order. Bling, Miranda thought, she would need to add that to her word sculpture. And cousin. "Jellie will look great in this dress tomorrow," Miranda said, gratefully changing back into her own clothes for the dinner party downstairs.

CHAPTER

19

FTER ALL THE GUESTS finally left the garden save for a few passed out in lawn chairs, Miranda and Scott surveyed the wreckage of the party. Selin picked through the piles of plates and discarded cups. She looked elegant even with a black plastic garbage bag billowing at her side.

"Go," she said, making a shooing motion with her hands. "I like this part best. Everyone is quiet, and I can finally enjoy the party. Omar and Roger will be back soon. They will help with the rest."

"But please, let us help," Miranda said. She moved to pick up a pile of used napkins.

"I'll not have it. You are guests, and tomorrow is a very important day. First, the town clerk, then the church, and then the reception. Which, praise be, is being held in a catering hall." Selin smiled at them. "Tomorrow night, I will be like that." She pointed to an older woman in a pink suit snoring loudly in a lawn chair. "My youngest son, married."

"Married," Scott repeated. It seemed to be one of his

favorite words this week. Each time he said it Miranda felt her skin get hot like her entire body was blushing. The word sculpture that came to her mind was the sappiest yet. Married. Ideal. Love. Forever. Ambrose would want her to write that down. She could see his email in her mind chiding her about greeting cards for weddings. If her phone worked, perhaps Miranda could see those emails and send along some of these sculptures. But really, she didn't want Scott to see them, especially not a humdinger like Married, Ideal, Love, Forever. Not yet anyway. Miranda hoped there would be time for that later.

"Go," Selin said again. "I'm serious. To bed."

Upstairs, they didn't quite know what to do. Each stood on opposite sides of the bed, the same side they each had claimed the previous night.

"I'm tired," Miranda said. "Big day. First tumors, then a baby, now a party. And the lying by omission. It really takes a lot out of a person."

"Randa, stop."

"Stop, what?"

"Being nervous. You don't have to do this. And we aren't going to do this." He made a sweeping gesture over the bed. "I've had years to think about this. And I don't expect things to just change in one day."

"You don't?"

"No, I don't. I've waited this long. I can keep waiting."

Miranda sat down on the bed, kicked off her heels, and settled back against the pillow. Her whole body sank deliciously into the soft, feather bed on top of the mattress. Either the bed was that exquisite, or she was just that tired. "I wish I had known you were waiting. I know I was."

"You were?"

Not even the comfort of the bed could hold her down. She bolted upright. "What did you think? I followed you around like a lost dog, oh, I don't know, my entire life. All I ever got for it was you with one of Avery's interns in a white bikini playing horse in the pool. In my own pool."

"That's unfair. I couldn't do anything about it. You weren't even out of school yet. How would that have looked to our families?"

"It's just that I thought college would change things, and then it didn't. And I knew I wasn't ever going to be like the girl in the white bikini. When you showed up right before my twenty-first birthday, I thought something had finally changed. That you knew how I felt. But then you vanished; it felt like losing everything all over again."

"I lost, too, Randa. After I explained it to my parents, they refused to speak to me. My dad pulled some maneuver that cut off the trust fund from my grandparents. I lost my job with the firm, and I was in Oregon. It took five years and them finally meeting Lynn to soften up. They didn't understand the whole thing with Lynn's mother. No one did; everyone I tried to explain it to called me crazy. I couldn't risk hearing that from you, too. No one understood."

"But you didn't even give me a chance to try. What is the deal with Lynn's mother? Who is she? Where is she? I don't want to mess this up. Whatever this is. Or whatever it could be."

"How would things between us mess anything up? And I don't see why Cassadee Parkins gets to have any more impact on my life than she already has had. Isn't what I am doing already enough? Why does she come up in this, too?"

"You're a dad now. And I've been in Lynn's place after my mom died, and Avery met Dad. I was already a teenager, so it didn't matter as much, but it still hurt to see him so happy again with his arms around someone else. And that was after knowing exactly what happened to my mom. What if Lynn doesn't get that chance? She's young now, so she hasn't pieced it all together, but what happens when she does? I don't want her to blame me for any of this. I don't want her to think I replaced her mother."

"How can you replace something that isn't even there? Cassadee never even wanted to be there."

"But do you know that for sure? Does Lynn know that?"

"I think Cassadee's actions speak for themselves. Lynn is only six. How could I explain any of that to her?

"But do you talk to her about it?"

"Why are we even talking about this? Miranda, I love you. I have since we were kids. I barely knew Lynn's mom. Cassadee was just someone I fooled around with once. We partied together in college. When she got her diagnosis and Lynn was born, I was the only one out of the crowd clean enough to show up. I'm sure she calculated the money factor, too. She knew that thanks to my parents, I would never starve. What more can I say? I can't say any of that to Lynn."

"How bad can Cassadee be if she knew to pick you?"

"She didn't know. She got lucky."

"Maybe she did know, Scott. Maybe she knew you were the best chance for Lynn. So far it looks like she's right."

"Sure, sure. It all worked out. Lynn is my kid. I love her more than anything. Every cliché ever written about being a parent rings true to me. But there's still other room in my heart, too, Miranda. Don't think we can't do this. I've waited too long to say these things to you."

"I know there is. But I don't want to ruin this. It doesn't seem right that Lynn doesn't have her mother. I think it makes me miss my own mother too much."

"But it isn't like that. Lynn doesn't even know her mother."

"But she should, Scott. A girl needs a mother."

"I think you would make a great mother, Miranda."

"What?"

"I saw you with Lynn. I saw the diary you bought her for Christmas. You met her once and understood her."

"That's because she's a great kid."

"She is. But you are great, too. I don't mean today or next week or maybe even next year. But I am committed to this. I want this to work for me and you and Lynn. I thought about you all those years and seeing you at Thanksgiving reminded me how much I wanted to be with you, how long I waited until you were old enough, and that I missed my opportunity. I wish I had handled it better that morning, but it scared me. As much I say I wanted to speak up, I've been alone with Lynn so long I didn't think it was possible to let anyone else in."

"You have no idea how many nights I stayed home just hoping that you would finally turn up again."

Scott settled down next to her, reaching over to pick up her hand. "Then what's stopping you?"

"Maybe just that, Scott. It's been years. And now there are all these other considerations. And I don't want to just ignore all that and be some stupid cliché of a woman who jumps at the first opportunity just because her best girl-friend is getting married. And Lynn matters to me, too,

Scott. We have to do what's best for her first." Her whole hand tingled under his touch making the words hard to say and even harder to believe. But they were true. She had wanted him for so long that she couldn't figure out if it was the wanting that kept her attention or the actual man.

"Randa, you know it isn't like that. I explained to you about your dad and waiting. And then Lynn and my parents. I have a reason for all of this. Can't you just trust me?"

"I used to, Scott." She rested her head back down on the pillow but didn't pull away her hand.

"Baby steps," he whispered. "I'm not going anywhere."

CHAPTER

20

ALARM CLOCKS BEGAN TO SOUND all over the house as the inhabitants and their guests began to ready themselves for the events of the day. Miranda's own alarm clock came in the form of Danielle knocking on her bedroom door wearing a black tank top with Bride written in cursive across the front in rhinestones.

"Gift from Jellie's mom, Deniz," she said, pushing into the room without an invitation.

Scott, still not quite awake, struggled to get up. "Just let me grab a few things, and I'll head up to Omar's room."

"Good," Danielle said. "You can wake him and be sure he is ready to go to the clerk's office by eleven. We have a noon appointment, but you need to plan everything with an hour's worth of delays. Turkish standard time, Omar tells me. He says I should just get used to it. Instead of getting used to it, I plan for it. He hasn't figured it out yet. I told him we needed to be there at eleven."

"Very wife-like," Miranda said. "You've been at this long?"

Danielle pointed at Scott and then put her finger over

her lips. When he finally left the room, suit bag and shoes in hand, she spoke. "Well, ten years of dating and the last five years of living here really cemented some key points in my game plan."

Miranda started to laugh. "You're too funny. And wait a minute, where are you going to live? Now you guys really need to work that out." Miranda asked.

"Ah, well, that is a tough question." Danielle walked over to Miranda's luggage and began picking through the make-up bag. "Blue eye shadow? Really? People still do that?" she asked.

"Yes, well, I just grabbed a bunch of stuff. It was kind of a last minute deal, you know. And hey, don't change the subject. Is he finally going to move into your apartment?"

"Omar got the promotion with a transfer."

"A transfer? Where? Tell me it's not Turkey. Tell me you're coming home."

"Well, not quite home. But Canada. An oil and gas exploration company. Engineering. They are even going to pay for us to relocate. But not until the summer. They want him to finish out a project here, and then start up the next one there. He found out last week but was waiting to tell me as a wedding surprise."

"Canada! You'll only be a few hours away by plane. And with the baby, too. I'm happy for you, but I am happy for me, too. This really keeps getting better. I'm glad I'm here."

"I'm glad you're here, too, but not glad enough to let you use blue shadow. Good thing I brought all my own make-up. Enough with this sappy stuff. Let's get dressed."

"Fine, no more sappy stuff, but can I get one hug before we start?"

Danielle stood still while Miranda wrapped her arms around her. She kept still for a few minutes until she finally returned the embrace. "I can't believe this is all really happening," she said. "I've waited a long time for this."

"I don't want to talk about waiting," Miranda said, regretting it immediately.

"What? What are you waiting for?"

"Nothing. Let's not talk about that today. Let's talk about your dress instead. Show it to me."

"Scott, right?"

"Yes."

"That's all you are going to say about it?"

"No. Yes. For now. Seriously, I don't want to think about that. I want to be a good friend and not a mess."

"You're never a mess. Though I might enjoy seeing that. There were hints of it with that Ronan fellow, but you know, the phone didn't give me the full picture of how regally screwed up you were." Danielle opened the bedroom door and pulled in a suitcase and two dress bags. "And it's dresses. One for the clerk's office and one for the church." The second dress bag billowed out so much that it looked like it contained a street vendor's full stash of balloons.

Miranda pointed at the bag. "Jellie?"

"Worse, Deniz. Wait until you see it. It's exactly like your dress only bigger. But don't change the subject. What happened to Ronan? And what is happening with Scott?"

"Ronan was just a thing, okay? I got carried away, then I went home for Christmas, and you called, and this happened, and Scott decided to come with me. Ronan blew a gasket. He wanted me to bring him instead."

"Why didn't you?" Danielle unzipped the smaller bag to reveal a trim Chanel style jacket and skirt, in white with gold trim. It wasn't something Danielle, whose wardrobe consisted of yoga pants and skirts bought from vendors in the parking lot of Phish concerts would wear, but anyone could tell it was beautifully made. "Selin," she said. "That woman is just amazing. If they say men marry their mothers, Omar is clearly confused on that point. I can't even figure out how she gets a manicure to stay on for more than two hours let alone everything else. And get this, she's also a chemical engineer. She stopped working when they moved back to Turkey for Roger's job. She's like Martha Stewart and Marie Curie combined. Omar says even when she worked full time she kept the house like this. What do I do? I teach English, under the table, and spaghetti with sauce from a jar is my signature dish. Let's not even talk about vacuuming."

"There's a learning curve. Maybe she will teach you how to cook." Miranda couldn't help but laugh again. "You're going to be fine. You haven't exactly hidden your true self from Omar. He's had ten years of spaghetti. Maybe he likes it."

"Enough of this. You still didn't answer me. Why didn't you bring Ronan?"

"Do I really have to answer that? It's embarrassing."

"Embarrassing? Hold on a second." Danielle yanked the zipper on the second dress bag. Layers of white satin and chiffon dotted with rhinestones spilled out and kept coming. With the bag finally on the floor, Miranda could see that the dress was indeed an exact copy of her own only times two. The skirt even had a flexible hoop built in, along with yards of crinoline to keep it encircling Danielle's legs at the proper diameter all evening long. She held it up to herself and swung her hips back and forth. "See? Embarrassing! But when you have a week to plan a wedding because you think you are dying, you tend to go with the flow. And I flowed right into Barbie's dream wedding gown."

"It's dazzling."

"Oh, you and your poet words. Don't think I don't know what you are really trying to say. Now spill it. Why was Ronan embarrassing? Was he short? Toothless?"

"No, God, no. He was gorgeous with an Irish brogue, and faint reddish stubble when his beard started to grow in after a night. Real cover of a romance book type. But that was it. I think maybe it was, well, physical." Miranda buried her head in her hands to cover up the blush that burned her face.

"But he was a poet. In your class. Didn't you have that in common?"

"It didn't ever come up."

"Oh, too busy with other things coming up were you?"

"Don't make fun."

"But was it fun?"

"Yes, oh, my god, yes." Miranda couldn't contain her smile remembering what those few weeks had felt like and all the things they did. "But I don't think it was enough. After all that, intimacy, you know, I couldn't even buy him a Christmas gift. Nothing. Not even a book of poetry. I couldn't find one single thing that I thought he would like."

"You broke up with him because you aren't a good shopper?"

"But I am a good shopper. I got Lynn the perfect gift that same day."

"But what about Scott? How does he factor into all of this?"

There was knocking on the door as it opened. Miranda and Danielle jumped apart as if they were caught red-handed.

"Daniiiiiii," said Jellie, who was followed by Deniz saying the same thing. They were like Turkish matryoshka dolls in matching aquamarine-studded abayas that swept the floor at just the right length so that only the toes of their silver, crystal-studded shoes peaked out. They nodded at Miranda but pounced on Danielle. Neither spoke much English, so Miranda stepped back and watched as they poked and pulled through Danielle's massive pile of brown wavy hair and wove and shaped it into a glorious up-do that could only be called a crown. Selin peaked in and nodded. Other cousins appeared, clucked a few hellos, and disappeared back downstairs.

"Is it okay if I wear this to the town clerk?" Miranda held up her best I'm-a-teacher dress.

"*Anne*," Jellie called out, forcing her mother to turn away from the supervision of Danielle's lipstick.

Deniz turned, lipstick still in her hand, and said, "No."

No, it turns out is one of the few words Deniz knows in

English. And she practiced saying it for every single thing Miranda pulled out of her suitcase. Luckily, when she picked up the green satin confection of the bridesmaid dress that, too, was met with a no. She wasn't expected to wear that to the town clerk.

The other ladies finished Danielle, turning her into a brunette version of a wedding day Barbie with her white Chanel suit. Not Chanel-style. Chanel for real, Miranda found as she handed Dani the jacket from the hanger. "Selin," Dani said, shrugging.

Deniz slapped her thigh and repeated, "Selin." Then she issued a directive to Jellie in Turkish so quickly that not even Danielle could translate. Jellie bolted from the room, and a silence fell over the cousins. They stood between Danielle and Miranda, but their focus was now on Miranda. They murmured under their breath, pulled out containers of blush and eye shadow, holding them up to the light. It seemed the group now realized Miranda was a lot fairer than them and even fairer than Danielle. Miranda bent down and pulled out her own make up bag and handed it to Deniz's second in command. She was a larger woman in an equally stunning pink abaya dotted with teardrop clusters of crystals. Her thick black hair was pulled back into a massive braid the size of a loaf of challah bread.

"Yes," she said, flicking an expert finger through the tubes and clamshells. She said something to Danielle next.

"They are going to do your hair first," she told Miranda. "Just let them. It will be for all day." As soon as Danielle finished speaking, the ladies pulled out two large cans of Aquanet. They blasted Danielle's hairstyle like fire fighters dousing a blaze.

In the end, Miranda emerged from the guest bedroom in a copy-cat hairstyle of Danielle's and a floating peach chiffon abaya. "I thought they were Christian," Miranda said. "Aren't these dresses Muslim?"

"That's just Turkish. Or maybe Middle Eastern. They are Christian. Well, Omar's parents are. Just wait until you see how the cousins dress at the reception. I don't think they are religious in any way."

"What do you mean?"

"Imagine your bridesmaid dress short."

"How short?"

Danielle slapped a place on her thigh a good three inches above where her white skirt stopped.

"Oh, this is going to be an adventure, isn't it?"

A surprising number of people fit into the local marriage registrar's office. Even though Miranda could tell from gesticulation alone that the secretary in the outer office only wanted Omar and Danielle and two witnesses. She kept putting up two fingers and waving them frantically at each new person who pushed to slip into the office. Of course, Jellie was last. When she pushed through this closing door, she exhaled with a loud, "whew." Everyone laughed, even the marriage registrar, who luckily didn't mind all the people.

The smell of perfume and cologne and the flowers Deniz had tucked into Danielle's hair at the last minute filled the small room, which was becoming increasingly hot. Scott stood on the other side of the room, in the gang of Omar's cousins. They could only be called a gang. They each wore the same cut of suit in dark blues bordering on black. Their hair, raven and gelled, stood perfectly coiffed an inch or two above their heads, swept evenly back like Ken dolls. They were a gang of Ken dolls. And Scott, even without the benefit of his summertime tan, fit right in. His hair was similarly styled, slicked back with a slight wave, though more brown than black. His suit must have been borrowed from one of them. He kept turning his eyes up toward her in between the punch lines of jokes the cousins were making. The youngest kept whispering in Scott's ear, probably translating. Scott laughed with his whole body, slapped his knee and tapped his foot, a one man band of joy. Miranda giggled to herself, not even knowing the joke.

The local registrar announced each form, holding it up for everyone to see, before reading it aloud completely in Turkish. Then Omar and Danielle signed, and Deniz and one of Omar's brothers signed. You wouldn't expect anything romantic about a crowded room and government paperwork, but seated in front of the registrar's desk, Danielle and Omar didn't glance down at the paperwork even once. They kept their eyes locked on each other, their smiles growing broader with each signature.

Finally, the registrar collated the stack of papers and stood. "Evlilik i lerinde ba arılar!" he said.

Miranda didn't understand at first, but the wave of clapping and cheering gave it away. Omar leaned across to kiss Danielle. He made it as far as her cheek, when his dad placed a hand on his shoulder. He said something quickly to Omar. Jellie, standing next to Miranda, translated, "The church first."

Danielle blushed and picked up Omar's hand and kissed it instead. Their moment was short, though. The room broke down into gender lines, and the men pulled Omar away. They would go off and have lunch while the women went back to the house to get dressed again. Miranda watched the men walk away; Scott blended into the group effortlessly. She focused on him, the cut of his suit jacket, the sway of his hips as he walked, the smile on his face as he turned to laugh so easily with strangers.

"You ready?" Selin asked, taking Miranda by the arm.

"Sure," Miranda said, looking over Omar's grandmother's shoulder as the men moved up the street, hooting and clapping like a pack of hooligans. Just as she started to turn to follow Selin, she took one glance back. Scott stood apart from the group, his hand over his eyes to shield against the sun. He scanned the crowd of aunts and female cousins, finally resting his gaze on her. Then he blew her a kiss. A real kiss couldn't have felt any better than that one. Then he turned and in a Gene Kelly move, jumped up clicking his heels out together to the side. The other men saw this and began attempting the move themselves. When one toppled into the other, a slight tussle broke out. Omar pushed the two boys apart and their merry party continued up the street and out of view.

"Boys," Selin said. "Eh, let them have their fun, right?"

Miranda didn't answer. She wanted to run after Scott and pull him away from the group. She wanted to duck down a deserted side street and kiss him for real. She wanted to make him click his heels again.

"Oh, you'll see him soon enough," Deniz said. "Come let's get changed."

At the house, all the ladies gathered together in the main living room. Danielle was arranged in a chair in front of the fireplace with the heavy mantel painted a gleaming white to match the rest of the trim in the room. A painting of two Turkish girls with ample bosoms lounging on stacks of woven rugs in brilliant colors filled the space above the mantel and echoed the colors of the plush rug under their feet. Miranda kneaded her toes into the silky fibers of the rug as she awaited Selin's directions. Cousins and aunts filled in the left side of Danielle, with Jellie crouched down at Danielle's feet like a faithful and beautiful hand maiden. Selin directed Miranda to Dani's right shoulder, then placed herself behind them. The other aunts and cousins, including Deniz, filled in behind. At once Miranda understood the pattern: Single, Left. Married, Right. She saw the word puzzle in her mind, throwing in the word Liar for her own part in the tableaux.

The photographer took several rounds of pictures. Then, he changed lenses, gesturing for them to get closer or separate. She felt her cheeks burn from the effort of so much smiling. If everyone weren't so close, she would have whispered things in Danielle's ear, the kinds of things that had gotten them into trouble in school. At one moment, Miranda looked down and saw that Danielle had placed her palm against her belly and was staring at her navel. The photographer kept chirruping something that could best be described as eyes up. Miranda kicked at the leg of Dani's chair. She dropped her hands to her side and smiled for the camera.

Released by the photographer, Danielle jumped from her chair tugging Miranda's hand as she went. They rushed from the living room and out of the kitchen, past waiting trays of pastries and delights, and into the back yard. Danielle finally stopped moving, but she didn't drop Miranda's hand, instead she pulled it to her stomach.

"She's kicking," she said.

Miranda felt the flutter under her hand and tears in her eyes at the same time. "Oh, Dani, I've never—"

"I know, me neither."

If it had been anyone else, they might have heard her approach. But the moment was too big to be on alert as well. Miranda stood there with her hands pressed on either side of Danielle's stomach; the two of them oohed and ahhed like fools as Jellie slid up right in between them.

"Whatcha doing?" she said in a clear imitation of a cartoon Lynn watched in Stanton's den. Something about inventions and summer vacations and boys with triangular heads. If only Miranda's mind hadn't slipped to the cartoon and stayed with the moment, she would have moved her hands away. But she didn't. At least not until after she heard Selin call out to Jellie.

Miranda turned to see Selin peeking out of the back-door. A glimmer of realization swept Selin's face. Her carefully painted eyebrows arched in surprise then settled into a thin, sharp straight line. Her beautiful, towering heels, the exact shade of her navy dress, banged out a swift tattoo as she marched over the stone patio. Jellie, obviously knowing that look, hightailed it back into the house.

"Are you okay?" Selin demanded. "Tell me now."

Miranda wasn't sure what she expected, but the Dani of her childhood, a PK as she called herself for preacher's kid, might have lied her way out of this. She once convinced her parents that she started a prayer study group in their garage. To explain the smoke, both legal and illegal, and the empties tucked into the plaid couch that used to be inside the rectory, Danielle told them how she wanted her prayer group to reach beyond traditional church youth, and minister to those who really needed it. If a cigarette or a Pabst Blue Ribbon got a boy to listen to the news of the Lord, wasn't it a tool of the spirit, she asked.

"The doctors found something yesterday," Danielle started.

Miranda leaned back on the heels of her shoes, swaying a little, both nervous and anticipatory; this story could be a good one.

"You know, at the clinic, they told me that I didn't have long and that I couldn't travel, that I needed to see the people at the American hospital."

"Yes, I thought you had an appointment next week." Selin said.

"I told Omar that because I didn't want him to be worried about it during the wedding. I wanted him to be marrying me not because I was sick but because he wanted to. So I had Miranda take me yesterday. I had to know what was wrong."

"That's silly. We've known Omar was in love with you since his first month at college."

"You knew?"

"I'm his mother, of course I knew."

"Why didn't you tell him?"

"I'm his mother. That's his business to tell me. In those affairs, a mother can only ruin things. But what is it now? What did the doctor say?"

Danielle's face lost its color. She inhaled deeply and closed her eyes. "I'm pregnant," she said. She kept her eyes closed.

"A baby?" Selin said pointing at Danielle's stomach. "For us?"

"For us?" Danielle repeated, her eyes snapping open.

"Yes, of course, for us. This family. You and Omar. Our

grandbaby. At last."

"At last? You were waiting for this?"

"We expected him to marry you and stay in the States and then he followed us to Turkey, and you followed him, and we kept waiting. He lived here, and we never bothered him about spending the whole night out or where he was going. But we didn't know why he kept pretending like nothing was serious. Omar was already eleven when I was your age. I wasn't sure how much longer you would wait for him. I guess God pushed things along."

"You aren't mad?"

Selin took Danielle's hands into her own. "I have been waiting for a daughter since I was nineteen. And now to get a daughter and a grandbaby in one day—only a fool would be mad."

Danielle started to cry. The tears ran over the make-up on her face but not a single drop of mascara ran.

"Deniz did your make-up?" Selin asked.

"Yes," Miranda said, answering for Danielle, who couldn't stop crying.

"Then you'll look fine for the wedding. Cry it out. The hormones do that."

Selin, gracefully like a cat, plucked her way across the patio stones in her glossy Loubatans and slipped back into the house. Danielle slumped forward into Miranda's arms. "Good thing I am not further along, or I could have gone into labor with that!"

The patio door quickly opened again. "Don't tell Omar I know," Selin said. "I want to congratulate him directly."

Miranda could have sworn that Selin winked at the last bit. "Directly," Miranda repeated. "Sounds like Omar may be in a bit of trouble."

"Poor Omar," Danielle said. "I'm just glad she isn't blaming me."

"Ah, you're pregnant. I think you get a pass until the baby is like three months old. Then you get to be the evil daughter in-law who takes too much of her son's attention and keeps the grandbaby all to herself."

"I can't imagine doing that!"

"Ah, you'll find a way. Be imaginative."

CHAPTER

21

I T TURNED OUT THAT Danielle did lie that day, about the hair and the make-up, at least. They slipped back into the kitchen and tried to make it upstairs to switch dresses undetected, never expecting the ambush of curling irons and eyeliner to be waiting in the guest bedroom. Their hair apparently needed to be increased in volume to match the skirts of their dresses. Even Jellie submitted to the torture, emerging like a Southern Belle on her way to a beauty pageant with her hair piled in a cascade of curls and loops and her dress, a miniature version of Miranda's.

"Nice dress," Miranda said to Jellie as they stood side by side watching how their skirts continued to sway back and forth even after they stopped walking.

Jellie smoothed her hands down the front. "It's beautiful," she said. "I can't wait to dance in it."

Lynn would love Jellie. She could see them racing off to the dance floor together and sharing a piece of cake. But it was foolish to think about Lynn that way. She wasn't Miranda's to think about. In her mind's eye, the word mother was laid down across the middle of the Scrabble board. Then "maybe" off the "m" in mother. If she were home, she would use the foggiest filter she could find to capture it, maybe doing a second shot with the word Step added in.

Not even several months of Cross Fit would have prepared Miranda for properly holding the golden crown over Danielle's head for the duration of the Eastern Orthodox ceremony. When Miranda's arms started to tremble, Danielle smiled up at her and whispered an apology. But the ceremony itself was beautiful; even though Miranda didn't understand a word of it—the symbols were clear enough. The rings, the wine, the circling the altar—each new moment caused tears to well up in Miranda's eyes. She didn't dare look for Scott in the pews. She kept her gaze focused on the stained glass of Jesus on the cross over the altar. The blood dripped from his body and blossomed into a rose bush that spanned all three panels.

Finally, the priest called, "Na zisete," and everyone in the room erupted with applause. Omar gathered Danielle up in his arms and kissed her firmly. Miranda saw Selin blush, and then brush away a similar kiss from Omar's dad. Miranda looked away, and then quickly back, just in time to see Selin give in. Miranda felt a pang of jealousy as she trailed behind the happy couple lost in the sea of relatives all speaking in Turkish.

The whole group spilled out onto the church's front lawn and out into the street. They walked several blocks to a giant banquet hall on the banks of the river. The terrace overlooking the river was festooned with flowers and tulle bunting all in the same green as Miranda's and Jellie's dresses. Jellie caught Miranda's hand and led her out to the dance floor where the DJ already played music that mixed current pop hits with traditional sounding beats and techno overlays. There seemed to be no formality; it was just a giant party. The crowd of people surged forward, spreading out over the dance floor and the rest of the terrace. Wine was opened and passed around. Waiters began circulating phyllo dough filled with all manner of savory delights. Tiny kebabs and pita with hummus came next. Luckily, Jellie liked dancing as much as Miranda did, though they did stop each time a new tray came circulating past. Miranda kept scanning the crowd for Scott, but to no avail. Instead, she grabbed a second glass of wine and kept dancing.

Finally, the caterers finished filling the banquet trays along one side of the terrace, and the DJ called everyone to the buffet. Danielle and Omar sat at a sweetheart's table at the edge of the dance floor. They fed each other from plates Selin brought for them. Miranda looked at the empty tables, unsure where to sit. Before Jellie could pull her back out to the dance floor, Scott materialized.

"Sorry," he whispered into her ear. "Lynn says hi. I had to call. Didn't mean to miss the start of the party."

"Here," she said, handing him her wine glass. "Catch up then. Lynn is okay?"

"She's great. Off the bunny hill and onto the big one, she said. I had to tell her all about the wedding. She's hoping you get to bring this dress home."

"You told her about the dress?"

"I texted her a picture."

"Ugh!"

"No ugh. You are beautiful. Lynn agreed—she said you look like one of the Christmas Barbie dolls."

"Nice. I guess I'll take that as a compliment."

"Randa, I mean it. You are beautiful. Come, let's find a seat."

Miranda felt the butterflies fly up in her stomach. He pressed his hand against the small of her back and steered her toward a table with the other younger men friends of Omar and a few of Danielle's students.

"You are her friend," the one guy, who introduced himself as Ted said. "I will practice my English with you tonight," he said.

"Leave her alone," another one said, punching Ted in the arm. "And you're name isn't Ted."

"It's Ted when I speak English."

"We're going to get some food," Scott said. "Be right back."

Miranda collapsed in giggles against Scott's chest as they waited in the buffet line.

"They've been going on like that all day. I keep hoping the wine will lighten them up, but it just seems to make them even more punchy. On the walk over, they were fighting about soccer. Before that it was whether or not a Ford is the best car. And before that it was something about a television program, a soap opera of some kind."

"We don't have to sit there," Miranda said.

"It's actually fun. And I don't plan on sitting much. You will dance with me, right?"

"Are you asking?"

"Yes, I am asking. Will you dance with me?"

They loaded their plates with rice and grilled chicken and vegetables and more hummus and pita. "You remember the first time we danced?" Miranda asked.

"Avery and Stanton's wedding. I guess I have a thing for girls in bridesmaid's dresses."

"Girls?"

"Well, you, really. I was so scared that night. You looked so grown up. I kept trying to figure out how you got older than me in one night's time."

At their table, the boys had cleared out already—they danced wildly to a hip-hop mix, pretending to break dance. Ted kept trying to spin himself around on his head.

"The whole time we danced, I was trying to keep my arms down, so you wouldn't see the sweat circles. Satin in June is killer."

"How about today?" Scott asked.

"All good," she said, lifting her fork over her head. "They make better deodorant now. So, something else will have to embarrass me. Probably my dancing skills."

"We could be embarrassed together then."

Omar and Danielle finally took the dance floor as the DJ played a slow number Miranda recognized from her prom. The boys from their table paired off, and began dancing together in a mock slow dance, feeling each other up. Omar's grandmother took her cane and swatted them off the dance floor. "She looks happy," Miranda said.

"Who? The grandmother? I know, right? She's been dying to hit someone with that cane all day."

"Not the grandmother," Miranda laughed. "Dani. She loves him so much. I can't believe everything that happened to them."

"Omar is a lucky man. He gets the whole package."

"Whole package?"

"You know, the wife and the family. All together. It's better that way."

"I don't know, you seem to be doing fine."

"Fine, sure. But it's lonely, Miranda. I want to share it with someone. I've really enjoyed being with you again. I missed this. It's easy with you. I don't have to explain everything—you already know the story."

"It is nice," Miranda said. "I can't imagine why you believed them when they said I didn't want to talk to you anymore. What made you think they could all of sudden speak for me?"

"Probably because at the time I didn't want to talk to myself, either. I screwed up. I did know Cassadee because of drugs. In college, I thought that money in the bank meant you could do whatever you want—party all the time. Getting that job with the firm just meant more money. Then that one phone call changed everything. I learned really quickly how wrong I had been. You were too good for me and my messed-up life. I was embarrassed, I guess, and overwhelmed."

"But I would have understood. I do understand."

"I know that now, but I didn't then. Do you forgive me?" He picked up her hand and kissed it.

"There's no reason to. Come on, show me your dance moves. Surely you must have learned something worthwhile from all that partying."

Scott stood up quickly and grabbed her hand. At the dance floor, with one deft maneuver, he spun her tightly against him with his hand on her waist. He kissed her cheek, then released her with a quick spin toward the other couples. Then he pivoted and pulled her back up against him.

"There," he whispered into her ear as they swayed close together.

"There what?" she said, smiling up at him, delightfully dizzy like after getting off a carnival ride.

"That's my dance move, that's it. Just that."

"That was pretty good."

"Well, when you only got one move, it has to be good. For the rest of the evening, you are just going to have to enjoy the sway."

"The sway?"

"Yup, you and me, side to side like we are on the deck of Linden's sailboat and a storm is about to come in. Back and forth, back and forth." He rocked her from side to side to exaggerate.

"Oh, do I get stay close to you like this?" She pushed her body against his, feeling the muscles in his thighs working.

He kissed the top of her head and slowed his motion. "I'd like it very much if you stayed right there."

The DJ switched to a fast Turkish pop song, one that everyone seemed to recognize. The younger people exploded into wild moves with whooping and jumping. Scott steered Miranda to the side of the dance floor, but they didn't release from their embrace. They didn't stop for cake or for coffee. Or even when Jellie attempted to take their picture with a camera she stole from the photographer. Fast or slow song, they remained paired tightly together.

"So, you go back tomorrow," Danielle said as they stood outside the reception hall.

"Yup," Miranda said. "With a layover in Paris."

"Paris, with your new boyfriend. You're slow to start, but once you get going, you really roll."

"I'm glad you're over the shock and back to teasing me about my love life, old married lady. It's just a layover, not some romantic vacation," Miranda said.

"I'm going to miss you more now that you have been here. Before, being in Turkey was different from my life in the States, like a dream or something. And now it's real. Really real."

"You're going to be a mom. That's as real as it gets. I wish I could be here for that part. I'd like to see it."

"I'm scared, Randa. Keep calling me, okay?"

"Of course I will. But only after your honeymoon."

Omar stepped outside and cleared his throat. "Love," he said. "The car is here."

Miranda hugged Danielle tightly. "Enjoy your trip! At least you don't have to worry about getting knocked up."

"Very funny. I could turn that around on you, you know?"

Miranda winced. "Ouch," she said. "Not yet, okay. I don't even know if we're dating."

"Oh, you are," Danielle said, turning to leave. She stopped at the door and picked up her bouquet from the table. "Here," she said. "Catch."

22

B UT IT'S ONLY A LAYOVER," Miranda said to Scott as they stood in the concourse looking at the departure board for their flight from Paris to JFK.

"Yes, a twelve-hour layover. In Paris. On New Year's Eve," Scott said. "You can't tell me that you have not once entertained a single fantasy about being in Paris. Me, I want to go see the Mona Lisa. And eat a croissant. And get a new poster for my classroom. Maybe of the Mona Lisa and eat another croissant. Or a crepe." He danced around in a circle. Miranda could clearly see where Lynn got her enthusiasm, though she danced much better.

"That all sounds good. I could do that. Especially the crepe part."

"But that's my Paris fantasy. We have time for yours, too. Tell me. Name one thing that would just scream Paris for you. On a schoolteacher's salary, it's not like I get this opportunity all the time, and what, you're a poet. Let's enjoy this."

"Let's get a cab to the Louvre and start there."

"Whatever," Scott said, dancing his jig up the concourse.

"We can start there, but you will tell me."

"Les Deux Magots," she called out to him.

He stopped and turned around. He cocked his head to the side and put his hand on his hip. "I'm listening."

She strode forward to him. "I want to write a poem at Les Deux Magots. While having a drink or a coffee or something. I hadn't thought that part out."

"Now we're cooking. I bet I could get my croissant there. Allez-y!"

"So now you speak French?" she asked, walking double time to keep up with him.

"Nope—just that, really, and merci. Which by the way, Merci. Merci beaucoup."

"You're welcome?"

"No seriously, Miranda, I haven't been on an adventure in six years. I've missed the way this feels." He put his arms to the side and fluttered them.

"Free?" she asked.

"Yeah, and light. I know she's safe with my parents, and well, I can just do this. And I'm not even going to think about the credit card bill until February." He repeated his Gene Kelly move.

"Oh, this," she said. Balancing one hand on her suitcase handle she approximated the heel click.

"I'll give you a seven for effort. We have to work on that."

Despite the chill of December, many patrons sat on the terrace of the café sipping espresso from tiny cups and enjoying all manner of pastries while the sun warmed the sidewalk. The waiters, in black coats and bow ties, with starched white aprons, moved deftly through the crowd, refilling cups and even pouring wine despite the early hour. The maître d' led Miranda and Scott to a table on the edge of the terrace, giving them a view of the whole café and the street that ran alongside it.

"Hemingway wrote here," Miranda whispered to him. "And Joyce, and Sartre, and Simone de Beauvoir. Picasso, too."

"And now you, too. Shall I order for us?"

"Do you do that in French, too?" Miranda asked.

Just then the waiter appeared. He introduced himself far too quickly for Miranda to understand. Scott opened the menu and pointed a few times and then held up two fingers. The waiter nodded and slipped off into the stream of other waiters entering and exiting the café proper.

"What did you order?"

"Well, I'm not sure. Let's just hope for the best."

And the best it was. A complete petit dejeuner with croissants, coffee, apple juice and some tartlets. Each morsel tasted better than the last. "Ah," Miranda said, a bit of croissant melting on her tongue. "This is wonderful."

Scott didn't bother to swallow before responding. "It is," he said, mouth full of tartlet. "I might need two croissants after we visit the Mona Lisa. But we aren't done here. You need to write your poem first."

Miranda winced. "It doesn't quite work like that. It's been so long since I wrote a real poem, you know with paper and pen. It might take me a bit. I don't want to waste our time in Paris."

"Would this help?" he said, pulling out the smallest travel Scrabble Miranda had ever seen. "I brought it so we could play on the plane, but I forgot. I got so wrapped up in talking to you and then we fell asleep. In Turkey, there was no time."

"You can say that again! I can't imagine that kind of wedding. Too much."

"Really? You wouldn't want all that? The big dress and the parties?"

Miranda took the Scrabble board from him and opened it. She started to select tiles and move them around the board. Even though it would be saccharine, she needed to start with Paris. Scott began to finger the tiles as well, making words for her to review like light and pastry.

"After my mom died, I didn't think I ever wanted to be in a church again."

"A wedding doesn't have to take place in a church." Scott laid out Seine.

"Seine—good one. I need Louvre. This will be real touristy. I know they don't need a church, but that's what my mom always talked about. We would go to other people's weddings, and she would say, 'When you get married, we'll decorate the pews with bows,' or 'The organist will play this.' You know, she planned everything."

"She did, didn't she? Always liked to know exactly what was going to happen next."

Miranda had Paris and Seine and Louvre.

The waiter reappeared. He leaned down and arranged love from the v in Louvre. "Pardon," he said. "L'addition."

Scott handed him a credit card and added, "Merci." The waiter again disappeared into the sea of tables.

"Good touch."

"Allow me," Scott said. He turned the board and took a picture.

"I know it's not done, but it's a start. I don't want to waste our whole time here. Let's go find the Mona Lisa. But wait—" Miranda fished through the letters again, adding Mona and Lisa. Scott snapped the new picture.

They returned to the airport with under an hour to spare and bags of posters and chocolates for everyone at home. They found a framed print of one of Degas' ballerina paintings for Lynn and the Mona Lisa painting for Scott's classroom. Miranda bought postcards to send to Dani and Omar and Omar's parents to thank them for the hospitality. They collapsed into the plastic airport chairs, exhausted from the last few days but buzzing from all the chocolate chauds and crepes they had consumed.

Their flight left at midnight. Scott looked at his watch. "Which time zone do you want to celebrate in?"

"Celebrate?" Miranda asked.

"New Year's Eve, silly. It's almost midnight here. Midnight already happened in Turkey."

The flight attendants emerged from a door next to the flight stand with three bottles of champagne in hand. "Everyone," they said, first in English then in French. "Before we board, let's toast to the New Year."

The mix of clearly exhausted vacationers lined up to receive their champagne in the tiny plastic cups. They counted down to midnight, "Dix, neuf, huit, sept, six, cinq, quatre, trois, deux, un." Then cheers of "Bonne Annee" went up over the loud speaker and then came the Choral des Adieux. Based on the music, it was clearly a French Auld Lang Syne.

Miranda wiped at her eyes. "Damn it," she said. "This always makes me cry."

"Here," Scott said, "let me take your mind off that." He leaned down and kissed her. He pressed the whole length of his body against her and wrapped his arms around her back. She moved her hands to rest on his shoulders and stood on tiptoes to meet his embrace.

She wasn't sure how long the kiss lasted, but she knew it was the first time she would remember a New Year's kiss.

"To many more?" Scott asked, raising his plastic cup.

"To many more," she said, lifting her own.

While they waited for their luggage, Miranda finally turned on her phone. The staggering number of email messages, mostly from Ambrose, overwhelmed her. Two hundred and fifty of them. She scrolled through the list, pausing at the subject line. Classes cancelled. Then the next one from the President of the College with the subject line, Request for Meeting. Then her phone faded to black. No battery. Again.

"Scott, can I borrow your phone? I think something has happened."

"What? Are your parents okay?"

"Yeah, yeah. Nothing like that. Something with Ambrose. And my job."

Just as Scott handed her the phone, the luggage conveyor belt fired up with several shrill beeps and an asthmatic whirling wheeze. The speed must have been set too high as the carousel spun rapidly, sending everyone's luggage and golf clubs wildly around. Some bags lost their purchase and flipped off at the feet of the people waiting. It became a mad scramble. Miranda handed Scott his phone back and began searching the wreckage for their luggage.

As they got to her car, Scott's phone rang.

"Lynn," he shouted. "We're back!"

Miranda watched the giant smile spread across his face as they loaded the bags into the trunk. She could hear the faint chirrups of excitement through the phone as Lynn told Scott all about snowboarding that day. Scott pointed at the phone and then pointed at Miranda. He pantomimed driving, his hands at ten and two on an imaginary wheel. She nodded and got into the driver's seat. As much as she wanted to call Ambrose and the president of the university, she wanted to listen to Scott try to get a word in with Lynn. The music of their conversation washed over her like sunshine. She watched his animated gesticulations explaining how tall the Eiffel Tower was and how many crepes they ate while walking around Paris.

Miranda navigated the car to the exit, paid for the parking, and stopped at the intersection with no idea which way to go—to her apartment and her laptop or to her parents' house where Lynn would be tomorrow morning.

It was strange being in her parents' house without them home. Lynn had told Scott on the phone that Avery and Stanton decided to come out to ski, too. "Only they don't ski," Lynn protested. "They just sit in the lodge and watch other people ski."

They dropped their bags in the foyer and immediately headed for the kitchen. Despite their French pastry bender, after the long flight, Miranda's stomach growled.

"Where're the take-out menus?" Scott asked. "I know Avery must have a stash that would rival a college student's."

Miranda pointed to the small desk in the kitchen. "Just get me something. Anything. I need a shower. And then a drink. And then some food."

The warm water felt good on her back and shoulders.

As she stood there, she tried not to think about being alone with Scott. But the idea of it was too much. Sleeping in the same bed for four nights. Pretending to be married. The kiss. She heard the doorbell ring downstairs. But she didn't want to move from under the shower or stop replaying the last week in her mind.

A knock on the bathroom door startled her.

"Yes," she said.

Scott cracked open the door. "I thought you could use this." His disembodied arm held a glass of white wine. The glass fogged immediately in the heat of the shower. "Wow, you like it hot," he said.

"Yes," she said resisting the temptation to say something like, I think you're hot or some other come-on. Every ounce of her body wanted to open the shower curtain and take the wine glass. Or maybe pull him into the shower with her.

"I'll just leave this here," he said. "Food's here. I'll put it out while you dry off."

The wine glass clicked on the marble of the vanity, and the door softly thudded back into place. Miranda stood there, hand poised to draw back the curtain, until the hot water finally gave way to cold.

The wine, cold and white, which she swallowed all too quickly, did little to relieve her feelings of what she would have liked to have happen in the shower. A jersey wrap dress in a blue color that Avery always told her highlighted her eyes hung in the closet. Avery would leave hand-me-downs there, and every few months Miranda would open her girlhood closet and find new treasures to take back north. She fingered the soft fabric, considering the dress. It would be low cut on her. But it wouldn't be her. Instead, she pulled open a drawer and pulled out sweatpants with the University of Connecticut logo peeling on the front and a flannel shirt from a high school boyfriend. The wine only made her more aware of her hunger.

Downstairs, she found Scott in much the same outfit,

only his sweatpants were from Yale. "I see you got the dress code memo," he said, reaching over to turn on the giant television in Stanton's study. Lynn's nature video, polar bears this time, filled the screen. "Do you mind if we watch something else?" he asked. "She makes me watch this all the time. And I get it, circle of life and all that, but I am so tired of watching all the animals struggle. I really don't know what she sees in it." He handed Miranda a takeaway container of fried rice and some chopsticks. "Plates seemed like too much. We were just in Turkey, right?"

"Yup, Turkey. And Paris."

"And you were my wife." He didn't look up from the television as he said it. He was flipping past the sports channels, finally settling on an NHL replay.

"Yup, I was," she said. The power play clock started, and the players on the ice fired up in frenetic patterns, hammering the goalie with shots. The goalie blocked one with his chest, caught one in his glove, and sent one back to the middle of the ice with a kick off his skate.

"I meant it all, Miranda. Please don't think being home changes that."

"It doesn't?"

"No, it doesn't. I am going to be more direct. I love you. I thought too much time had passed, that it was just part of being kids together. And then at Thanksgiving, it all came back. I couldn't stop looking at you. And then you got that text at Christmas, and I just about lost my mind. The idea of you and that guy, a guy who would send a wonderful, smart girl like you dick pictures, I couldn't stand it. When Danielle called, I knew I had to go with you. Miranda, I love you. I wouldn't say it if I didn't mean it; there's too much between us to risk wrecking it on just a throw-away relationship."

"You don't have to do this. This isn't some fairy tale. You have your own life with Lynn and your school. We're not on vacation anymore."

Miranda didn't move her gaze from the television. The

power play finished, and the other team, now whole, attacked the forwards with vicious blocks and thrown elbows. She couldn't trust herself to say what she needed to, or rather wanted to.

"There's a Montessori school affiliated with your university. I checked. And I still am a lawyer remember. They don't take it away just because you screw up the rest of your life. I can work in other places besides New Jersey. And Lynn needs you just as much as I do."

"You didn't screw up."

"Okay, maybe that's not the right word for it, but my life certainly isn't going the way I had planned."

"What did you plan exactly?"

"Well, not this. I thought at 29 I'd be married and maybe be close to making partner in a firm, maybe even Stanton's firm. I'm not unhappy with my life. Lynn is amazing, and I love every minute with her. I just didn't expect this. I didn't plan this life. I teach elementary school, Randa. Me with beeswax crayons and circle time."

Miranda tried to hide a laugh. She imagined him at the head of his classroom goofing around to make some point about American History or multiplication.

"No, go ahead. Laugh. It is funny. You can only imagine what my friends from law school say. I don't even bother to hang out with them anymore. My parents often offered to take Lynn for the weekend, so I could go catch up with my friends, but it wasn't worth it. You are the only person who knew me before who didn't laugh and who talked to Lynn like a human being and not some alien."

"But Lynn is awesome to talk to. She's just so open to everything. And excited. Really, really excited."

"They just can't get their heads around being a parent. They just don't see it. But you do. I know you do. Miranda, I want you to do this with me. Lynn needs a mom. I want a wife."

Miranda set down her Chinese food. "But she has a mom."

"Barely. Cassadee calls once a year, three, four weeks after her birthday. Likes the pictures I post of her on Facebook and then asks for money. That's not a mother."

"Scott, do you just want a relationship with me because of this?"

"How could you even ask that?" He reached out and grabbed her hand interlacing his fingers with her own. "Don't you remember what this felt like? Since as long as I could remember, holding your hand is the only thing that felt like love to me. I don't know when it started, but I have yet to feel this with anyone but you. Maybe your dad was right to shut me down at the time, but I swear to you, Miranda, this isn't about Lynn. This has been going on between us forever."

"Avery once told me that our moms planned our wedding the minute the doctor announced it's a girl."

"I know; my mom told me that they even had their dresses planned. They would wear something matching, my mom in baby blue and your mom in pink. They wanted people to ask them why, so they could tell the story of how they knew we were just meant to be. They tried to keep it a secret from us, but after Aunt Louise died, my mom wanted me to know. But she made me promise not to tell you unless it came true."

"How do you know it's coming true?" Miranda asked.

"It is, isn't it? Don't you feel it?"

"Scott, we aren't even dating. One trip in six years does not a courtship make."

"Maybe this will." He slipped off the couch and knelt before her. From the front pocket of his pants, he pulled out a ring. A single emerald cut diamond the size of a pinky fingernail, winked up at Miranda. She knew this ring well. It was her mother's.

"How?" she asked.

"I asked Avery before we left for Turkey. I carried it with me the whole trip, but I kept thinking I wanted to wait until we were home, together as a family to ask. But I can't hold out anymore. Miranda, will you marry me?"

The trip, the wine, the food, the ring. A lifetime of imagining this moment. She felt herself swell from it all, threatening to burst, if she didn't say it. So she said it. "Yes." And then she said it again and again and again.

"Do you love me?" he asked.

"I always have," she said.

He slipped the ring on her finger and then reached up and held her chin in his hands. He brought his lips to hers with the lightest touch, so close that their breath moved between them in a soft whisper. The hair on the back of her neck stood up, and goose bumps ran down her arm. She pushed harder against him, letting her body sink to the floor. They knelt there in a tangled embrace, exploring each other's bodies with hands, and lips, and tongues. She could have kissed him all night, but then he stopped and leaned back.

"I might kick myself for this tomorrow, Randa, but we should stop. Wait."

"Wait?" she asked. "Wait to get married? Of course. We don't have to rush that. This is more than enough for right now."

"No, not the getting married part. I want to wait until we get married to make love."

Miranda chuckled. "It's not like I'm a virgin. And I'm pretty sure you're not, based on how Cassadee made you think Lynn was biologically yours. I'm almost thirty; I don't really care what my father says. And plus, they aren't even home to worry about it."

"Don't make a joke; this is important to me."

"Okay," Miranda said, using every ounce of air from her lungs to get the sound out.

"Don't take it that way. It's not like that. I just want better for us. I've made a lot of mistakes. I want this to be right," Scott said.

"It is right. Is this some sort of cold feet, Scott? Did you not expect me to say yes?"

"I want this to be more than physical," he said.

"More than physical? We've known each other our entire lives, and we've only kissed what—maybe once before today?"

"Exactly. I don't need to make love to you to know that I want to, or to know that I am going to want to for the rest of my life, Randa. You and I don't get a lot of firsts as a couple. I already have a kid. We've already had a lifetime of holidays and vacations. We lost your mom. We even lost each other. But this one thing, this waiting, it's the one thing we can do in the right order. May I have this gift?" He picked up her hand. The engagement ring glittered despite the circumstance.

A gift, she thought. She wondered if she would ever feel on steady footing with this man in the room. She bowed her head against his chest. A calm washed over her. A golden feeling of light and love so much deeper than a sexual charge. As much as she wanted to press herself even more against him, to feel his body all over hers, inside her, she wanted that feeling more.

"Yes," she said, "yes, to all of it."

CHAPTER

23

WHEN SHE FINALLY WOKE UP, it took Miranda a minute to remember. The trip home, the wine, their conversation. The engagement ring on her finger. She pulled herself out of his embrace. In the dim light, she could still make out the glimmer of the familiar diamond. She remembered her mother giving it to her father before the last time she went into the hospital. The three of them stood in the foyer of their old house.

"Take this, Stanton," she said. She slipped a necklace from her neck and let the chain puddle around the ring in his palm.

"Lou, please," he said. Miranda heard her father's voice break.

"I don't want to be buried with it. You know that. Miranda knows that. Let's not discuss it."

"Lou, you aren't dying," he said.

"For a smart man," she said. She reached up with her thin, bony hand and stroked his face, now damp with tears. "Miranda, please go wait in the car."

The door closed behind her, and Miranda heard her

father let out a wail. It was the last time she heard him cry. When they came back from the hospital that night without her mother, the ring remained on the hall table. It stayed there until her dad sold the house and moved to this new house with Avery. Miranda chose not to say anything about the ring; she knew Avery would have put the ring somewhere safe, and at the time, Miranda was in no rush to see it again. Now on her hand, it meant something else.

"Hey," Scott murmured. He leaned up and snuggled his face into her hair. "It's a beautiful ring, Randa. I'm glad you're wearing it."

"It is beautiful. My mother loved it."

He picked up her hands and folded them into his. "I love you. It's more intense than I thought it would be to say it out loud."

"It's more than I thought it would be hearing it. Scott, I love you, too. But I have a very important question; does Lynn know about this?"

Scott held up his phone. "Already texted her." On the screen was a picture of her hand, engagement ring glinting, resting on Scott's chest. "I woke up a bit ago and couldn't resist. I figured she'd tell all the parents, too."

"Well played," Miranda said, kissing him deeply on the lips.

"We're home," Lynn shouted, racing into the den where Miranda and Scott sat having coffee. "I made them leave early."

Avery and Stanton stumbled into the door, dragging a few bags each. "Very early," Stanton said. "While I want to shower you with congratulations or whatever it is that might be appropriate for this situation, I first would like a shower and a nap."

"I second the wisdom of my husband," Avery said, blowing them both kisses, as she mounted the stairs. "Bunny said it was too early. She'll call when they get back to New York. And she said to tell you, Randa, welcome to the family, but that it sounds funny because you've always been family."

Lynn ran up to Miranda and grabbed her hand. "You said yes!"

"I did, I said yes."

"This is big," Lynn said.

"Very big," Scott said. "Are you thinking what I'm thinking, Lynn?"

"Pancakes!!!" she shouted.

"I can see I made a very wise decision saying yes to your proposal, especially if it will be celebrated with pancakes. Is this common?"

Scott stood and extended a hand to Miranda, pulling her into a tight embrace with one swift motion. "My dear— all good things are celebrated with pancakes. Come let us show you how."

Before the batter was even mixed, Lynn started with the questions. "Will we have a wedding? Do I get to be a flower girl?"

Miranda stopped shoveling the coffee into the filter and looked up at Scott. He stopped cracking the eggs and looked back at her. "Yes," they said together.

"Do we get a cake and dancing?"

"Yes," they said again. Scott stopped cracking the eggs and moved behind Miranda at the counter; he wrapped his arms around her, squeezing her even more tightly than before. "I love you," he said. "This makes it even better than before. Better than I imagined."

"Wait," Lynn said. "Look at me. I need a picture."

They both turned to look where Lynn finally stopped spinning. She held her Dad's cell phone, camera pointed at them. They beamed at her, hugging tighter together.

"We need to announce this on Facebook," she said. "Nothing is real until it's Facebook real."

"What kind of school do you send her to?" Miranda asked.

"It's not school," Lynn answered for herself. "Miss Kendra told me."

"Miss Kendra?" Miranda leaned back from Scott's embrace and turned her head to the side. "And who is Miss Kendra?"

"My babysitter. She's sixteen, and she comes when Daddy goes to basketball." Lynn didn't look up. She was deftly maneuvering through screens on her dad's phone. "There," she said. "Miranda, you need to accept Daddy's engagement request online."

"Okay, I will."

"Now?" Lynn asked.

Miranda held up her phone. "Out of juice."

"You'll do it later. Promise?"

"Of course. It has to be Facebook real."

Lynn raced the length of the kitchen and wrapped herself around Miranda's legs. Scott wrapped himself around them both.

"Family hug!" Lynn shouted.

The questions didn't stop. Over Jenga, Miranda was drilled on possible wedding colors and whether or not Lynn could wear high heels. Finally as dusk began to settle, she hit the biggest question. "Where are we going to live?"

Scott took a heavy sip of his coffee, then another. Miranda froze, her hand hovering over the Jenga tower.

Then Lynn saved them. "It's doesn't matter, though, right? As long as we're together."

"Together. Yes. But tonight, I need to go back to New York."

"And we have to go back to New Jersey, pumpkin. We all have school in the morning."

Then Miranda remembered the emails about her classes being cancelled and the request to call the president's office. She felt this fairy tale slipping away from her. "Can you guys finish the game without me? I need to ask Avery if I can use her computer for a second."

She found Avery in the office upstairs, fighting to keep her eyes open while staring at a stack of legal documents.

"Contracts," she said. "I'm sorry I haven't been much fun today. I'm glad you snuck away. I wanted to be sure you are really okay with everything."

"Of course, I'm okay," Miranda said. "Why wouldn't I be okay? This is like a dream come true."

"It's a little fast, isn't? When he asked for the ring, I wasn't sure what to say. I let him have it because I knew Bunny would—" Then she stopped. "Never mind."

"You knew Bunny would what?"

"Get it back if he flaked out."

"Oh," Miranda said. "Well he didn't flake out."

"No, no, he didn't. And we're happy for you. I'm happy for you. I just wanted to check in, you know. Maybe it's just the lawyer in me."

"Not like I need a pre-nup or anything."

"Well, your dad already has one. He and Linden have been hammering out the details."

Miranda rolled her eyes. "It's not like that."

"Tell me what it is like?"

Miranda sank back into the chair and closed her eyes. "I've always been in love with him. There I said it. But I never really thought about what that meant. And now here we are, all grown up, and there's Lynn to think about."

"Have you thought about that? It's not easy, you know."

"But you did it."

"Yes, but you were a teenager. And I had the Book."

"The Book?"

"Yup, your mother could never leave anything to chance. She wrote the equivalent of a Supreme Court case brief on you. She prepared briefs about everything in your life from when you were first born to that awful boy that was mean to you at summer camp."

"Joseph Groton? He was in there?"

"Your mom was an amazing lawyer. The best. She had everything laid out and organized. Every trick or turn, she anticipated. No one could shake her. When I first started with the firm, I would go to her trials just to watch them unfold. She had everything documented. Other firms hated going up against her. The lawyers that worked under her dreaded the hours of mock trials she would hold. No surprises. She even had that hanging over her desk."

"No surprises? I didn't know that."

"Not even this would surprise her. She knew this would happen. I always thought that Joseph would come around, but your mother knew best."

"Joseph? Really? I think he is doing time for selling prescription drugs to minors."

"Maybe you can't plan everything."

"But you can try. My mother did apparently," Miranda said.

"She was a great woman, Miranda. I never tried to replace her, I hope you know that. I just always wanted to be here for you. With Lynn, it might be a different story. You don't know much about her mother, do you?"

"Scott won't talk about her."

"That isn't good, Miranda. You can't just pretend she doesn't exist. You aren't some replacement mother. The girl has a mother. For better or worse."

"But I don't know anything about her."

"Do you want me to look into it? You should really know what you are getting into."

"You'd do that?"

"Of course, I'd do that. It's probably nothing. Bunny mentioned the mother had a drug problem. Avery spoke the last bit using Bunny's high-brow accent. "Maybe if you knew a little more, you could draw Scott out in conversation. Make some sort of plan for the future. No surprises and all."

"You sound like my mother," Miranda said.

"Don't talk like that. You'll make my mascara run."

"Fine then, can I use your computer? I need to check my emails, and I left my phone charger in my apartment. I haven't checked in a week."

"That sounds nice. A week without a cell phone! Are

you sure you want to check now?"

"Yeah, it's just work and stuff. You know."

"Oh, I know. I'll go order us some pizza then."

After logging in, the screen flooded with emails. The one from Facebook asking to confirm her engagement, which she clicked on without pause, thinking of Lynn's excitement downstairs. Many from Ambrose. And then the two from the college. She clicked on those first—all her classes were cancelled, and the president of the university needed to see her. He left his assistant's cell phone number with instructions to call immediately.

Picking up the house extension on the desk next to her felt alien. She used to spend hours on this very phone, sitting at this desk playing solitaire on the computer while talking to Danielle about such important topics as which bathing suit to wear to Avery's party and whether or not Scott would be there. Now as she punched the buttons, she focused on more important details than bathing suits and parties; she wanted to know if she still had a job. She was one year out from tenure. As the phone rang through, one thought filled her: Ronan. She tried to shake the image away. He wouldn't have filed a complaint. But then she remembered his anger, his hurt.

"Hello," Kathleen said. Miranda knew her from social things at the university. Wine and cheese things where the faculty who were deemed important for the moment mingled with visitors at the president's invitation. She favored navy blue twin sets and skirts with ballet flats. Her hair, a silky golden color, was always tied up in a bun. Miranda's cheeks burned with embarrassment; what would someone like Kathleen think about her and Ronan?

"Yes, hi, Kathleen. This is Miranda from the poetry department. I was just in Turkey, and I've received an email telling me to call you and—"

"Yes, yes. What do you have for tomorrow? The president must see you immediately."

"Immediately?" Miranda asked.

"Of course, this must be handled properly. Is nine too early?"

"Nine. No, not too early at all. President's office?"

"No, no, the residence, please. I'll send over breakfast. See you at nine."

Miranda couldn't bear to open the emails from Ambrose yet; she couldn't make him any more word sculptures tonight any way. The hundreds she already sent would have to be enough for a few days until she sorted out this mess with the university. Whatever this was. Words began to swirl in Miranda's mind. Paris. Hilton. Tape. Played. In the corner of the board, she imagined including herself with a "me" tucked into the triple word score.

"Ronan," she said softly, "what did you do?"

Scott knocked lightly on the open door frame. "Pizza's here." He stepped inside the room. "Hey, you okay? You don't look so good." He picked up her face in his soft hands and looked into her eyes. "God, I love being able to do that," he said. "I get to touch you. Look at you. But I'm sorry, love, what's the matter?"

Miranda stretched out her arm and clicked away from the email screen. She didn't want to mention Ronan—not today—but there was an extremely high chance he had just cost her her job. Today was supposed to be about them and the future. "Nothing," she said. "I have a meeting at nine in the morning tomorrow. And I don't want to go. I don't want to be away from you."

"It's okay. How about this? How about Lynn and I drive up on Friday? Then we can stay until Sunday night. If we're going to do this, we have to start figuring things out. Wait, that's not why you're upset, is it? It's only six months until school's out in June. And we have Spring Break and lots of long weekends. We'll have time together. We'll make it work."

He pulled her to standing and pressed his whole body against hers.

She let herself melt into it and began kissing him in return. "No," she whispered. "This is perfect."

"Enough already." Stanton's voice boomed up the staircase. "The pizza is getting cold."

"I guess we have to go," Scott said.

"Wouldn't want to upset your future father-in-law?"

"More. You forgot the more. I believe I have already upset him quite a bit. He hasn't been downstairs all day; I am starting to be afraid."

From downstairs came her father's muffled, "Well, I'm not waiting anymore."

Miranda tilted her head and shrugged. "Maybe it would be a good thing to be a little afraid of him. He does have a history of forming opinions about you. You go on ahead; I just need to log out."

At the table, she chewed every bite of her pizza at least twenty times. She nibbled delicately on the crusts. She took long pauses for tiny sips of soda. She had a fourth slice even though her stomach protested by straining the top button of her jeans. The longer she took to eat, the longer they would be together. Avery had pulled out the Scrabble board along with the pizza delivery. Miranda and Lynn teamed up; Lynn leaned in against Miranda and wrinkled her nose at the letters they had.

"I hope you're good at this," Lynn said. "Spelling isn't my best subject."

Everyone laughed.

So far they had the lead, making use of "qi" on a triple letter score. The only time Scott's hand left her lap was when he moved to place his tiles on the board. She had never seen him make Scrabble decisions so quickly before.

Stanton was a master at filling in the spaces between words with single and double letter combinations that resulted in three- or four-way scoring, and he soon caught up to Lynn and Miranda's score while making it almost impossible for anyone else to place words. For once, Miranda was grateful for her father's strategy. The game crept along very slowly.

"So," Avery said, as Stanton plotted another thwarting placement of an e and an x. "Will you be staying the night again? We have to get up early in the morning, but you shouldn't hear us."

"I have to go back tonight," Miranda said. "I have an appointment in the morning."

"And I have school," Lynn said. She pursed her lips together and sank her chin to the table. "I used to love school, but now I'd rather be with you guys."

"Well, Miss Lynn, you are welcome to come back any weekend. Our house isn't just open on holidays. And now, well, it looks like we will officially be family. After the wedding, we'll be your grandparents, too. Oh, Stanton, did you realize that?" Avery said. "I'm too young to be a grand-mother!"

"My mother said the same thing," Scott said. "Then she got over it. She likes to bring up having a granddaughter in conversation in places like restaurants or in lines at the store. The waitress or the cashier undoubtedly chimes in with, oh, not you, you're too young to be a grandmother. Gives her the biggest smile."

"Better than Botox," Lynn adds. "At least that's what Grandma Bunny says. I wouldn't want to shoot poison in my face. Yuck."

"Yuck, indeed," Stanton said, finally placing his tiles. "That's it, I'm out, and there are no tiles left."

Lynn looked down at the tally sheet. "You won!"

"I always win, dear one," Stanton said. "Just look how lucky I am. And before I forget to officially say it, Scott, I'm glad you finally stepped up. I was beginning to think I scared you away for good."

"No offense, sir, but I don't think that would have been possible."

"Congratulations to you. All three of you." Stanton raised his can of soda high. They all followed suit, clinking cans across the table.

"Thank you, Daddy," Miranda said.

Miranda helped clean up the paper plates and pizza boxes, while Lynn twirled around Scott begging to stay one more night. Miranda imagined putting her arms out wide and spinning, too, letting her oversized University of Connecticut sweatpants billow away from her body. She'd hold back her head, a broad grin across her pale and freckled face, and let out a chorus of please, please, please directed at the universe herself. Please, please, please let us just stay together in this house. Please, please, please let me skip the meeting with the president tomorrow. Please, please, please let us start being a real family right now.

Scott folded up the last of the pizza boxes into the recycling bin. "Well," he said.

"Yup," she said, her eyes still turned up toward the ceiling, still imagining spinning under the halogen lights that illuminated Avery's carefully chosen granite countertop. She felt tear drops rim her lower eyelids and kept her gaze up.

"Hey, pumpkin," Scott said. "You know what time it is, right?"

"Vitamins." She spit out the word.

"And?"

"All, right, I'll go. Randa, you won't leave while I'm upstairs, will you? I need a hug goodbye."

"No, of course, not. I'll wait right here."

Lynn dragged herself out of the kitchen.

"Come here," Scott said. He pulled her closely against him. She buried her head into his shoulder, inhaled his Old Spice scent, and finally let herself cry. Her body shook from the effort of at once holding it back and finally letting it go like a car stalling. He sighed and hugged her tighter. "It's going to be a long few days," he said. "You'll keep your phone charged?"

"Of course," she said gulping for air. "You'll call?"

"Yes, and text. You won't be able to teach your classes."

"About that," she said. "They cancelled my classes. I

have a meeting with the university president in the morning."

"Why didn't you tell me?"

"I really just found out before dinner. I'm not used to telling anyone anything."

"It's probably nothing."

"Or Ronan."

"Oh," he said, dropping his arms down at his side. He tapped his faded green Chuck Taylor against the ceramic tile. "But that would be fine. You could come to New Jersey right away. We wouldn't have to wait."

He picked her up and spun her around.

Wouldn't have to wait, she thought to herself. All of sudden everything felt much too fast like the ride at the shore that spins and spins until all you see is the streaky blur of the other carnival rides and people waiting for their turns. You go so fast that the music almost doesn't catch up; you stop hearing the words and only feel the beat as it mixes with your heart.

CHAPTER

24

T₁ HE CAMPUS WAS UNDENIABLY beautiful. She would miss this if she lost her position here. The sky was a perfect blue for the clear and cold weather. Even in winter with the trees bare and piles of black-tinted snow melting at the corners of brick sidewalks, it was beautiful. The whitewashed campus buildings sparkled in the sun. Miranda plunged her hands into her pockets and hugged her arms close against her body.

In a blinding realization at four in the morning, Miranda decided that she would beg for her job. As much as she wanted to marry Scott, she didn't want to give up her whole life. It's not like a poet could get a job just anywhere. She and Scott could use the money when they finally got married; having a kid meant needing money—even Miranda, in her limited experience with children, knew that much. And she liked her job. She liked sitting in the loose circle of her workshop classes, nodding along as students read through their work and began to debate about the second or third stanza. She loved seeing students with the sparks of inspiration, the fever of creation burning rosy on their cheeks as they stopped by her office. And she loved this place, the beautiful cold campus that she struggled to get across in time. Lynn and Scott could love it there, too. The woman didn't always have to give everything up for the man.

The president's residence was as you would expect. It was a tall building in the middle of campus, white with green shutters, and a long sprawling porch on the front that rose up from ground level by an impressive set of marble steps. Miranda steadied herself with one hand on the railing as she picked her way up the stairs. She looked at the door and suddenly wasn't sure if she should knock or just go in. During the regular term, the front of the residence served as an office space for the assistant and any specially commissioned committees. People came and went at will, but today, the college was closed. She stopped at the top step, unwilling to go any further and risk making a mistake that would damn her case further.

As soon as she stopped, the front door sprung open, and President Jonas Nicholls himself beckoned her inside. "Thank you for coming," he said. "I wish it were under better circumstances."

He ushered her into a sitting room just off the main hallway. Fine leather chairs in the college's hunter green surrounded the fireplace that had a white marble mantle. A surprisingly large fire filled the hearth. The rug under her feet was so plush that with each step her footing gave way in a slight slide. She stopped walking and stood in front of the fire, pulling off her coat and folding it over her arm. Not knowing what to expect, she didn't want her coat to be too far away from her.

The president entered, carrying a tray with two cups of coffee, milk, sugar, and some breakfast pastries. The joke around campus about meetings was that if the president was there the food would be great. From the look of the cheese Danish with sugar icing, the joke was true. "Please take a seat," he said. He motioned to a chair next to the fireplace and sat the tray down on a low table in front of it. "Coffee?" he asked.

"Sure," she said, reaching for a cup. Normally she took sugar, but Miranda couldn't imagine the awkwardness of opening the sugar and stirring. To do so, she would need to set down her coat. Instead she took a sip of dark bitter liquid and smiled.

He cleared his throat. Then he clasped his hands in front of his chest, raising his shoulders, before exhaling the words she most feared hearing. "There's been a complaint."

"A complaint?" Miranda choked out.

"Yes. I am sure you can guess the origins of this issue." Miranda swallowed hard.

"In light of the man's age and current status, we are left with a certain amount of leeway here. Leeway is also afforded by the secondary set of circumstances you seem to have found yourself in. Apparently, you have been quite busy in the last few months."

Miranda shifted in her seat. His tone dug at her, and he didn't stop looking at her, eyeing her up and down as if he were imagining the details Ronan must have provided.

"Apparently, the internet celebrity driving your current fortunes extends to the university as well. The IT people tell me hits to the website are up 65%. Applications are up 35%. Even from top-tier high schools, which I personally would have thought immune to the cult of the Internet." The president rolled his eyes and set down his coffee.

"Yes," Miranda said, more a question than an answer. What current fortunes, she wanted to ask. Did he mean Blocked Poet? Suddenly, she wished she hadn't skipped those emails from Ambrose.

"While you were not asked to sign a waiver to your creative works when you were hired, we do feel that in order to restore you in good standing to the community, some reparations, if you will, some service would be in order. You have placed us in a very delicate position. We do not wish to terminate your employment given your current circumstance, but misconduct as alleged in the complaint, no matter the student's age or standing cannot be tolerated. Do you understand?"

"I'm beginning to," Miranda replied.

"We have drawn up some papers, an agreement that outlines certain service expected of you in your new capacity as, what do they call it? Scrabble Poet, is it?"

"Blocked Poet," Miranda said.

"When Mr. Reed first reached out to me, I must admit I didn't understand. I don't do much with the Internet except email donors and read the newspaper. I didn't understand that anyone could cause the stir that you have and so quickly. Mr. Reed quickly educated me, though, and when I told the trustees—they all understood immediately. As your classes were already cancelled for this disciplinary action, we saw no reason not to request that Mr. Reed extend your trip, at your expense, to include certain stops beneficial to the university in terms of donors, etc."

Mr. Reed. She nearly choked on the last sip of her coffee. A trip? What trip, she wanted to ask. What expense?

"Additionally, Mr. Reed assured us that you would be able to create volumes dedicated to the university with the proceeds directed to us."

Miranda nodded.

"Let me be clear. You must meet these obligations to be reinstated in your position. Additionally, we expect the utmost in confidentially about this issue. We will settle things with the complainant in a timely fashion once these documents are signed." He handed her a stack of paper with a rainbow of tiny sticky notes indicating where she should sign.

"I'll leave you to review those, but I must caution you that this is not open for negotiation." He rose and left the room, his feet made no sound on the heavily padded carpets. "You can leave them on the table when you are finished and show yourself out. Mr. Reed already has a copy."

She didn't even need to beg; instead, she signed.

CHAPTER

25

H₄ ER COMPUTER SCREEN FILLED up with three hundred emails from Ambrose. The last one, sent just ten minutes before, read, "Call me," in all capital letters and a font that blinked from a normal black to a bold red so rapidly that it could induce a seizure.

She pressed call on her phone.

"Miranda," Ambrose said. "Let's talk about your schedule. I trust the meeting with the President went as well as could be expected. I tried to contact you about this, but I figured you would probably want to keep the position. Internet fame is so fleeting. But really, a student? Must have been hot, right?"

He didn't wait for her reply.

"Well, anyway. As the merch rolls out, I have scheduled different events for you. I started with smaller cities. Plus the events the university demanded; I figured you would want to placate them. So anyway, you will have two or three days in each. First a college bookstore or a seminar, talking about poetry, writing in general, and about the university-themed volumes in the Blocked Poet collection. Then you will do another session at a local Barnes and Noble or indie store or community center. Each stop will get a package with ten Scrabble boards. The idea is that you will show people how to play with words. These have been billed as interactive events. People pay money to see their "poems" photographed by you at these events and posted on the Blocked Poet feeds. Tickets sales have been through the roof. You will also need to sign books. Have you seen the books?"

"I haven't seen anything!"

"There's been some television. You didn't see that? Not even Good Morning America? We had a rough fight for the afternoon talk time. Ellen won. That's your last tour stop in Los Angeles, February 14th. I didn't bother booking New York; I figured you could do that after you got back. Baltimore, Charlotte, Atlanta, Gainesville, Birmingham, New Orleans, Santa Fe, Phoenix, Las Vegas, Portland, and Los Angeles. You fly out of Newark tomorrow—I saw the engagement pop up on Facebook yesterday—congratulations—and then I had my assistant change the flight plan—figured you want to say goodbye to the new lover boy. I must say, you do move fast. I also need your financial information, you'll want an accountant to keep track of taxes and your deductions, but you will be pleasantly surprised how much this has already made. There's an ad feed on your website, and the ticket sales, books sales, coffee mugs, tee-shirts, and earrings. Links to copies of the e-books should be in your email."

"Website?"

"Oh, dear, you haven't read any of the emails have you?"

"I just got back."

"They have Internet in Turkey. It's not Patagonia. Shoot, they even have Internet in Patagonia."

"I didn't think I needed to check."

"Can you check from now on? That's how you'll know the schedule. We may add stops."

"Add stops?"

"Miranda, really? Scott said you were bright. Do try to keep up."

Miranda looked at the suitcase she still had yet to unpack from Turkey. It already had her best outfits. They were dirty, yes, but there were laundry machines all across the United States from Baltimore to Los Angeles. The chance to see the country, flying from city to city, would have once filled her with ecstasy. Instead, she studied her phone, unsure what to text Scott.

Finally, she typed. "I need to tell you something." Then she deleted it. "Text me your address," she typed.

The address Scott returned was two hours and fifty-six minutes straight down I-87. She steered the car carefully to the interstate, then accelerated as quickly as she could, going as fast as she could without thinking too much about speeding tickets. The all rock music station blared "A Get the Led Out" tribute to Led Zeppelin. And she sang along with the music, letting the lyrics and guitar fill her mind instead of thoughts about the tour and her job and her future. She would think about that later, after she saw Scott and told him, after she made sure he hadn't changed his mind, after she made sure that all of this would be okay. That they would be okay.

"Screw it," he said in a whisper. They sat on Scott's living room rug, print-outs of the itinerary spread around them like a couple of teenagers doing homework. Lynn sat on the white leather sectional, looking down over their shoulders as she pretended to color in a worksheet on the life stages of a caterpillar. "Lynn, why don't you go watch television in my room?" he asked.

"What can I watch?"

"Anything," he said.

"Even Cartoon Network?" she asked.

Scott sighed. "Yeah, even that."

"Daddy hates Cartoon Network," Lynn explained before running upstairs.

"Forty-two days. Extra stops to keep your job?"

"Yes," Miranda said. "But it's not all about the job. It's a book tour. I'm a poet with a book tour."

"More like blackmail."

"Well, it is more than that, but if I want to keep my job, these are the terms."

"Then screw the terms. Quit."

"Scott, I don't want to quit. I want to keep my position."

"You do? Even after this?"

"These types of positions don't grow on trees. I'm not exactly qualified to do anything else. And bottom line, I like teaching there. How else could I support myself?"

"I could support you," he said. "You could move here. Like right now. We wouldn't have to wait."

"You know it's not that easy."

"My mother did it."

"Did what?"

"Stayed home, took care of things."

"That's hardly fair to say. She did that while your dad brought home a lawyer's salary."

"I could go back to it."

"And then we would never see you. What would be the point? You said you could transfer upstate; you said they had a Montessori school, too."

"You wouldn't want to stay home?"

"Be a stay-at-home mom?" Miranda caught herself before she laughed out loud. "I wouldn't know anything about that."

"I thought you would like it," he said.

"What would make you think that?" she asked.

"I don't know," he said. "I feel like I don't know anything anymore. This suddenly feels like a lot to figure out."

Miranda felt the bottom of her heart give out. "At least we'll have some time to figure it out," she said, hoping to sound lighthearted.

"Yeah," he said. He patted the space next to him. "Can we just enjoy being together for a minute first?"

She pushed herself against him and rested her head on his shoulder. She sighed, trying to release the tension from her body. The excitement of the last few days leaked from her; dreams never matched reality. While she wouldn't want to give up this feeling, she didn't want to trade away the last six years of her life and all she had worked for. Being a stay-at-home mom never even entered her thinking. Her mom worked as a trial lawyer until she got so sick that she couldn't stand for longer than ten minutes. And even then, she took calls and consulted from home. Bunny's idea of staying at home meant running every charity auction and playing tennis at the club every afternoon. Avery made a few stabs at putting dinner on the table, but at fifteen, even Miranda with her limited kitchen skills could cook dinner more safely than Avery. With relief, Avery turned back to her work, and the remaining domestic tasks were outsourced to a variety of services and hired staff. Miranda wasn't the type of woman to swoon at babies or get excited about new recipes. She loved books and teaching, the way her mother loved the courtroom and the law. With her Blocked Poet work, Miranda could see glimmers of her old joy for writing, which by all accounts would be difficult to do while watching Dora the Explorer or waiting to carpool the soccer team. If Scott wanted that kind of life, that kind of wife, he picked the wrong person.

Then the doorbell rang, startling them both to their feet.

"Shit," Scott said.

"What is it?"

"Kendra," he said.

"Kendra?" she asked. "Is there something you haven't told me?"

"I have basketball. Kendra is the sitter. Remember with the Facebook. I'm such a jerk to cancel now."

"That's not a problem—I'd like to see this basketball you speak of," Miranda said.

"You would?"

The doorbell rang again.

"Yes, I would. Or is it weird for me to come? Do girl-friends go?"

"Girlfriends? Sometimes, but you are more than that. You're my fiancée."

Miranda felt her stomach flip over when he said it.

"I'd love for you to meet my friends. I'm sure this is all going to throw them for a loop. It will be fun to watch. You can make fun of me. They all do."

"I couldn't possibly. I'll be your cheerleader."

"You may want to rethink that after you watch him play," Lynn said, rushing past them both to get to the door. "There's a reason that I stay with Kendra. That and the pizza. Daddy, can Kendra and I get a pizza?"

Kendra was exactly what you would expect from a babysitter except in addition to the snapping gum and cell phone, she settled her AP Organic Chemistry book loudly on the table to shake Miranda's hand. "Nice to meet you," she said.

"You, too. That's quite a book."

"Yeah, I think the book is a warning sign that the class will kill you. Three of my classmates started seeing a chiro-practor after starting this class! Two got eyeglasses. I've escaped the curse so far, but I do have a callous on my index finger from writing so many notes." She held up her finger for Miranda to examine.

"Wow," Miranda said.

Kendra snapped her gum.

Scott hustled into the room in basketball shorts and the most garish neon green sneakers. He handed Kendra twenty dollars. "Pizza is cool. Just don't let her order the anchovies. She says she likes them, but she doesn't."

"I do, too," Lynn said.

"You do not. We'll be a little later tonight. I'm going to

have to take Miranda for dinner after this to make it up to her."

"Make what up to me?"

Scott pointed at his shoes and then the safety strap that he was attaching to a pair of yellowed, wrap-around glasses he pulled out of his pocket and affixed to his head.

"Oh," Miranda said. "Well."

"Don't worry, I'll change before dinner."

Scott drove them slowly through the streets of his very quaint town. The main street, lined with both shops and houses, looked like something from Currier and Ives—all white clapboard siding and shutters in respectable colonial colors like hunter green and burgundy. The church, Dutch Reformed, was a giant stone structure with a triptych of stained glass documenting the passion of Christ over the glossy, red front door. The door itself was so massive, Miranda couldn't imagine it even opened.

"You play in there?" she asked.

"Well, not in there, around back."

Behind the stone church stood a glass and metal edifice that rivaled a modern art museum. "You play in there?"

"Yes, it's like a Y."

Women in high end yoga gear streamed out of the building, slipping into BMW and Lexus SUVs. Inside, they were greeted by a perky girl with dyed red hair wearing an all-black spandex suit.

"Kind of like a Y?" Miranda asked as Scott showed his identification and signed in.

"Well okay, a gym. The church had a campaign about bodies being the temple of God, and some of the members got together and created a gym. They opened it to community membership to help defray the maintenance. The pastor said yes because it meant they could spread the word of God to more people."

"At a gym?"

"Yeah, all the treadmills replay the Sunday sermons.

And the muzak is all hymns. Other than that it's like a regular gym."

"A regular gym with Bible verses on the wall," Miranda said, pointing to First Timothy, 4:8 inscribed over the reception desk. "'For while bodily training is of some value, godliness is of value in every way, as it holds promise for the present life and also for the life to come.' Very valuable advice. Exercise now for the afterlife."

"Don't knock it until you try it. It's nice here."

"I know, I know," Miranda said. "It's certainly modern." Everything glistened from being both new and clean. They walked past a room of treadmills and elliptical machines. People of all shapes and sizes, eyes fixated on the screens on top of their machines, walked, ran, and climbed to their own rhythms.

Scott opened the next door, which led to a cavernous gym with yellow wood floors that squeaked under your shoes just like in high school. Miranda was grateful that instead of the classic bleachers, the sides of the court were lined with stadium seats. "A local movie theatre closed and donated the seating. If you sit up there long enough, you can still smell the popcorn."

On the far side of the court, five men dribbled and shot in a frantic rush. They bobbed and weaved around each other, each playing against his own invisible opponent.

"Finally," the tallest and widest man, sweat already soaking through his oversized sweatshirt called. "Oh, I see, a chick."

"Not just any chick," Scott bellowed back. "My fiancée."

The other men stopped dribbling and trotted the length of the court to circle them. They stood panting, blatantly eying Miranda up.

"So you did it," the bigger man said. "You really did it."

Miranda held up her left hand and wiggled her fingers. "Yup," she said. "He did."

The big guy grabbed her up into a hug, lifting her feet off the ground. "Congratulations," he whooped. Putting

BRANDI MEGAN GRANETT

her down, he extended a hand, then pulled it back, wiping it on his sweaty shirt before extending it again. "Pastor Dan, welcome to the gym of the Lord."

"That's not what it's really called," the shortest man in the group said. His sneakers were a blinding fluorescent orange. "I'm Rabbi Irv. And mazel tov."

"Let me guess," she said to the next man. "You're a priest?"

"No, close though, I'm a lawyer. Jonah. Nice to meet you."

The next man, with the most ebony skin Miranda had ever seen, put out his hand. "I'm Francis. I'm the priest."

"Geesh, guys. Congratulations. I'm Albert, house painter."

They stood there staring at her, not saying anything.

"I'm sensing a joke here," Miranda said. "But I am not sure how that would turn out. Nice to meet you all."

Pastor Dan didn't waste any time. "So are we going to play or what?"

The men immediately separated into two groups. Pastor Dan looked at his watch, fished a whistle out from under his shirt, and blew it hard. Miranda found the game tough to follow. After a few minutes, she pulled out her phone and began scrolling through the emails from Ambrose and now from his assistant, Kristen.

She immediately liked Kristen's style. The woman favored a single K to the word okay. Though an English professor by trade, Miranda liked when the language went feral and changed. That these changes were taking place during her own time amused her. If the text-speak dialect had longer words, she would use them in her word sculptures.

Miranda kept scrolling with Kristen taking over more and more as Ambrose's plans sprung into life. She ordered books and hired editors. She booked all the travel reservations and kept Miranda's itinerary up to date in a Google document that everyone could update. Her flight tomorrow was at one from Newark. Non-stop one hour and fifteen minutes. It seemed extravagant to fly to Baltimore, but the next stop was Richmond, and then Atlanta. She couldn't keep her car for the entire trip, and it was probably safer in Scott's driveway than racking up over a month of parking lot fees while she was on some lark of a trip. When she got deeper into the emails, she finally saw the first one marked Completed Book. She hovered over the link.

Pastor Dan blew his whistle to signal a foul, and Francis took over the free throw line. Miranda watched him miss all but one of the three shots. Then Dan blew the whistle again, and the men scurried to and fro in some pattern not quite discernable to Miranda. She waved to Scott, who locked eyes with her and smiled. Distracted, he missed a pass from the Rabbi.

"Nice work, Lover Boy," Albert razzed, elbowing Scott in the ribs as he passed by, ball in hand, clearly a traveling foul from Miranda's viewpoint.

She bent back down over her phone and clicked on the link. A stark black cover with the words Blocked Poet on a Scrabble board took up the full width of the tiny screen. She clicked again to open to the first page; she cringed a little seeing one of her first poems there, but she kept clicking. Ambrose had kept the formatting she used for the photo. She liked the way the images were sharper and how the poems were organized together to weave a sort of story. When she got to the last one, she realized she was crying.

"I know I play like shit, but you don't have to cry. It's only a once a week pick-up game. I can stop anytime, really I can," Scott said.

"What?" Miranda said, looking up, wiping at the tears on her cheeks.

"I'd cry if I were marrying him," Albert said. "Nice meeting you." The other men waved as they filed past and out into the lobby.

"No seriously, Randa, you okay?"

"I'm better than okay; look at this." She handed him

her phone with the cover of her book on display. He clicked through, just as she had.

He reached a sweaty arm around her and pulled her to her feet. "Let me try to make up for before. Let's go celebrate properly."

"Hold on, let me send this to Danielle."

"You do that, and I'll change."

Miranda looked up from her phone in time to watch him walk away. Watching him now was different than in Turkey; this time she knew he would come back and keep coming back. And she thought it was funny how as much as everything had changed between them, it hadn't. As much as she wanted to kiss him and more, he still felt like her friend, the boy she grew up with. She felt a smile spread across her face. He turned and winked at her from the other side of the gym before slipping into the locker room.

Her phone buzzed in her hand. She half expected it to be a text from him, but it was Danielle calling. It must be four o'clock in the morning in Turkey.

"Is everything okay?" Miranda said, skipping the hello. "It's almost four in the morning where you are."

"I got tired of waiting you out."

"Waiting me out for what?"

"To invite me to be your bridesmaid. I saw the picture on Facebook. And what's this book you just emailed me? You've been keeping things from me."

"Oh, Dani, I didn't want to bother your honeymoon. I figured you had enough of my relationship drama."

"But this isn't drama, is it?"

Miranda felt her smile grow even larger. "No, it's not. It's really not. It's perfect."

"So tell me all about it."

So Miranda told her all about the day they got back, about her mother's ring, and how excited Lynn was. Then she told her about the book, the university President, and the tour.

"But enough about that—how's the honeymoon?"

Miranda asked.

"Things are nice. In two more hours, we have plans to take a sunrise cruise on the Mediterranean to a private island where we can sunbathe and snorkel all day."

"Then why aren't you sleeping?"

"Because I've been worried about you. And because this baby won't sit still. It's like she's on American time."

"She?"

"I don't know that or anything. I just hope so. A girl would be nice."

"It would. I'm so excited for you."

"I'm so excited for you. You'll keep me informed, won't you? Oh, shit," Danielle whispered. "I think I woke Omar up. He'll be nuts if he finds me out of bed. Says I need my rest."

"I better let you go," Miranda said.

"Yeah, I'll just pretend I was going to the bathroom. Call me next week, okay? We'll be back home then."

The line went dead before Miranda could answer. She liked the idea of her fearless friend sneaking phone calls in the middle of the night. And she liked the idea of Omar caring about Dani getting enough rest. Her friend was finally settled. And safe. After all their years together, it shocked Miranda to find that instead of Dani rushing off to do something crazy, it was her turn.

Instead of moving the car, they walked two blocks to an Italian restaurant with red and white checked tablecloths and wine bottles corked with candles that melted over the sides of the bottles, a living, breathing Italian restaurant stereotype. But the grandmother who came out from behind the counter and pinched Scott's cheeks was anything but inauthentic. With her thick accent, she cried out, "Where is the bambina?"

"Lynn's with Kendra," Scott said.

"Oh, Kendra. Bright but trouble." The grandmother leaned around Scott to peer at Miranda. She squinted her eyes and then leaned back. "You bring a girl? You?"

"Not any girl, Maria Rosa: my fiancée, Miranda."

"No, you didn't propose without me meeting her first? You couldn't have."

"I had to; I couldn't let her get away." Scott wrapped an arm around Miranda and pulled her in close to him. "And my mother picked her out for me when she was a baby. I had no choice. You have to do what your mother wants."

"Smart boy. Lucky girl. Table by the window?"

The grandmother led them to a two-top next to the window that looked out on the main street. She didn't give them menus. Instead she turned and tottered back to the swinging door that led to the kitchen; she shouted, "Antonio," as she pushed through the door.

"Maria Rosa took a liking to me when we first moved back here. I wasn't very good at cooking, so Lynn and I ate out a lot."

"She seems lovely."

"She is. And her meatballs are to die for."

Antonio appeared from the kitchen with two glasses of water balanced in one hand and two plates of salad on the other. "Nice to meet you, Miranda," he said as if they had already been introduced.

"Things are a little casual here. And Maria Rosa won't let me order. After a month of coming here, she told me that you don't order from your grandmother's kitchen."

"Do things like this just happen to you? Are you naturally charmed?"

"Maybe I'm charming? What do you think? Randa, am I charming?"

"I'm not sure." She reached across the table to pick up his hand. "Captivating maybe. Enchanting? I know I'm smitten."

"Smitten, eh? I could like that. Wish I could talk you out of leaving. What would it take to get you to just stay?" He picked up his fork without letting go of her hand.

"Scott," she said. "I thought we were supposed to be celebrating."

"Yes," he said. "I'm sorry. Well, no, I'm not sorry."

"Well, I'm sorry this bothers you, but that doesn't change anything. The rest of my life didn't stop just because of this." She held up her hand; the ring glimmered in the candlelight.

"I'm not asking for your life to stop. Maybe just pause for a minute. I just thought we would have more time—weekends at least. Something. But tomorrow you're gone. Did you see that schedule? You don't even have a day off between stops because of that blackmail."

"It's not blackmail; it's an agreement. I signed."

"I wish you could unsign."

"If I unsign, how would I support myself?"

"What if I could prove to you that it would be fine? What if we went back to my place and ran the numbers? Treat it like a merger."

"A merger?"

"You know what I mean—I could call on all of that management consultant legal mumbo jumbo and do the numbers, make up the deal sheet? If I can prove it with the deal sheet, would you stay?"

"But this isn't about just the numbers, Scott. It's about my book. It was in the New York Times; they talked about it on Good Morning America. I'm scheduled for Ellen."

"So do Ellen—what does Ellen have to do with the Wakeforest Community Center or the El Paso Texas Book Shoppe? Or some alumni tea in East Someplace I haven't heard of? Will you just hear me out? Can we just try and see what it would take on paper to make this happen?"

He looked up at her so desperately, she found herself nodding in agreement. She would look at the numbers, maybe it could all be okay. Maybe he was right about El Paso and the alumni tea. Maybe they could all go to California together.

"She tried to wait up for you guys, but I finally convinced her to wait in bed. I checked after five minutes, and she was out," Kendra said.

"Thank you for watching her," Scott said. "Same time next week?"

"Yup. And congratulations on the engagement. Lynn told me all about it. It's wicked cool that you've known each other like forever. See you next week."

Kendra let herself out, leaving Scott and Miranda standing in the main room just looking at each other. Miranda looked around. Lynn's coloring book rested on the coffee table in front of the monstrous white leather couch. The tangle of wires around the entertainment center. The absence of art on the walls. It took her breath away to think about what the next few months would bring. How would his house and her apartment become theirs? She never imagined her life looking this way. Becoming someone's wife? Someone's mother? At the same time. She turned to him and said, "Scott—"

He raised a finger to his lips and pointed up the stairs. "Come with me," he whispered.

The door to Lynn's room was cracked open a little. He nudged it open a tiny bit more with his toe, just enough so that they could watch her sleep. The glow of her night-light cast a halo around her head. The diary Miranda gave to her lay open on the pink comforter next to her. They stood there, holding their own breath, watching her breathe.

He leaned slowly forward and pulled the door shut, before tugging Miranda gently into the room across the hallway.

"When she was little, I would get this weird panic in the middle of the night, and I would have to just go and watch to make sure she was still breathing. Now I think I do it out of habit. Go ahead, make fun of me."

"I can see the appeal of it," Miranda said. The word sculpture formed in her head without even thinking about it: Sleeping, Pretty, Young, Girl, Love.

"Well, I see the appeal in you," he said. "Let's try to work this out. I don't want you to go. But first I need numbers."

"I don't want to leave either—but it's not about leaving you, Scott. It's about this opportunity and keeping my job and paying my student loans.

"You don't have go right now; you could call Ambrose and have him reschedule the whole thing."

"Scott, please—how about you work on those numbers first then we'll talk?"

She downloaded all of her bank statements, printing them off from his ancient desktop computer in the living room. Then she found her student loan statement online. And her credit card bill. And the car payment.

"Stanton didn't pay for graduate school?" he asked.

"Frankly he didn't much like the idea of a poetry degree. Frivolous, he said. Tough love. He finished up the lecture saying a good parent wouldn't let you waste your life and talents on nursery rhymes."

"Oh," Scott said. "That's harsh."

"You know, I didn't mind. I wanted to be my own person for once and not tied to his bank account and lectures."

"I felt that way with Lynn. I didn't want to rely on my parents to rescue me. All of a sudden I felt like I had to do it on my own. But, wow, look at those numbers. School cost that much?"

"Yeah," she said. "I told you I needed to work."

"Yeah," he said, opening another spreadsheet on his laptop.

None of the numbers supported his plan. The column of bills never matched the single number in the earning column.

"Ambrose said I could make money on Blocked Poet," Miranda said.

"Yeah. Could. And for how long?"

"And going on the tour is how I can make that money."

"It's like a weird maze," Scott said. "We have to stay in it to get out of it."

She leaned over his shoulder. It felt so good to be that

close to him. She kissed his ear. Then a number on the screen caught her eye. Four hundred dollars in an unmarked column.

"Wait," she said, pointing it out on the computer screen. "I think you have an extra number there."

"Really?" he said. He kissed her quickly on the cheek, then looked at the column. "Oh," he said, his voice deflated. "That's not a mistake. Well, it is, but not one that I can correct."

"What's it for? That would cover the student loans and your car payment. With some left over."

"Cassadee," he said.

"A month?" she asked.

"I told you, she demands money. I try not to pay, but when I push it too far she dangles the whole paternity test and mentions the paperwork I want her to sign. See here." He clicked open his email.

"Pay or say goodbye," read the body of the first email.

"Do you think they would let you keep a child from its mother? Especially with your own past out here—remember, I know all the charges," read another.

"I'll sign nothing except for the back of a check," read a third.

He moved to click on another.

"No, that's okay," Miranda said. "I've seen enough. How could she even say those things?"

"I told you Randa; she isn't right. She doesn't care about anything except for herself and her next score. Me, Lynn, we're just a means to an end with her."

"I just don't understand."

"It took me a long time, too. I just didn't think people could really be like that. We weren't raised that way, and I don't want Lynn to be either. So I pay. And keep paying. And while it pained me to do it before, seeing how much more it costs us kills me. I want to be able to beg you to quit your job and move here. Right now. But I can't. Maybe if I took on some tutoring after school," he said. "I'd have to give up coaching the soccer team, but maybe, I could. And I could go call my father, go back."

She put her hand over his. "Please, stop. It's only forty-two days; this isn't forever."

"And what are we going to do after you get back? Forty-two days doesn't change the distance between your job and my job."

"But I am out for the term; they cancelled all of my classes. I wouldn't have to be back until June for the summer term. That gives us a lot of time to think about this. Figure it out. Come on, Scott, please try to just be happy for me. It's only a trip. Six weeks. Not even two months."

"Randa, I left you once, and I thought it was going to be for a week, and it turned out to be six years. I don't want something to change along the way and ruin this."

"Do you really think that is even possible?"

He closed the laptop screen and stood up. "Actually, I don't want to think about it at all," he said. "How about we go upstairs instead?"

"Hold up—what happened to waiting?" Miranda asked.

"That doesn't mean we have to wait for everything," he said.

CHAPTER

26

I N HINDSIGHT, they probably should have pulled on some clothes before going to sleep. Luckily, they were quick with the sheets and blankets as Lynn bolted into their room seconds after Scott's alarm clock chirruped with sounds of a sportscaster discussing the Giants' dismal possibilities in the playoffs. And Scott was even quicker with the redirection. "Lynn," he chimed. "Quick, go see if we have pancake mix. We could have a special breakfast for Miranda's going away party."

She spun before she could even approach the bed and fully take in their bare shoulders let alone climb up and jostle any strategically placed blankets. The minute they heard her footsteps scamper down the stairs, they began pulling on their clothes.

"Wait," Scott said. He opened a drawer and pulled out a tee shirt and some sweat pants. "Put this on. I don't think you should go down in last night's clothes. We need to make this seem above board. You know, like proper."

"Proper? Like you only have sleepovers after you're engaged?"

"Exactly like that. Or how about you only have sleep-overs with romantic partners after your father is dead? How about that? What could we say to convey that message?"

"Wow, now you are channeling Stanton to a tee, huh?"

"I learned from the best."

"After what I've been finding out, I am not sure it is the best. Unless you're into that whole 'father knows best and manipulates everything' routine."

"Don't be so hard on him," Scott said. "It's not easy being a dad."

Lynn's only concern was why she couldn't skip school to take Miranda to the airport.

"Sorry, girlie, you can't miss school today. We only just got back from break, and it looks bad if I let you stay home."

"But you aren't going to be at school," Lynn protested.

"Miranda and I will drop you off together, and then I will take her to the airport, and then I'll be back to teach."

"Can I show her my classroom?" Lynn asked.

"Sure," Scott said.

"Can I show her your classroom?" Lynn asked.

"Sure," Scott said.

"Can I—" Lynn started.

"Eat your pancakes? Sure you can. Finish up. Then go get dressed."

"Can I use the shower?" Miranda asked.

"Sure. Let me just come up and show you something first."

Scott waited while she got her things from her suitcase and followed her to the bathroom. He closed the door behind them and then loudly announced. "I'm just going to brush my teeth while you get a shower."

"Okay," she answered back just as loudly.

He giggled and pointed at the door. Miranda shrugged and turned on the shower. She slipped out of her clothes while he watched before following her into the shower.

"Brushing your teeth, huh?" She turned her back to him letting the water from the shower soak her hair.

"Allow me," he whispered. He took her shampoo bottle from her hand. She listened to the pop of the lid and air escaping the bottle as he measured the right amount. When he placed his hands in her hair, she shuddered. He massaged her scalp deftly.

Then he rinsed it out and took up a wide-toothed comb from the shower ledge and the bottle of conditioner. Like a salon expert, he combed the conditioner through her hair lifting it in sections to both rinse it and keep it tangle free.

"Do you do cuts and color, too? I'm beginning to feel like I'm in a spa." She leaned back a little. "Well, that's something they don't have at the spa."

"I wish we were getting married today," he said. "Waiting is hard."

"That's not the only thing," she said, giggling.

He picked up the soap and began lathering her back.

"Let me," she said. She took the soap and returned the favor. Savoring the opportunity to just touch him, all parts of him, she took her time. Behind his ears, the backs of his knees, his belly button. When he was a completely covered in soap, she took him in her arms again and shimmied back and forth, then turned around and repeated the motion, laughing as she did so.

"See. Two for one."

"You really are smart," he said, kissing the top of her head.

Lynn began singing loudly along to a Justin Bieber song on the radio. "That's our cue," he said. "Can't be late for school."

The school looked more like a sprawling ranch house than an elementary school. Ivy, green swaths of fungus, and an accumulation of last fall's leaves concealed the low, sandstone-colored walls of the building within the landscape.

Tall pine trees encircled the sprawling complex, the thick smell of their dropped needles hovered in the air.

"It's like a Hobbit house," Scott said. "We focus heavily on nature and how it can teach us almost everything we need to know."

As if on cue, Lynn turned to face them as she skipped backwards up the school path and recited Joyce Kilmer's poem, Tree. Miranda dropped Scott's hand and skipped ahead to join her, chiming in on, "Poems are made by fools like me, But only God can make a tree."

Then Lynn stopped and looked up at Miranda. "I wish you didn't write poems," she said. "If you were just a regular teacher like Daddy, you wouldn't have to go anywhere."

"Oh, Lynn, I'm going to miss you, too. But you promised that you would text me, right?"

"And Facebook," she said. The smile started to inch back across Lynn's face. "You'll be like Ford Prefect in the Hitchhiker's Guide, sending us updates."

"The Hitchhiker's Guide?" Miranda asked.

"Daddy read it to me at bedtime," Lynn said.

"I had to start her young," Scott said, shrugging his shoulders.

Miranda laughed, the sound carrying under the pine trees. Teachers and students still making their way from the parking lot stopped to look at them. But she didn't care.

"Family hug," Scott called, just as loudly, and the three of them huddled forward for the sweetest embrace Miranda had ever enjoyed.

"What's this, what's this?" an older woman in a purple tweed suit and very sensible loafers said.

"Dr. Long," Lynn said. "I want you to meet Miranda."

"I'm Patricia," said Dr. Long, extending her hand.

"I'm Miranda, but you probably know that."

Dr. Long slid her glasses off and squinted. "I know you," she said. "You're that Scrabble board poet, aren't you?"

"Yes, it appears that I am."

"Patricia, that's why I needed the sub this morning. I'm

taking Miranda to the airport. She's going on a book tour. Forty-two days."

"Forty-two days—you must be quite popular for a poet," Patricia said.

"That's what they are telling me, but we were in Turkey when all this happened, so I am just now trying to figure out what it all means."

Dr. Long extended a long plainly manicured finger and tapped Miranda on the nose. "It means, dear, that you are very lucky. Maybe when you are done being a famous poet, you could come back and teach here?"

"Oh," Miranda stammered. She looked about at the tide of children parting on either side of them, with their loud talking and big backpacks. "That's something I never considered," she said.

"I think one elementary school teacher in the family is enough," Scott said.

The bell for classes rang, and Lynn sprinted off with the last pack of stragglers. "Bye, Randa," she called. "Come see my classroom." The sea of big backpacks swallowed her up and pushed her into the building.

"Duty calls," Dr. Long said, picking up the hand of the last wayward child that seemed more interested in the cracks in the sidewalk than entering the building.

"So you do this?" Miranda asked.

"Five days a week."

"And you love it?"

"Some days I do. Some days I don't. But I wanted to be near Lynn. I wanted to make sure she was safe. I couldn't do that working twelve hours a day to protect other people's money. Now, come see what I do so that I can get health insurance and apparently afford little else." A bit of a harsh tone crept into his voice.

Scott's classroom looked much like any other class-room. Tables with diminutive chairs cluttered the area in front of a whiteboard. A carpeted area in the back of the room was littered with bean bag chairs and stray books.

But instead of having bulletin boards featuring the spelling word of the week, the walls of the room were lined with music posters for various bands from a variety of venues from the 1960s to present. A Kiss poster, complete with Gene Simmons' tongue, loomed over the white board. A poster for Jimi Hendrix in San Francisco abutted the light switch. Dave Matthews Band hung out with Willie Nelson by the coat rack. Cyndi Lauper in a plaid mini skirt graced the space over the reading nook. Five boxes of Scrabble sat on the shelf over the cubbies. Next to the door to the courtyard sat an entire stack of Frisbees. His classroom captured the essence of him. Miranda could see clearly what this place meant to him, and what leaving this wonderful school might mean for him and Lynn.

"Beautiful, isn't it?" Scott said. "I play all of those bands for the kids."

"And you're allowed? On the Road Again? From the Watchtower? Girls Just Wanna Have Fun?"

"It's a really progressive school. As a school, we vowed to include all the banned books we can into our classes. Student lunches are nut-free, and no plastic is allowed."

"But a little Hendrix is fine?"

"Rock and roll never hurt nobody. Plus the hipster parents like it."

"Are you a hipster parent?" Miranda tapped his chest, before quickly stealing a kiss.

"It depends, are you into that sort of thing?"

"I don't know yet. I never really considered the options. I only knew the lawyer variety. Where are the kids?"

"They have Feelings and Dreams Assembly on Wednesdays. Everyone gets together to talk about how they feel and what they want to accomplish."

"And Linden knows this is what you do for a living? He doesn't freak out or anything?"

"Lynn wore my dad down. If it's for her or about her, he doesn't care. If I told him she needed me to be a circus clown, he would buy me the giant shoes and the big red nose. Although, leaving the family business did burn him a little; my great-grandfather started that firm. I think maybe he was jealous. He always wanted to own an ice cream store."

"I remember that. He was going to open it up in the Hamptons, but stay open all year serving whiskeys instead of ice cream in the winter."

"Can you imagine? My dad scooping ice cream?"

"Not really. But I couldn't imagine this either. Can I come back another time when the kids are here? I want to see you in action. But right now, we probably have to go."

"If we don't peek in on Lynn's room, I won't hear the end of it."

Lynn's class was still at Feelings and Dreams. Her teacher, Mrs. Kells, favored maps on her walls. Not any old maps—transit maps. From the Boston T to the London Underground to the Paris Metro. She even had one for the bus lines in Berkeley. "She's a bit of a travel nut. One of those people who can take a backpack and passport and amuse themselves in Central America for three months. She thinks the world's problems would be solved if we just travelled together," Scott explained.

"They would be solved," Mrs. Kells said, entering the room with the pack of first-graders behind her. "Class, what values does public transportation provide?"

"Cost savings, environmental benefits, and community," the class called in unison as they found their way to their chairs. Lynn could barely stay seated in hers. She leaned forward waving her arm frantically.

"Yes, Lynn," Mrs. Kells finally said.

Lynn let out a puff of air and a rush of words. "Can I introduce you to Miranda? She's a poet, and she's marrying my dad."

"Wonderful and welcome," said Mrs. Kells. "Our tiny community could always benefit from another artist in residence."

Miranda suddenly felt her mouth go dry. All she could

do was politely nod and wave as Scott pulled her gently toward the door.

Scott pulled the car off the highway and started the circle loop around Newark Airport. He signaled left for the short-term parking.

"No, don't," Miranda said. "Just drop me off."

"But I can go in with you. I don't have to be back to school until noon."

"If you get out of the car, I don't think I'll be able to leave. And I want to go. Every writer dreams about this trip."

"I wish it was me you dreamt about," Scott said, kissing the back of her hand.

Miranda watched a man in a crisp navy blue suit hand over his luggage to the skycap and then stride away purposefully. She used to be jealous of people like that. People who could just drop all their baggage and walk away with nothing more than a couple of credit cards and a Chapstick in their pocket. Imagine if she had done that at Thanksgiving. If she had called Avery and cancelled and jumped a plane to Ibiza, then none of this would be here. None of this would be happening.

She couldn't look at him, so she kept her eyes on the automatic doors that swallowed up a group of Korean tourists and more men in suits. "I've dreamt about you for as long as I can remember. My whole life I kept wishing you would notice me. See me not as your friend, not as Uncle Stanton's and Aunt Louise's daughter, but as me. When you came to my apartment, no prompting from our parents, I thought this is it, this is him finally seeing me. Then you disappeared. I watched for you online. I sent you a friend request that you never approved. I still waited. I still dreamed."

"But you weren't waiting. You dated Ronan."

"I slept with Ronan. I didn't really date him. And that was after Thanksgiving. After I saw you again and you freaked out on me about Lynn's vitamins and not wanting any help. I thought okay, that's all ruined, might as well start paying attention to someone who will notice me. But then everything changed. And as much as I want to stay in this story, I want to get on that plane today and find out the next chapter of that story. It's like I want to read two books at exactly the same time."

Scott reached over and touched her shoulder. She finally broke her stare at the automatic doors and looked at him. "This story doesn't end because you get on that plane. This story didn't end because I disappeared. This story doesn't end because you slept with Ronan. This story doesn't end."

"All stories end," Miranda said.

"You can't tell me that you really believe that."

"Maybe I do."

Scott settled back into his seat. "Does this mean you don't think this is real? You don't think that we are real?"

Miranda didn't want to answer that. She never wanted to believe in anything as much as she wanted to believe in this. But it all seemed too good to be true. "Scott, look at me," she said. "Let's be honest about this. Where will we live? What about Lynn and what's best for her? We have to do this right. And that means there's a lot we need to talk about first. Even this morning, what if Lynn had found us naked? Or worse, last night after we went to bed? What would we do then?"

"We would have, I don't know, explained something. People do this all the time."

"But they don't do it right. And none of this changes how I feel about you. About this." She gestured to the space between them. "I've always wanted this to be real. Can that be enough for now?"

"I guess it will have to be. Can you promise me that you know I'm going to be here when you come back?"

"You better be. How else will I get home from the airport?"

"Oh, I see how it is. Kiss me, funny lady."

One kiss turned into two and then three and then four. Finally a stretch limo pulled alongside them. Miranda looked up and saw that the driver was staring at them.

"I think we have company," she said.

Scott turned his head and waved at the guy, and then kissed her again. "So you really want to do this?"

"I do," Miranda said. "As much as I want to stay here, I want to see what this whole famous author deal looks like, too. I'll email you the itinerary and text you all the time. And you'll call me. A lot. Like we're teenagers."

"Hey, that's something we didn't do as teenagers. We didn't talk to each other on the phone."

"I would have died of embarrassment calling you."

"You're over that now, right?" He tucked a strand of her hair behind her ear.

"Yeah, pretty over that."

"So," he said.

"So," she said. "I'm gonna do this." She put her hand on the handle but didn't move to open it.

They sat like that for a while until a Port Authority cop pounded on the trunk. "Keep the lane moving," he hollered. "No parking."

She leaned over and kissed him one last time and slipped out of the car. He jumped out and got her bag from the trunk. "I'm just going to turn and walk away," she said. "Otherwise I won't be able to go. I'll text you once I get through security."

"Okay," he said. "I love you."

"I love you," she called over her shoulder. The first tear fell like a raindrop, staining her blouse. With her free hand, she wiped them away and kept walking.

CHAPTER

27

I₁N THE CAB FROM THE AIRPORT to the hotel, Miranda composed an entry to Lynn. On the plane to Baltimore she devoured the Hitchhiker's Guide in an attempt to discern Ford Prefect's style. Writing to Lynn felt a bit like submitting a poem to the New Yorker or Harpers, like she had her whole career riding on its acceptance. "A note on American Planes," she started. "They are crowded and loud, but the honey mustard pretzel bites are not to be missed. Within the airport, a mystery develops. Did your baggage arrive? Will it spin out on the baggage carousel, the big sister of the carnival's wheel of fortune."

After she checked in, her phone binged with Lynn's reply. "Do you like carnivals? What about the shore? Daddy says he is a pro at balloon popping. Says he used to win. All the time."

Miranda remembered walking the boardwalk with Scott and begging Linden and Stanton to part with a few more dollars to just play one more game. No matter how hard she tried, he always popped more balloons, knocked down more milk bottles, or scored higher in skee ball. She quickly typed to Lynn all about this.

"But he always shares. So don't be upset when he wins."

The first stop in Baltimore, an independent bookstore, featured a tall stack of Blocked Poet books alongside a collection of board games and thick heavy books for toddlers about farm animals.

The bookseller shrugged her shoulder at the odd arrangement. "There are three things that sell well right now—things derived from the Internet, board games, and books for babies."

Miranda smiled politely and sipped at the slightly bitter latte the woman had given her. "I guess it makes sense."

"Does anything make sense?" the bookseller asked before walking away to tend to a customer at the counter.

Her first event wasn't a reading in a traditional sense. It was more of a live writing session, according to the emails sent by Kristen. Each stop would provide a Scrabble board. Miranda would talk about her process and any rules or order she used, and then she'd create a few samples. Kristen had even created some samples for her for each place. Baltimore had: Charm, City, Orioles, Crabs. Miranda envied the local color touch and sent Kristen a note of praise. It was up to Miranda to then photograph and post the specific creations, using the "appropriate filter" and "social media application" as per Ambrose. The crowd would be invited to throw out topics for Miranda to create from which she would then photograph and send out accordingly. Unlike most readings, tickets had been sold for many of the events, and Kristen collected some requests ahead of time. Each city on the stop had a cloud document listing the place and the possible subjects she might encounter. So far the one she couldn't wrap her mind around was Sheep Dogs. Apparently neither could Kristen; this entry was followed by a question mark.

Miranda had arrived at this first event an hour too early. She texted Scott about the board games, toddler books, and lattes. He and Lynn were watching her nature video. He photographed a baby polar baby and its mom from the screen and sent it to her.

"They reel you in with the baby animals," he wrote. "Then they switch to the killing. I should never have let her watch this."

When her phone rang, Miranda stepped out onto the sidewalk in front of the store.

"Hello, Miranda," sang an overly chipper voice. "Kristen here. Just checking to see how things are going. You're there, right? Everything fine?"

Kristen said so much that Miranda wasn't sure when or if she was supposed to reply. Instead, she found herself nodding into the phone. When Kristen finally took a breath, all Miranda could manage was, "Hi."

"Hi," Kristen said. "So, tonight you are at the Nuclear Books. Tomorrow you do a teen event at the Boys and Girls Club—that is a fundraiser for the local literary project. Then you are on to Richmond. Same deal there. Bookstore then fundraiser. Oh, wait, there's also the book festival there. Ambrose has documents for your CPA about the tax deductions on your fundraising participation. This should offset some of the revenue from the books. But as I said in the email, we need your CPA to sign off. And soon. I need to start cutting the checks on your payments."

"CPA?" Miranda said.

"An accountant. You have one, don't you?"

"I don't," Miranda confessed.

"Oh, silly, you should have said so. I will hire one. Do you need anything else?"

"Anything else?"

"Yes, dinner reservations. Information about museums. Show tickets. Whatever you need, you reach out to me, and I make it happen. Ambrose calls me the magician."

"The magician?"

"Yuppers. I am at your service. Anything you need.

Anything. The weirder the better, in fact. Gives me something to blog about. Kristendoes.com."

"You have a blog?"

"Yes, that's why Ambrose hired me. It's like double marketing for the firm."

"The firm?"

"Oh, geesh, Miranda, you are really not informed. You need to read all the emails I sent."

"I will." Miranda said, counting how many steps it took to get from one side of the bookstore's storefront to the other.

"Do you promise? Pinky swear promise that you'll read the emails and let me know if you need anything."

"Pinky swear." Miranda couldn't help but smile saying it. It sounded like something Lynn would say.

"Then we are good to go. Signing off," Kristen said, disconnecting the line.

The bookseller poked her head outside the door. "There you are. We're ready for you."

Miranda hadn't noticed the stream of people enter the store while she was on the phone. All the folding chairs were full, and a few people milled around behind the book row. They all had copies of her book in their hands. The stack next to the latest role-playing game about dragons now only stood two books high. She was almost selling out.

And at the end of the event after such winning poem themes as spring training, Ford trucks, and many requests about Ocean City and vacations, the crowd applauded her loudly and two people scooped up the last two books. The bookseller shook Miranda's hand and invited her back for her next book.

The whirlwind feeling of it all wore off on the cab ride back to her hotel. It was a mid-level chain, nice enough to have a marble floor in the lobby with a fish tank along one wall, but not nice enough to have room service. As she sat alone in her room contemplating a dinner of macadamia nuts and Milano cookies from the mini bar, the loneliness of this whole adventure really struck her. There were forty-one more days to go.

CHAPTER

28

EACH DAY SHE SAID to herself that she would get up early and go see some of the sights to create her own list of local color words, but each night she stayed up for hours talking to Scott on the phone.

"I wonder what our life is going to be like," Miranda whispered into the phone, her voice hoarse from talking for the last two hours already, recounting the people she met at the bookstore event like the lady with pink hair who wanted a board done with all the names of her cats and the man who just crept around the back of the event taking her picture with his cell phone.

"What do you mean?" Scott asked. "It's going to be awesome." He too whispered, not wanting to wake up Lynn, who had already interrupted the call twice to tell Miranda about the new bunny in her classroom and why long division is difficult.

"No, like specifics. Like imagine it's Sunday morning. What do we do? Do we read the paper? Do we eat waffles?"

"Well, waffles take too long. So it's pancake city. I've got a griddle that takes up two burners on the stove."

"I love that you cook," Miranda said.

"I love that you eat. Especially pancakes. I probably shouldn't tell you this, but they are the best thing I make."

"Surely you can make other things."

"Mac and cheese. From a box. I microwave a good, organic chicken nugget. And I can roast a ham."

"A ham?"

"Yup. You just put it in the oven. No fuss, no muss."

"What do you eat with the ham?"

"Mac and cheese."

"From a box?"

"Yup. I'm a regular old Julia Child here. We probably don't read the paper on Sunday morning. Let's just say that you only get about twenty minutes of sitting still when Lynn's in the room. Especially on a weekend. School wears a kid out, but by Sunday, they are recharged and ready to go."

"Oh," Miranda said.

"Oh, you didn't anticipate that?" Scott asked.

"Not that, I'm recalculating. We will eat pancakes and then go to the zoo to walk them off."

"Run them off, you mean, but okay. The zoo, I like that. I was afraid you were going to say church."

"Well, maybe church, we'll see about that. Maybe your basketball games count for that. But let's start with the zoo. What animal would you be?"

Scott didn't hesitate. "Otter," he said.

"Otter? Tell me why. I have to hear this."

"They swim and have fun; have you ever seen a moping otter at the zoo? Never. They swim. They play with balls in the water. And people love them. Think they're cute."

"I think you are cute."

"See, I'm already half way there," he said.

"I love you, too. That's it. You must be an otter," she said.

"Then it's a done deal. I will be the otter. And you my dear, you are a giraffe."

"A giraffe? How did you get to that otter man? Why can't I be an otter, too?"

"You are more majestic than an otter. You rise above, beautiful. You see things."

"I see things?"

"Yup, that's why you are a poet. You see the things other people miss."

"I miss you," Miranda said.

"Oh, baby, I miss you, too. I've been missing you for far too long in this life. I can't wait for that Sunday to happen. It's going to be a three-Red Bull day tomorrow"

He yawned.

She yawned.

The clock read three fifteen.

Most nights, they fell asleep with phones on until their batteries died.

In the morning, still thousands of miles apart, she sent him articles about the dangers of energy drinks. In response, he sent her pictures of his students in various states of chaos with baking soda and vinegar volcanoes and red clay models of the founding fathers.

"Touché," she replied back. To be cheeky, she had Kristen ship a case of Red Bull to the apartment. He took a picture of that and posted it on Facebook announcing to the world that romance was no longer dead.

She replied with a word sculpture on the Blocked Poet feed. Bull, Love, Red, Devoted, Yours.

Ambrose replied to that. "Keep doing this. Corporate loves the love. Selling rights."

Kristen sent a new contract the next day, which offered better payouts than a B-list celebrity's. Every post with the corporate sponsor's name earned a flat rate of ten thousand dollars. Click-through rates applied to each liked or shared post. If someone used the embedded coupon code, the click-through rate when up by twenty-nine percent. With her followers expanding every day, even a poet could do the math and see the value enough to sign.

Miranda spoke at another store, school, community center, hotel banquet room. Then she got on a plane and did it again and again and again.

The car Kristen arranged dropped her off in front of a house that made her parents' house look like a child's toy. The driveway wound so far back that Miranda had mistaken it at first for just another road. The house, three stories tall, featured grand columns out front like Tara and outdoor double staircases winding up either side to the front door on the second floor. Festive greens dotted with red berries flanked the doorway with a pineapple at its pinnacle. Miranda knew it as the colonial symbol for welcome and that it stood proudly on the university's main gate. This was obviously the right place.

She took the stairs to the right and examined the door unsuccessfully for a bell. Instead, she lifted the heavy brass ring that hung from a lion's mouth on the center of the door. As she lifted the ring, a chime rang out Pachelbel's Canon in the interior of the home. Footsteps quickly followed, and Miranda found herself enveloped in a hug from a petite brunette in a red business suit.

"Hello," said the woman. "Did your driver find the place okay? Well, silly me, obviously, or you wouldn't standing there. I'm Ellie," she said. "Class of '88."

"Hello," Miranda said.

"Well do come in—everyone's waiting for you."

Miranda was led down the center hallway past the grandest staircase ever. They continued past a series of doors all shut until they reached a set of double doors at the end of the hallway. Ellie opened both at the same time, and the two women stepped into a glorious glass-walled room filled with game tables and beautiful potted plants. Foursomes of women played Scrabble. Wait-staff circulated the room with pots of coffee and trays of cookies shaped like Scrabble tiles.

"The conservatory I call it," Ellie said, making a sweeping gesture with one hand, "but the only thing I conserve here is my sanity. Without these gatherings, I think I would just die of boredom. When I heard you were at the university, I called up there to have them send you down right quick. You are just the type of thing I like to have here."

"You do this often?" Miranda asked.

"Oh, yes," Ellie went on. "I have all sorts come and visit and share their talents. Musicians, scholars. Why once I even had that man from the television, the one who yells at people who own restaurants poorly? I had him come down and do a cooking demonstration."

"Here?" Miranda asked.

"Indeed, my husband, class of '86, had a whole television kitchen brought in. We filmed it and gave out the DVDs to our friends for the holidays that year."

"So what do you want me to do exactly?" Miranda said.

"Oh, you know, your usual. I was told you will make up poems on the spot. They're going to collect the pictures from your website and make a special book for my friends. But first, please eat something. The buffet is still set."

After her meager evening meals of food gleaned from hotel mini-bars and snack stations, Miranda did not need to be asked twice.

"Lisa," she said to one of the passing servers, "Please show the Blocked Poet to the buffet—see she gets what she needs, then seat her at the head table."

On the other side of the room, on a raised platform was a table for one with several Scrabble boards waiting for her. Miranda indulged on a variety of things from California rolls to sliders with bacon and bleu cheese. Despite Ellie's small size, she appeared to understand food. Miranda mentally took notes to share with Avery. The shot glasses of tomato soup with little rounds of grilled cheese on top were simply too whimsical not to share. She considered taking out her phone and snapping a picture, but she wasn't sure of the etiquette. After all, she was the help.

After the ladies finished up their Scrabble games, Ellie lauded the redhead who earned the highest score of anyone in the room, giving her a floral quilted purse filled with lotions and soaps. "Just a little something," Ellie said. "Now for our main event. The Blocked Poet."

Miranda ran through her samples, and then opened the floor to requests. Quite a few equestrian themes, one unexpected about NASCAR, one about Paris that she could barely contain her composure for, and many, many on friendship and debutantes and cotillion—the last two breaking her seven-letters rule.

"It's okay," a blonde in Barbara Bush's pearls and pale pink twin set told her. "It means more if it's about what we want."

Ellie herself asked for one about orchids. The group luckily pitched in on that one calling out different types and colors until finally Miranda was able to fill the board.

After all the sculptures were complete, another buffet table was unveiled with tiny cups of cappuccino topped with delicate sugar cookies and pies the size of half dollars on lollypop sticks. Miranda mingled through the guests, answering their questions about two-letter Scrabble words and their favorite poets.

At the s'more station, Miranda found herself next to a six-foot-tall woman who announced herself as Ellie's sister.

"Sister?" Miranda asked, looking the tall woman up and down.

"In law," the lady said. "Class of '85."

"Oh, how nice, you all went to the same school."

"Yes, nice. For those of us who earned our place and didn't flounce in on legacy."

"Oh," Miranda said. "There's something to be said about tradition."

"Tradition. Speaking of that, I really wanted to ask you about that student of yours."

"Which student?"

She leaned in to speak to Miranda and wound up hovering over her. "Aren't you coy? You know. The one that landed you here. Rumor has it you bedded a student for an entire year." The woman accepted her s'more from the attendant. She popped the whole thing into her mouth and then licked the marshmallow off one finger at a time. "Was it worth it?" she asked.

"I don't know what you're talking about," Miranda said.

"Oh, you know, based on the email the student sent to Jonas, it sounds like you knew every inch of his body. What was it you said to him, "Put out or get out? Isn't that quite the poem?" She leaned back and called out over her shoulder to the table of the women behind them who were pretending not to eavesdrop. "That's right, girls. That's what she said. "Put out or get out. To a student."

"He wasn't a student," Miranda said.

"So it is true," the woman said springing back. "I knew Ellie wouldn't have been able to pull this off otherwise." She reached over and took the s'more the attendant was handing Miranda and floated off, waving the treat in the air. "Ellie," she called out. "We simply must talk about what I just learned from your little poet."

Miranda's cheeks burned with embarrassment. The car wouldn't be back for another half an hour.

Instead she skulked about the edges of the conservatory, hiding among the various orchids and ferns, talking to the few guests who hadn't yet heard the rumors burning through the room like a wild fire. The ones who had heard just winked at her or raised their cups of coffee in a mock salute. After her sister-in-law pulled her aside, Ellie left the conservatory and didn't reappear. One of the waitresses fetched Miranda when the car finally arrived.

She dialed Scott the minute she reached her room, her ability to hold back her tears dissolving the minute he answered.

"Randa, slow down," he said. "Slow down. What is it?"

She told him everything. The house. The food. The tall sister-in-law. The stolen s'more. The utter crushing embarrassment of the whole thing.

"The rotten shit," he said. "How could he share that? That violates several different employment and student privacy statutes. We could sue."

"I don't want to sue," Miranda said, her voice clogged with tears. "I just wanted to keep my job."

"I told you this was blackmail. Now it's worse than that. It's blackmail and punishment. What the hell? You don't even have to keep on doing this."

The more he went on the more Miranda felt herself unable to focus. She didn't want him to fix it. She just wanted him to listen. Instead of feeling better, she felt worse—first embarrassed and now lectured.

"Scott, please," she finally said. "Listen, I need to take a shower. I have some early events tomorrow."

"Tomorrow," he said. "How can you even think of continuing?"

"I gave my word; people are expecting me."

"Well, I'm expecting you, too," he said. "I love you."

"Scott, why are making this more difficult? I just wanted you to listen to me."

"I am listening to you."

"Then why don't you understand that I want to be on this book tour, that I want to be doing this, that I want to keep my job, and that I never wanted to be just a mother."

"Never wanted to be a mother?"

"Not that—just a stay-at-home mother. I want to keep my job."

"But you didn't say that—you said mother. What are playing at? You know what Lynn means to me. You knew this was a package deal."

"Of course I do. You're not listening. You misunderstood."

"Maybe I didn't, Miranda. Maybe you said exactly what you meant to say. And I'm done listening to it." He hung up.

She tried calling back, but each time it went to voicemail.

CHAPTER

29

I N THE MORNING, she only found Kristen's latest update to the schedule, nothing from Scott. No email, no text, no call. She had to be to the airport in an hour; the tour began to make its way west. Next stop, Phoenix.

On the way to hotel, she dialed Danielle. "Tell me I'm not crazy," she said before Danielle could even say hello.

"Wait, first tell me I'm not fat."

"You're not fat."

"I'm sorry then, you are crazy; I am so fat I can't fit into my yoga pants. My stretch yoga pants."

"Come on, don't be hard on yourself, Dani."

"They split up the butt. While I was working. The only thing that saved me was that my shirt covered my ass."

Miranda tried not to laugh. "I knew you were having a girl," she said. "Girls make your butt bigger."

"Oh, so the torture of parenting a girl starts early. All this, and then she turns sixteen and only comes out of the bathroom to yell at me."

"You were sixteen once; it isn't that bad."

"Exactly, I was sixteen. I remember. So tell me why are you crazy?"

"It's Scott."

"Oh, I know you are crazy about him. What are you two lovebirds up to?" Danielle asked.

"It's not like that. That's the problem. We keep fighting."

"Fighting?"

"Well, maybe not fighting; we're just not on the same page. He really wanted to me to quit my job and just move to New Jersey."

"That's it—you should throw him to the curb. New Jersey! Who wants to move to New Jersey?"

"Dani, this isn't funny. He thought I would be a stay-at-home mom. He wanted me to back out of the book tour. Still does."

"Ugh, I wouldn't have thought it would be like that. You guys have known each other for so long. Why does he want you to back out?"

Miranda told her about the party and the tall sister-in-law.

"That was cold," Danielle said. "She took your s'more. But I do see Scott's point. Why subject yourself to that? What does it get you?"

"It gets me my job back."

"Okay, it's a job, though, and last I checked you were pretty into Scott, engaged and all, right? Isn't that more important?"

"I wish it were that easy. I've got bills and student loans, and I've never—"

"Miranda, you are talking to someone who followed her boyfriend to Turkey. Do you know how long it took me to get out of default on my student loans? I'll have bills until I die, but I knew I wasn't ever going to have another Omar."

"It's just I never thought I could do this."

"Do what?"

"The whole thing—be a wife, a mother. Count on someone else to care about my student loan payment. Count on someone else to care about anything I did or didn't do. After my mom died, my father's way of caring about me was to go behind my back and arrange things or make proclamations about what would or would not happen on his dime. It never felt like it was about me—just some generic principles on raising economically productive children that he picked up somewhere."

"But Scott isn't your father."

"But he's Lynn's father."

"Yes, and so? You like her, don't you?"

"More than like her."

"Then what are you so afraid of?"

Miranda stared out the window. Rows of identical brown houses with terracotta roofs lined the interstate. "Losing it all," Miranda finally said.

"Isn't that what you are making sure happens? Work it out with him, Miranda. I've known you since we were fourteen. I know you love him. And her."

"Dani," Miranda said, "How does your head feel?"

"What? What are you talking about?"

"It sounds like pregnancy has made you go soft. Are you feeling sentimental?"

"Very funny, Miranda."

"Would it help if I told you that you were right, Dani? I do love him. I do want to work it out. I'm not sure how, but I want to."

"Good, then go figure it out. I gotta go. I'm suddenly very hungry. I think I need Omar to bring home some baklava."

"Cravings, eh?"

"If I'm going to get fat, I might as well enjoy myself."

Miranda would have thought that each part of the country would have offered some distinction, something to let her know that she had just travelled several hundred miles and a time zone. But the hotels all looked alike. Sometimes exactly alike, as if they had been renovated at the same time. She would leave her hotel room looking down at a text message or email, look up and be on the completely wrong end of the hallway.

The front desk had a package from Kristen. Inside, Miranda found four specially made Scrabble tiles with two exclamation points and two question marks. For the local color pieces, her note read.

Luckily, Phoenix had the Suns basketball team—it should be easy enough to work that in. And the bird Phoenix. And really hot weather. Cacti.

The next day a contract arrived from the NBA. It doubled all the Red Bull terms and extended to every team in the league. An email from Kristen identified a new procedure for making word sculptures for the NBA—they'll hire an internal team to make sure every match-up featured at least two boards to place on Twitter, Instagram, and the Blocked Poet Facebook, which the interns would maintain. Miranda would maintain creative control and approve all boards first, if she agreed. Which she did, sending in this new contract immediately.

Ambrose followed up with a simple text: "Keep doing this."

"Sure," she said to herself, plunking down on another identical bedspread. "At what cost?" She looked down at her phone. Still no return call. The twenty texts she sent remained unanswered.

CHAPTER

30

OREGON WAS KNOWN for its rain, but when she emerged from the airport in Portland, the sky was such a spectacular blue that she almost thought she had taken the wrong flight. But the green Prius taxicab that ferried her to the hotel downtown clearly echoed the eco-friendly reputation of the Pacific Northwest. And by the time she emerged from her hotel to head to the event, a light misting drizzle frizzed her wavy hair into an untamable tangle. At least the scenery matched her mood.

At the last stop, in Seattle, Scott had broken his silence only to ask for "some time to think about things."

"Okay," she replied. "I love you. And Lynn."

"I hope so," he answered.

She stood outside Powell's, staring at her reflection in the door trying to pat down her hair to some respectable form when a hollow visage appeared next to her own in the glass. "Oh," she exclaimed, bouncing back and knocking into the lady's walker. Luckily, the nurse aide, a woman in navy blue scrubs with a print of tiny rainbow hearts, steadied both the lady and Miranda. "Sorry," Miranda said.

"Thank you."

The lady with the walker stood rigidly upright. A bandana held back thin wisps of blonde hair. Her skin was pale, white like paper, with the blue of her veins clearly visible on both of her arms. Her eyes were sunken with deep purple circles ringing them. Despite her obvious frailty and short stature, the woman was downright regal. A queen.

"Let me get the door," Miranda said.

"You're too kind," the lady said. She moved slowly forward with the aide trailing in her wake.

The event went well. Plenty of people attended. The local color word sculptures featuring espresso and hippies elicited enough laughter that Miranda blushed and looked at the floor. She noticed the Queen standing in the back, a cup of coffee in her hand. The Queen raised her cup while everyone else applauded at the end. This event also featured a book signing. It seemed the whole room stayed to get their copy signed, from a few older hippy ladies wearing flowing yoga pants with their gray braids hanging squarely down their backs, to a new mom with a baby in a sling, to a pack of hipsters with their skinny jeans and ironic Fedoras. The Queen, though, didn't get in line. Just as well, Miranda thought. The line was long, but she couldn't help personalizing each book. Sometimes, if the person had a request during the event, she would draw in their word sculpture on the back page. The mother with the baby loved that; the book was a gift for her twin sister, who also had a baby the same age at home. "Sisters, mothers, friends, tired," it read.

She packed up her bag, helped the clerk box up the Scrabble boards to be sent on to the next location, and said her goodbyes. When she reached the front door, the aide blocked her way.

"She wants to speak to you," the aide said.

"Oh," Miranda said. "Sure."

The Queen was arranged on one of the overstuffed

couches that rested in niches around the store. She lay with her legs stretched out across the couch. With a slight wave of her hand, she motioned for Miranda to take a seat on the footstool next to her.

"Congratulations," the Queen said.

"Thanks. It's a fluke really. I never thought I would have a book, or at least not a book like this."

"No," the Queen said, "not that. This." She pointed her bony index finger at Miranda's engagement ring.

Miranda felt her cheeks blush again; she still wasn't quite used to the attention the ring attracted; when Stanton had purchased it, his motto was bigger is better. In the florescent lights of the store, the ring exploded with sparkling light. Despite everything, she didn't want to take it off. She still wanted to marry Scott. "Oh, this, yes, just got engaged. It was my mother's," she added quickly. "I'm afraid it is quite obvious. Especially in light like this."

"No, love, that's not it. I know you. Well, not personally, but I know you all the same. You're marrying Scott Cramer. The Scott Cramer."

"What? Do you know Scott?"

The Queen let her head drop back as an enormous cackle escaped her. She laughed until it turned to a cough wracking her body with tremors. The aide quickly handed her some water and the tube to a portable oxygen tank she had strung over her shoulder. Miranda hadn't noticed the tank before.

"So, you don't know who I am?" the Queen asked when she finally regained her composure. "No idea. You aren't here for some reason."

"No, Ambrose, the publisher set this up."

"Oh, Ambrose, I know him, too. Was always quite the big shot. Bit of a nerd, but that seems to have worked out for him. Unlike myself and my current state of being. Maybe I should have hit the books more instead of other things."

"I don't understand," Miranda said. And then it hit her. The color of her hair, the shape of her eyes, the slight dimple on her chin. Lynn. "Wait," she said, "you're Lynn's mom."

"I am. Or rather I was. I guess that's your job now."

"It's not like that. Being a stepmother is different."

"Wait a minute," The queen said. "You don't want to be Lynn's mother?"

"No, it's not that at all. I love her. It's just, you are her mom."

"Not really, Love. I check in from time to time, but Scott does a pretty good job keeping me away from her. Can't say as I blame him, things being what they are, but well, I'm sure you have lots of questions."

"I do have lots of questions."

"Well, I have lots of answers. Just not now. I could be free tomorrow."

"I can meet you tomorrow," Miranda said.

"Of course you will," the Queen answered.

She texted Avery to see if she had looked into Cassadee. "Sure," Avery replied. "I was waiting until you got back. Emailing now."

The email contained multiple court documents. The final page, a summary sheet, listed offenses Miranda knew best from watching crime dramas on television. Intent to distribute. Accessory after the fact. Resisting arrest. Public intoxication. Prostitution. Attempted assault and battery. The sheet showed lots of addresses and a few aliases. On one drug charge from around the time Lynn was born, Scott Cramer appeared as a known associate. She read through Cassadee's statements to a variety of judges and parole officers. In each, she always clung to her innocence. "I didn't do nothing," was the most common phrase. Nothing in those pages could ever help Lynn understand or know her mother. Somehow Miranda had expected something different, like a dossier from a spy movie or an FBI profiler report—something that said who Cassadee was as a person and not just what law enforcement charged her with doing.

The last page detailed her release on parole to hospice care.

Miranda didn't feel right letting this woman just waste away without having something to pass on to Lynn. One day Lynn would ask, and Miranda would want to have answers. Her father, Avery, Bunny, and Linden didn't just wipe away the memory of her mother; they celebrated her birthday, raised toasts in her honor, and talked about her all the time. Scott picked Lynn's middle name for her. No one ever let her be forgotten. But despite all their best efforts, being without her mother felt like walking around with a shard of glass up against her ribs. If she hugged something too tightly or moved with too much excitement, the sharp edge pierced and stabbed her. It made her hang back, observe, wait. She didn't rush in or get too happy. If Miranda could feel that way with twelve years of her mother's love and attention, what could Lynn feel with none? Miranda imagined double the loss when Lynn finally found out that Scott wasn't really her father and was just some guy Cassadee picked for the job. What could it feel like to lose both your parents without ever even knowing them? Not for the first time, Miranda wished she could climb into the window seat next to her mother's chair and ask her. She would beg her to tell all about how exactly you prepare a child for loss.

As she climbed into hotel bed number thirty-something, Miranda listed the things she wanted to ask. The things no rap sheets contained. Where did you grow up? What did your parents do? What is your favorite color or album? What was her father like? What was his name? Why did you give her up? The last one was probably the biggest question of all. Miranda couldn't imagine any answer that would justify why someone would walk out on that child. She let the questions flood her mind until sleep finally took over.

She made it through the event the next day without spotting the Queen. Her absence came with relief; if Scott knew she even talked to Cassadee, he would probably never forgive her.

Miranda helped the staff with clean-up and hung back chatting with them about ideas for her next book. A petite young woman, maybe all of eighteen in a cardigan with pearl buttons and cat's eye glasses proposed erotic word sculptures. After the girl said it, she covered her mouth with her hand, and her cheeks blazed red. One of the hipster boys from the coffee bar made it worse by saying, "Jill, will you come over and read it to me?"

Miranda couldn't believe it possible, but the girl flared an even deeper shade of red. But something about the way the hipster boy looked at her, and she at him, told Miranda that they would write those poems themselves soon enough. A pang of longing for Scott filled her. She wanted to be looked at like that. Then Miranda felt a light touch at her elbow. She wheeled around and was startled to find Cassadee's aide.

"Ma'am," she said. "Dee is waiting in the car. She really shouldn't have come out today. It's not a good day for her."

"Not a good day?" Miranda asked.

"I shouldn't say nothing," the aide continued. "But she's really sick and won't listen to reason none. The girl could sell a lady in white gloves ketchup popsicles. Just because she convinced me to take her here doesn't mean I have to go all along with it. You should know."

"Thank you. I'm Miranda by the way."

"Oh, I know who you are. The minute that engagement photo popped up on Facebook, it's all she could do to not talk about you. You be careful miss. The wounded are more dangerous."

Miranda nodded as if she understood, only she didn't.

Cassadee the Queen waited outside for them in the driver's seat of an old Volkswagen Golf. The aide turned at the car and disappeared up the street with a little wave of her hand.

"Get in," Cassadee said through the open passenger-side window.

"You're driving?" Miranda asked, looking at the oxygen tank, moving it over to make room to sit. She kept her door open, not wanting to go anywhere with Cassadee. Not yet any way. Something about the whole thing didn't make sense. Cassadee had lost some of her composure from the day before; she moved her head from side to side like she couldn't keep her eyes focused on any one thing.

"Nah, but I could. I kept my license. Never got popped while driving. Only walking, and you don't need a license for that. I just like to sit up here. I like to imagine getting on the highway and cruising all the way down to Baja. I'd like to pull up next to some surfer beach and lay out in the sun smoking a bowl." Cassadee leaned her head back and took in a few deep breaths that shook her whole body. She stayed like that for a few minutes, obviously transported to the place in her imagination. "Ah, that's real nice," Cassadee finally said. "So you had questions?"

"Yes," Miranda said. "I was hoping to know more about you. I think Lynn should know you; Scott seems to think that you didn't want to see her. I just can't believe that's true."

"So he trusts you and everything, right? And vice versa?"

Cassadee's pupils were dilated, and she couldn't hold eye contact; her gaze kept darting to cars passing in the street and a couple walking by with a dog.

"I was just hoping to know more about your life, things from when you were little, like Lynn is now. I want to get to know you. I want Lynn to know you." Miranda said.

But it was like Cassadee hadn't even heard her. "But the thing is, I need money. And I think it's your fault I'm not getting it," she said. "Because you see, he used to trust me. We were friends. If I called, he came. Well obviously, but I mean even after the child. He really kept up with me. I think he even forgave me for lying and saying the child isn't his. He's like that. Good. But something has happened.

Won't talk to me."

"Lying?" Miranda asked. "Lying that he is the father?"

"Don't you contradict me. I lied that he wasn't! I said what I said. To keep him on his toes and keep him sending the money. I saw how he looked at the child. If he thought for a minute he could just have her without me, poof, there goes my chances. The hospital helped me right good without even knowing it. Telling him the child was early. Pennies from heaven that was." Cassadee made a fist and started tapping it against the steering wheel. "But, yes, it's your fault. I get no money, and you stole the child. You steal her, and you don't pay; that's not right. I need that money. They don't give me all I need. There's things I need, you see. Things." She exhaled the last word so sharply that her spittle splattered all over the windshield. "Without my things, my brain doesn't work right. I shake more. They don't understand the power of alternative medicines. They are so close-minded. It's not like it's going to kill me now. I'm already dead."

"But she was premature, she couldn't have been his. The dates don't line up. He said so."

"That baby was not premature. I remember every damn month of that shit. I had morning sickness that July. August, too. So sick I couldn't even party. Nothing would stay down. Then in September I got fat. Could barely score looking like that. Forced me to fuck some junkie to get some and got the HIV, too. That child ruined everything for me before she even took her first breath."

"He's her father. Like really her father?"

"The computer said you were some kind of professor, but you sure are acting stupid. I just said he was. I wasn't some kinda slut just running around sleeping with every-body. I like me a good time. But my good time is chasing the dragon. I just hooked up with him because he was where the party was. Mr. Dollar Bills."

Miranda sat there, unable to speak. All these years, Scott lived in fear of Cassadee testing Lynn's paternity for no reason.

"Don't just sit there like that. You should feel more responsible, don't you think? If not for you, maybe he would have taken more of an interest? Even back then we all knew he had a thing for a girl back home." Cassadee's nostrils flared on either side of the oxygen tube. She pounded the steering wheel to emphasize each word.

Miranda knew Cassadee didn't have the strength to physically harm her, but she also didn't need to listen anymore.

"Oh, you'd leave me like this. You're just like him. That's how they must make you all back East. You think money keeps you clean, keeps you safe. Why don't you share some of that with me? Why don't you tell your precious Scott that the mother of his child has needs, too? That he can't just push past and forget the little people behind him. I've got to have my medicine. Not that shit the doctors give but my own. You hear me. My own."

Miranda stood quickly, dizzy from the motion and the sunlight. The aide appeared from the shadow of the bookstore. "Ma'am," she said, rushing forward. "You go on and get out of here, ma'am. Dee ain't in her right mind any more. I can't settle her down if you are here."

Miranda nodded at the woman before striding headlong down the street. She didn't look back, wouldn't look back; she didn't want that angry darkness to follow her any more. She knew then everything Scott had said about Lynn being better off was right. She dialed Scott's number, praying he would answer.

"Cassadee lied," she said instead of hello.

"What are you even talking about?"

"Cassadee, Scott. I just saw her."

"Miranda, I don't understand what you're saying. I asked you for a few days to think about things, and you go find Cassadee. What were you thinking? I don't even want to know."

"Scott, please, I'm sorry."

"Sorry. Nice. How sorry can you be? Why would you sneak off behind my back like that? Yeah, we're having a problem right now, but that's low. What were you even thinking?

"I didn't find her. She found me. I need you to listen to me for a second."

"I need to listen, so that you can just go and do whatever you want without thinking of how it impacts me? Us. If you even want there to be an us. I don't get you, Miranda. Didn't you listen to me—she could take Lynn away from me!"

"That's just it. She can't. She says you are the father. She lied about the other guy to keep you paying."

"What do you mean?"

"I didn't even ask about that. She just confessed it. She said she lied about it so you would pay her money. She says she was pregnant in July."

"But she's a liar, Miranda."

"Scott, she was the worst person I have ever met in my whole life, but I swear to God, I don't think she lied to me about this. She was boasting about how she used it to make you pay up. She got mad at me when I challenged her. And frankly, she is so sick that I don't think she would live long enough to make it through a court case."

"She's that sick."

"She's in hospice, Scott. Oxygen tank. Nursing care."

"Hospice? As in dying?"

"Yes. I don't think we have to worry about her anymore."

"You said, we."

"I'm sorry. You. You don't have to worry about her. She said Lynn's yours. I believed her, Scott." Words tumbled out of her mouth like an avalanche. Nothing could stop them.

"Don't be sorry. Unless, you don't mean it. I want you to mean we. I thought no one would want to be my partner and help raise her. I never imagined there could be a we when it came to Lynn. When you said you didn't want to be a mother, that all came back for me. I thought all my fears were confirmed."

"But it has to be a we. I didn't just say yes to you. I said yes to both of you. To all of it. I just didn't think it meant giving up my job; I thought we could talk about it—make some kind of plan. I want it to be us together—the three of us. But I wanted to do it right."

"I want that," he said. "And you. And everything that comes with it. But I need us to be on the same page. Or figure out how to at least listen to each other better. We can't keep arguing like this. And we need to be upfront about things. I can't believe you talked to Cassadee."

"I just wanted what Avery had. My mother made an entire book for whoever my father married. I wanted to be able to tell Lynn where she came from, to show her that she was loved."

"But, Miranda, what if that's our job and not Cassadee's?

"But it's not like that. I don't want to replace her mother, Scott. Avery didn't replace my mom."

"That's because your mom loved you."

His words hit her. While she would have given anything to have her own mother back, the woman in the car wasn't Lynn's mother and wasn't capable of even thinking about anyone but herself or the drugs she wanted. Maybe she wouldn't have all the information Avery had to guide her as a stepmother, but she was going to have the same kind of love Avery always offered. And that would have to be enough.

31

C₃ HECKING IN," she said, as she approached the Platinum Member's desk at the hotel in Los Angeles.

"Name," the clerk, a blonde girl with features so perfect you would put her in the dictionary under model working a day job until she makes it big.

Miranda gave her name, slipping the credit card across the desk.

Perfect painted pink nails glided over the keyboard. She smiled, revealing straight teeth, which glinted in the pinpoint halogen lighting that was supposed to be illuminating the portrait of the hotel's founders. She processed the keys and slipped them into a powder blue envelop embossed with the word RELAX! as if the exclamation point could force you to unwind. Miranda turned to find the elevators; she knew exactly where to find them without directions at this point, when the model said, "Wait, we have something for you."

The model bent down low and then emerged with the largest vase of roses Miranda had ever seen. They blocked the girl's entire torso from view. The model heaved them up and over the tall desk. "There's a card," she announced as Miranda turned to find the elevator again.

"Thanks," Miranda said.

"But there's a card," the model repeated.

"I know," Miranda said, "It's right here." The creamy beige envelope stood out obviously against the deep red of the roses.

"Aren't you going to open it?" the co-ed asked.

Miranda dropped the handle of her suitcase and spun around. "You want me to open it here?"

"Well, we were just curious is all. Who sends roses like that?"

"Probably my fiancé," Miranda said. "We just got engaged. We had a bit of an argument. This might be his reply."

"Awww," she said. "So old fashioned!"

"I know, right," Miranda said. "Okay. I'll open it." She walked back across the lobby and set the vase back down on the counter. She opened the card. Took one look at it and put it back in the envelope. "You know," she said. "Why don't we leave the flowers out here so everyone can enjoy them?"

"You can't. They're yours. They'll make your room special."

"No, the rooms are too small. And air tight. I might get allergies."

"Are you allergic to flowers?"

"Nnnnn ... yes, I am. Can you keep them here?"

The model looked from Miranda to the flowers and back again. Then she shrugged.

"Great. Thank you." Miranda squinted to read the girl's name badge. "Thank you, Kaylee."

"Thank you. I just might pretend to my boyfriend when he comes that someone left these for me. A secret admirer maybe. He never does anything special like this. You are lucky to have your fiancé."

Only the card in her hand read, "Good Luck on Ellen,

Yours, Ronan."

"Yes, lucky," Miranda said, finally making her way to the elevator.

She sat on the bed of her airless hotel room, her stomach rolling. It wasn't like she thought Ronan would disappear off the face of the earth entirely; she just thought he would disappear off the face of her earth. Her mind vacillated from being upset about the flowers to being upset with herself for being upset. She didn't do anything wrong. She didn't owe Ronan anything. Not a phone call or an explanation. Their relationship wasn't meant to be anything of consequence no matter how many grand speeches he gave about wanting to leave his mark on America. He had a plane ticket before they even spoke outside of class. Yet some part of her felt guilty for how quickly she left off with him and took up with Scott. She knew what it looked like to Ronan. But she didn't want that hanging over her head anymore. He had done enough damage already.

She left a message for Scott. He couldn't call back for at least an hour when school let out. Instead of pacing around her hotel room, she pulled on the yoga clothes she optimistically bought in the Atlanta airport of all places, and soon found herself walking along a nondescript road where sidewalks led from office park to office park with the occasional strip mall featuring a nail salon or karate studio to break up the monotony.

Just past the second strip mall, her phone buzzed with an incoming call. Without looking at the screen, she answered, "Scott."

"Sorry, dear. Not him am I," Ronan said. "I see I failed miserably and still fail anew."

"Ronan," she said.

"One in the flesh. And how are you my fine lass? Or should I say Scott's fine piece of ass?" He drew out the s on each word in a long slur.

She gasped, unable to reply.

"The email says you got the bouquet. Don't you have any thanks for dear old Ronan? Or are you too far beyond that? A book. A new man. Television shows."

"Why are you calling? Haven't you done enough? Emails to the university? Almost getting me fired? Why would you do that?"

"Why?" he said. Then he repeated, it again. "Why, why, why, why?" Until he dissolved into a guffaw, then a choking cough.

Part of her wished for a brief second that he was really choking, but then he didn't stop coughing. "Are you okay?" she asked.

"Ay, a question even better than the last. Why would I be all right? I am stuck in this God forsaken village and the woman I thought could save me from all this tossed me over like yesterday's rubbish."

"Save you from what?"

"From being sent away. From this place. You were supposed to love me, Miranda. You were supposed to beg me to stay. Instead, you walked away. No wait, you flew away. With him."

"I don't understand what you are saying, Ronan."

"I speak plain enough. Think on it. You could have prevented this."

"But you already had your ticket. You were leaving."

"Tickets cost money. Exile costs time. Wasted, wasted time."

"Exile. What are you talking about, Ronan? I really don't understand. You aren't stuck in Ireland. It's a free country."

"Ay, I am without a Green Card, dear Miranda. You couldn't have just fallen for me a little. Just a little and let me slip in. I would have been good to you. We would have had some good years. How hard could it have been to give me just that? I gave you enough, didn't I? You enjoyed it all well enough, parting your legs with ease."

"I won't listen to this. It wasn't like that. It was just a thing."

"Oh, a thing was it. God bless your intended. May he keep you forever from other things. Faithless woman. Enjoy your time on the television. I'm sure it will be memorable." And then the line went dead.

She dropped her phone as if it were hot. It sputtered across the sidewalk and landed on the grassy median between the sidewalk and the street. She stared it, imagining the wild tangle of invisible networks that linked that tiny rectangle to the rest of the world; this web of connections both cradled her world and shook it like an earthquake.

But then her phone binged. Lynn sent her a photo of her day's artwork from Scott's phone. Three figures stood on top of a blue crayon mountain with jagged lines drawn on the top to show snow. Each figure wore a scarf and goggles. The character's names were penned in green crayon: Daddy, Lynn, Randa. They each wore skis as well.

"I don't know how to ski," Miranda texted back.

"I will teach you," Lynn said. "Daddy says I'm a good teacher."

"I'm sure you are," Miranda said.

Miranda scrolled through the options that she didn't ever use on her phone and found the emoticons. She found a penguin and entered it three times followed by a heart.

"Can you hand Daddy the phone?" she asked.

"Soccer practice. No phone rule," Lynn texted back.

The dots indicating another incoming message came up quickly.

"I forgot. No phone! Love you, Randa."

"Love you, too," Miranda texted back.

Scott wouldn't be available for at least an hour. She thought about calling Danielle. But neither one of them could tell her how much damage Ronan had done this time.

32

, HERE," Kristen said, answering her phone.

"Miranda, here," Miranda replied. "I think I have a problem."

"I'm here to serve," Kristen said. "Shoot."

"There might be a problem with the Ellen Show. I think Ronan, you know the one—"

"The one from the university? The student?"

"Yes," Miranda said, swallowing hard. She didn't want to argue the point. She was in no position to argue anything right now.

"Oh, that, so you got the email, too?"

"The email?"

"Yes, the one to the producers at Ellen; they sent it over yesterday for confirmation."

"What did you say?"

"We have a policy of always staying in front of these things. Admit, Accept, and Move on."

"You told them?"

"No, he told them. I confirmed. Admit, Accept, and Move on."

"Does Ambrose know about this?" Miranda asked.

"Of course, it's his policy."

"What did the Ellen people say? Is she going to ask me about this?"

"They said thank you. We never get to approve the questions before hand. Some of these producers still feel they are journalists."

"What am I going to do?"

"I sent you the itinerary, right? Just be ready when the car comes, Miranda. This is huge. Be sure you have a dance prepared."

Twenty minutes later, after she finally made her way back to the hotel, Ambrose texted her. "Scandal drives sales. Whatever it is, roll with it. And don't forget to dance."

Instead of going up to her room, she took a seat at the lobby bar for the first time on this entire trip. She ordered a bottle of Shiraz and tried to figure out the best way to prepare Scott for what he might see on the television the next day. The wine did little to improve her problem-solving abilities. With the bottle empty, she had even fewer ideas than before. She thought about ordering a shot of Tequila or maybe Jack Daniels or something Technicolor from the mirrored-shelf behind the bar. Instead, she decided to do what she promised to do: share her life with him.

He listened carefully, saying uh hum, and okay at all of the right places. "Dancing?" he finally asked.

"It's a thing on Ellen," she said. "The guests dance in."

"How bad could it be?" he asked. "If they have you dancing, it's not a hard-hitting news show. What time is it on?"

"The afternoon. Like three or four."

"So not prime time?"

"Nope."

"So they aren't going to ask about sex, Randa. There might be children watching. You'll be fine."

"But soap operas are on in the afternoon. That's all sex."

"I'm just trying to be helpful."

"Helpful. Okay," she said. "I'll go along with you. But what if they cancel?"

"That's your last stop, right?"

"Yes. Just the show and then I am done."

"Then you come home early. I see no problem there. I will move heaven and earth to meet your plane. Even if it's early."

"Early, huh? You ready for me to be back?"

"More than ready. I never wanted you to leave, remember? You'll do fine."

"Hmmmm—" Miranda said. "So it's going to be fine, you say?"

"It already is fine. You still love me, right?"

"Of course," Miranda said.

"Good. I still love you. What else matters?"

Between the wine and his sweet talk, Miranda agreed.

The next afternoon, Miranda messaged Lynn from Ellen's Green Room. "What dance should I do?"

"Your best one," Lynn replied. "Or wait, maybe just spin like a ballerina. On your toes." Lynn sent the emoticons for a ballet slipper and smiling face with a pink bow on top.

Before Miranda could find the emoticon for a horse, the animal she felt would most closely mimic her dance style, the stagehand signaled her out on stage. Taking Lynn's advice, Miranda stumbled out on to the stage, faked a pirouette and spun a few times to Ellen's couch.

"Before we get any further," Ellen started. "We have to clear this up. You're a cheater."

Ronan, she thought her stomach threatening to erupt its contents over the stage. She locked her eyes on Ellen, pleading with her silently not to go any further.

But Ellen continued anyway. "You play Scrabble by yourself, without any rules. Do you really need to win that badly?"

The punch line. A joke.

Miranda felt her shoulders creep back down into place. The interview went well from there. A staffer brought out a Scrabble board, and Ellen called on audience members to give themes for the Blocked Poet. Miranda tackled Pembroke Welsh Corgis and the Tampa Bay Rays, before an older lady in a navy blue pantsuit stood up and took the microphone. "I couldn't say it out loud, but they told me I could write it down, and you would do it."

A staffer appeared behind Miranda and handed her a note written in the most delicate cursive. Jeanine, the woman in navy, wanted to propose to Sue. The note explained that after twenty years together, gay marriage was now legal in their home state.

Miranda quickly arranged, Marry, then Me off of that and Sue off of that. The cameraman focused his camera tight on the puzzle, and it filled the screen behind Miranda and Ellen.

Sue bounced from her seat and threw her arms around Jeanine.

"Yes, yes, yes," she screamed.

A staffer led the couple, who refused to let go of each other's hands, down to the stage. Ellen photographed this sculpture, posting it to her own Twitter and Instagram, tagging Blocked Poet in each. The music cued, and another staffer led them all off to the green room.

Miranda showed Jeanine and Sue her own ring. "I just got engaged, too," she squealed with them, excited for their happiness and for not being on the stage anymore.

"When's the wedding?" Jeanine asked.

"I don't know. We haven't gotten that far yet. There've been other things to take care of." She gestured to the room around them.

"Well, we aren't waiting," Sue said. "I reckon we will do it tomorrow when we get back home."

"So soon? Don't you need to plan anything?"

Jeanine picked up Sue's hand and kissed it. "We already worked out the hard part; why wait? You never know what's going to happen tomorrow. You can't really plan for that—you only think you can."

"Ladies," a staffer interrupted. "Ellen wants to see you now."

Jeanine and Sue stood up straight and clasped hands. "Thank you for doing that for us. We're going to blow up the picture and frame it for the living room. Right over the fireplace. Thank you," Jeanine said.

"It was my honor. Congratulations."

"Oh, you might want to check your phone—it was buzzing terribly before," the staffer said.

Alone in the green room, Miranda fished out her phone. Then her phone hummed with the alerts from Ellen's Twitter and Instagram. Thousands of new people started following both her accounts and then lingered on them, liking and re-tweeting past entries. She thought immediately about Ambrose. And sure enough, he texted, "Kudos, Blocked Poet." This right before Lynn texted, "I need to teach you how to dance before the wedding." And Scott texted, "I love you. If I had known all I needed was a Scrabble board to propose, maybe I could have done it sooner."

Miranda flagged down a girl with a clipboard and a headset walking by. "Can I have one of those Scrabble boards?"

"Um, sure," the staffer said. "Can I get one of those games back?" she said into her radio.

Miranda paced the length of the green room, counting each time she touched a wall. At one hundred and fifteen, another person with a headset popped into the room, Scrabble board in hand.

"Last minute inspiration?" he asked.

"Something like that," Miranda said.

She flipped open the box and started pulling out tiles. The staffer didn't move to leave. She stopped and looked up at him.

"Oh," he said. "Just holler if you need anything else."

"Thank you," she said.

With the door shut behind her, she quickly arranged, Marry me, Friday on the board. She pulled out one of the question mark tiles from Kristen's special order to finish it off. She sent the photograph to Scott. Within seconds, her phone rang

"What do you mean by Friday?" he asked. "Which Friday?"

"You know, the one tomorrow," she said.

"But what about all the plans?" he said. "I know that Bunny and Avery could work wonders, but you don't even have a dress or flowers or anything."

"I don't need any of that. If I set it all up, will you do it?"

"Will I marry you tomorrow? Is that what you are asking?"

"Yes, that is what I am asking."

"Do you think you even need to ask? Will you even be home tomorrow?"

"I will, but I am still waiting for your answer."

"Yes, Miranda, I will marry you tomorrow."

"Good, then you better let me go. I have some phone calls to make."

She started to Google the church, the one where she last saw her mother. But she stopped and opened an email instead. She told Kristen all about the church, asked for the next flight to Newark, a car to take her to said church, and a pastor to marry them.

As Miranda slipped from the building into a cab bound for the airport, Kristen replied with her singular, K. Twenty minutes later, she replied with, Done, billed to Blocked Poet accounts. Then her phone buzzed again.

"Invites?" Kristen asked.

Miranda stared at her phone as the city whirred past her cab. Then she replied just three and sent Kristen the email addresses for Lynn, his parents, and her parents.

Then she turned off her phone and surrendered to the last leg of one journey and the start of the next.

THE END

Acknowledgments

I'M ALWAYS AFRAID TO WRITE an acknowledgements section because I don't want to leave any one out. But I wouldn't be able to think up the crazy things I imagine to write down and send out into the world without the help of some pretty wonderful people.

There's my family. It goes without saying without the people who raised you wouldn't become a writer. Some people might think that is a jab, but in this case, my family always loved me for who I was, even if I am weird. To be a writer, you need someone to love your odd self from a very small age.

Then there's my friends, the people who choose to love me even though I am weird. Without them opening their hearts, homes, phone lines, Facebook feeds, and lunch calendars, I might have self-destructed long before the book ever saw the light of day. Heck, before I even saw the light of day; sometimes a lunch date is the only reason I shower.

There's a subset of friends called archers. This group taught me some amazing stuff like working for your dreams and never giving up. While we never talked about writing (busy, shooting!), they sure showed me what it takes to get where you want to go. My heart is filled with gratitude for my coach, who taught me thoughts are things. His guidance is so much deeper than bows and arrows.

There's another subset of friends called Secret Facebook Groups. I won't say any more about that, but y'all know who you are and why this line is in here. Your safe spaces make moving through the world easier and a heck of a lot more fun.

Then there are the writers: the AWP Mentors and Mentees, the Yale Summer Group, the Key West Literary Seminar, the beautiful Tall Poppies, and the lovely writers who choose to work with me on their own projects. Thank you for pushing me with your examples and holding me up with your support. You all make me want to up my game and tweet about your books.

Among the writers is my amazing publisher, Nancy Cleary at Wyatt-MacKenzie. I thank you for giving *Triple Love Score* a beautiful home and seeing Miranda's journey the same way I did.

And finally to Moose and Big Man. There are not enough words to thank you both for the wonderful home we share. The stories we make up, the meals we eat, the arrows we shoot, the drives we take (probably to get food or shoot arrows) fill me and make each day better than the last. I can't wait to see what our next chapters hold.